AF485279

Necromancers
and
Navy Grog

Published by Blackridge Publishing, LLC

ISBN 979-8-9925139-4-3(eBook)

ISBN 979-8-9925139-5-0 (paperbound)

Fiction/Fantasy

First edition May 2026

After you reach a certain age, they think you're over.

Well, I will never be over.

— **Dolly Parton**

Chapter One

THE MORNING FOG BURNS away as we crest the hill on Third Street, the bay and the wharf spread out before us. Masts of the ships crowding San Francisco Bay poke through the mist like the bare bones of dead leviathans in the distance.

We descend Berry Street into the crowd, the stink of Mission Creek rising to assault us. The morning's low tide amplifies its aggressive pungency. The "creek" is little more than an open sewer, carrying blood and offal and Lord knows what else from Butchertown. Sailors complain it will peel the paint off a hull in a day and swear you'd be dead in two minutes flat if you fell in.

"Tell me again why we're chasing ghost stories?" I ask, lifting my skirt above the muck with my good hand.

My temporary partner Loosh, or Agent Aloysious Temple if we're being formal, pulls a handkerchief out of his breast pocket and dabs at his forehead, despite the cool morning. His breathing has been labored since we started out an hour ago. "Because Captain Garret needs to keep the brass happy. Because the mayor's sister-in-law swears to seeing the dead walking near Meiggs Wharf."

Loosh's been my unofficial nanny since I reported to my assignment at the Anti Death Magic Division of the Bureau of Magical Investigation last fall. My boss, Garret, who didn't like my history and had no idea what to do with me—a female agent with a problematic service record—had bestowed me upon Loosh, a part-time agent approaching retirement.

"The dead walking." I snort. Since I'd been assigned to Loosh, he and I hadn't uncovered more than whisper of death magic. "More likely a prank. Or worst case some poor shanghaied bastard making a break for it."

No one gives us a second glance as we push our way through stevedores, sailors, and merchants. Wagons clatter over the cobblestones to our right. The ships and piers to our left swarm with sweat-drenched men loading, hauling, and unloading cargo while swearing, singing, or conversing in what seems like every language known to man. I reckon a person could learn to curse creatively if they applied themselves for a single day of eavesdropping.

"Maybe." Loosh tucks the handkerchief away, his craggy face creasing into what passes for a smile these days. "Though the description in the report was rather...colorful. 'Pale as fish belly, moving like a man with lead in his bones.'"

"Sounds like someone who's been locked in a ship's hold for a week or two," I say.

"Indeed." Loosh nods, smile widening. "Perhaps this is our opportunity to free some prodigal Odysseus, return him to the bosom of his loving family."

I shoot him a sideways look. Loosh's background as a Classics professor sometimes leads him to flights of fancy. "Too much Homer before bed?"

"Never enough Homer, dear girl!"

We push through the mayhem, my blue riding skirt swishing against my boots. A concession to my sister Julianna's propriety. Technically, there are ordinances on the city's books forbidding women to wear men's attire, but they're only enforced when someone in power gets pissy. Even so, I wore the skirt to soothe my sister's sensibilities.

Loosh pulls a small notebook out of his coat pocket and scans it. I take advantage of the pause to steady myself against a stack of crates and use the hook replacing my left hand to adjust the stocking bunching at my ankle. The steel tip catches on the knit and threatens to tear; I'm sure Julianna would argue it's another reason for a nice ladylike prosthetic, easily concealed in a fashionable glove, but I prefer the utility of the hook. Terrible things, stockings, with their garters. Yet another nod to feminine decorum foisted upon me by my dear sister.

A passing stevedore flashes me a grin. "Need a hand there, ma'am?"

I bark a laugh. "No hand needed. Thanks all the same." I wave the hook in his direction, and he chuckles, shaking his head as he moves on. Stink aside, that's why I like the wharf. No one here gives a rat's ass about a missing hand, your past, your manners, or *feelings* as long as you do your job and mind your business.

Loosh glances around, then indicates our destination is the organized bedlam of Pope & Talbot's lumberyard across the way. "Our witness is foreman there," he says.

The lumberyard is swarming with men and boys gawping at the schooner in the Talbot's slip, its crew working to unload a massive redwood log into the yard. It's easily eight feet across and forty feet long, dwarfing the men maneuvering it. The trunk hangs from complex rigging halfway between the ship and the work yard. I'm drawn closer to watch. I still can't quite believe trees this size are real, what after the scrub oak and pinion of my last home in Trinidad, Colorado.

There's an eddy of activity on the ship's deck. Workmen's voices rise in pitch. An older man, maybe the captain, standing near the rail starts cursing "Back, BACK, you idjits." He waves frantically at the men on the ground. Next thing, the end of the redwood closest to the prow drops from the rigging with a horrendous creak and a rope snaps, sending the log swinging wildly.

Even as I gasp, the free end crashes to the dock below. It bounces once before coming to rest. Shouts fill the air. I feel death coming for some poor soul under that log. I glance back for Loosh, see if we should go in, but I've lost sight of him as the crowd gathers at my back, drawn to the excitement of the accident.

Turning, I fight my way clear to see Loosh disappearing into an alley.

I curse under my breath and shoulder my way through the growing mob. Men press forward to get a look at the damage, their voices rising in excitement and concern. I push past them, my skirts catching on rough hands and tool belts.

"Loosh!" I call out, but the din swallows my voice.

I break free of the crowd and sprint toward the mouth of the alley where I last saw him. The narrow passage between two warehouses is dark, crates stacked haphazardly. My eyes adjust to the gloom as the excited cries fade behind me.

But ahead...voices. Low and urgent.

I slow my pace, my boots silent on the packed dirt. A familiar reverberation slips past my defenses and starts up in my bones, a new sensitivity to old death. This hum has been plaguing me for months, an unwelcome gift from the dark ritual in New Mexico last year. Now I sense death magic residue like a dog smells rot. Can't turn it off, can't ignore it. Just one more way that business marked me.

"Told you he'd be sniffing around today," a voice drifts from deeper in the alley. "Boss wants to see him."

"Don't see why we can't just gut him here and be done with it."

My blood turns cold. I edge forward, keeping to the shadows cast by the overhanging eaves. The alley opens into a small courtyard behind the warehouses, cluttered with broken crates and rusted iron.

There's Loosh, his white hair stark against the dingy wall, bowler at his feet. Three men in filthy clothes have him cornered. Hollow-eyed and gaunt, with the pallor of people who haven't seen sunlight in weeks.

Hopheads, sure enough. But not the usual sort. Hoppies ain't violent. And they surely don't go dragging Bureau agents down alleys.

"Now, gentlemen," Loosh's saying, his voice steady despite the circumstances. "I'm certain we can reach some sort of accommodation. Perhaps we could discuss this over a drink?"

"Ain't gonna be no discussion," the tallest one says. "Boss says bring you, so that's what we're doing."

The thrum in my bones gets louder. There's death magic here. It clings to these men like smoke, no way they're normies.

I step into the courtyard. "Afternoon, boys."

They whirl toward me, and I get a good look at their faces. Sweet Christ. Whatever they've been smoking, it ain't just opium. Their skin has a waxy sheen. But their eyes burn with an intensity that has nothing to do with poppy dreams. I wonder if these fellows account for the zombie sightings we've been hearing about.

"Well now." The tall one grins. His mouth is a graveyard of blackened stumps where teeth used to be. "Look what wandered in. Pretty little thing, ain't she?"

"I ain't little," I say, keeping my voice level. "You best let him go."

Another one pipes up, burn scars stretching over his skin. He takes a step toward me. "You got spirit. Boss might like that."

"I doubt it." I blink slowly. "Let *Agent* Temple go," I continue, hoping the reality of law enforcement will send them scurrying. "The Bureau of Magical Investigations doesn't take kindly to folks roughing up their men."

The three exchange startled glances. Scarface's eyes widen. "BMI? Shit. You're with the Beemers?"

Loosh winces, shooting me a look that could curdle milk. I realize my mistake too late. He wanted to stay on the down-low.

"Boss just said grab the old man from Meiggs," Toothless mutters to the others. "Didn't say nothing about him being no law."

The annoying magical hum becomes more urgent. Whatever's wrong with these men, it's sending my new death sense into high alert. The corruption I'm sensing isn't old. It's alive, slowly eating them from the inside.

"Walk away, lady," Tall and Toothless says. "This ain't your business."

"Afraid it is."

"Mary Catherine, perhaps discretion—" Loosh starts, his tone tight.

Ignoring him, I launch myself before anyone can react. The Bureau doesn't allow me to carry firearms, but I've got other advantages.

My hook catches Scarface across the jaw, tearing flesh. He staggers back, blood streaming down his chin. The other two rush me at once. Damn it, I expected them to run as soon as I fought back. Hopheads never stand and fight.

I duck under a wild swing from Toothless, grab the short one by his greasy hair, and slam his face into my knee. The crack of his nose breaking echoes off the warehouse walls. He drops like a sack of grain. My knee numbs from the impact.

They're faster than they should be. Stronger too. Toothless backhands me across the face hard enough to rattle my teeth. Maybe I was too hasty in my approach? I stumble, my vision blurring.

"Mary Catherine!" Loosh shouts.

A fist catches me in the ribs. Pain explodes through my side, and I grunt, rolling with the blow. Whatever's in their systems, it's made them vicious and fearless.

Loosh grabs a broken crate slat from the ground and swings it at Scarface. It connects with his shoulder and splinters. He barely flinches.

"Hold her!" Toothless yells.

Scarface lunges for me. I sidestep, but my heel catches on my damned skirts. I go down hard on my ass, my palm scraping against the ground.

He's on me in an instant, his hands around my throat. His fingers are ice cold, and when I look into his eyes, I freeze. They're not just hollow. They're empty, emotionless. Like looking into a well at midnight.

"Should've minded your own business," he snarls.

I drive my hook up under his ribs. The metal punctures something soft, and he gasps. "Stupid bitch." His grip loosens.

I scramble backward out from underneath him until my shoulders hit the wall and pull myself to my feet, scanning for Toothless. The hum is so loud now it's like standing next to a steam engine.

Toothless is grappling with Loosh across the courtyard, trying to pin him against the wall. Loosh's got thirty pounds and at least six inches on the hoppy, but Loosh is old and tired. The hoppy's hands close on Loosh's throat, so I do the only thing I can think of. I run at Toothless and tackle him low.

He stumbles, off balance, and crashes into the cargo hook protruding from the warehouse wall behind him. The curved iron punches through his back and out his chest, just below his collarbone.

For a moment, he just hangs there, suspended on the hook like a piece of meat. Then his eyes roll back, and breath rattles out of him. Before the opportunity passes, I lay my hand on his chest and call the Gleaning.

Chapter Two

THE MOMENT MY PALM touches his chest, the world narrows, him and me connected. His animus flares beneath my hand, sickly pink threaded with violet, pulsing like a bruise. Wrong. Corrupted. The Gleaner surges, thirsty for the death, eager.

Toothless's final breath breaks foul across my face and I'm falling through the moment of his dying.

Sprawled on a filthy mattress in a basement that reeks of piss and rotting fish. My bones ache. My teeth hurt. Everything hurts.

Need it, need it, need it.

The craving tears through me like broken glass. Not just for opium. Something else. Something that makes the poppy seem like candy.

Flash.

I'm standing in a doorway, rain pelting my face. A man in expensive clothes steps from a carriage. His face a blur, but his eyes shine violet in the lamplight. Wrong color. Wrong everything. But he's got what I need.

"You want more?" His voice slides over me like oil. "You bring him to me."

Another flash.

I'm stalking Loosh. The way he favors his left leg. How he stops to catch his breath. The route he takes through the wharf.

The violet-eyed man presses something into my palm. It burns cold against my skin. "This will make you strong. Fast."

I take it and swallow it whole.

The hunger gnaws at my insides. I'd sell my mother for another taste. I'd kill for it. I will kill for it.

My link to Toothless snaps as his Animus Mortis rushes through me, hot and bitter. Corrupted. This isn't clean death. It's poisoned by whatever was in that vial. His energy scrapes against my nerves like sandpaper, leaving me shaking and nauseous.

The courtyard spins. My knees buckle and I hit the ground hard, bile rising in my throat.

Every living thing's got Animus. Call it a soul if you're feeling poetic. It's tethered to the body by invisible chains. When something dies, those chains snap. That breaking, that split second between alive and gone, releases a surge of pure energy. Animus Mortis, the scholars call it. Death energy.

My Gleaner, this knack I was born with, lets me ride that breaking. Absorb it. Store it up like bullets in a chamber, ready to unleash as pure kinetic force when I need it. Been doing it since I was a girl.

Something, a flicker of movement at the periphery of my vision. Just a shadow, slipping away like a wisp of smoke. The hoppy's shade? It hovers just out of reach. It's a fleeting echo of a life snuffed out in darkness. Trouble with Gleaning is, in addition to the dying bastard's memories flooding through me whether I want them or not, sometimes their shades stick around to haunt me after.

But Toothless ain't gonna stick. Got nothing tethering him to the physical plane; he's as much a shadow in death as he was in life. I blink rapidly, shaking him off.

"Mary Catherine!" Loosh's voice seems to come from miles away.

I retch into the dirt, my body trying to purge the tainted energy. But Toothless's animus surges through my veins, hot and electric. I feel every heartbeat in a three-block radius, sense the fear and excitement from the crowd still gathered over at Talbots. My muscles sing with stolen strength.

Hands grip my shoulders. "Agent McClellan, look at me."

Loosh's face swims into focus, flushed and slick with sweat. His breathing is ragged gasps, and his hands shake against my shoulders.

"What the fuck was that about, Loosh?" My voice comes out raw. "Those men knew you. They were hunting you."

His face pales beneath the flush. "I... What do you mean? They were just—"

"Don't." I struggle to my feet, the world still tilting. "I heard them. 'Boss wants to see him.'"

His eyes dart away from mine. "I haven't the faintest idea what you mean."

"Come on, Loosh." I gesture at the body hanging from the cargo hook, then at Scarface, who's clutching his bleeding chest while trying to crawl away. "These weren't random thugs looking for an easy mark. They knew you. They mentioned following you from Meiggs."

Loosh's face goes pale beneath the red flush. "Perhaps they mistook me for someone else."

I study his face. But before I can press him further, Scarface makes it to his feet and limps toward the alley mouth, blood seeping from his chest. I'm on him in three strides, bumping the back of his knee and knocking him to the ground.

Loosh fumbles in his coat pocket for his manacles. His hands shake so badly he drops them twice before managing to hand them off. Scarface groans as the metal cuts into his wrist. The short one just stares at nothing, blood crusting around his broken nose.

"We need to get these two to Captain Garrett," I say, hauling Broken Nose to his feet. "Let him sort out who sent them and why."

"Mary Catherine, wait." Loosh's voice creaks. "Perhaps we should reconsider."

I stare at him. "Reconsider what exactly?"

"Well, it's just…" He wrings his hands, his eyes darting between the prisoners and the mouth of the alley. "Captain Garrett has been under considerable pressure lately. From the mayor's office, from the city council. Perhaps it would be better if we simply turned these men over to the regular police. Let them handle it as an assault."

"Assault?" I can't keep the disbelief out of my voice. "Loosh, these men were magically corrupted. I can smell it on them. Feel it. This is exactly what the Anti Death Magic Division is supposed to handle."

"Yes, but think of the paperwork. The questions. The complications. You'll have to explain to Garrett how one of the suspects died and you…benefited." He's speaking faster now, the words tumbling over each other. "Wouldn't it be simpler to just…let us investigate ourselves?"

I study his face. The man who tries to teach me Latin and shares beers at Calpurnia's looks older than his sixty years. Fragile…frightened?

The deathly reverberation has faded to a whisper, but I still sense the residual corruption clinging to our prisoners. Whatever they'd been dosed with, it ain't natural. And it ain't gone.

But Loosh never complained about being saddled with me. Never made me feel like dead weight or a charity case. When other agents whispered about me, the Gleaner who killed a federal marshal, Loosh treated me like a partner. Like someone worth talking to.

I look at him. Really look. This is the terror of a man who knows he's in over his head.

Maybe I owe him this much, help him get out from under whatever he's gotten himself into.

"Regular police," I say finally. "Random assault."

"Thank you. Truly. I know this puts you in a difficult position."

I help him hoist Scarface to his feet. The man's jaw hangs at an odd angle where my hook caught him, but he's conscious enough to shuffle forward when I shove him toward the alley.

"This better not come back to bite me in the ass. And you're gonna tell me everything."

"I will but later. It's a long story and I've got to take care of something in Sausalito this afternoon. Monday, we'll sit down together and I'll tell you everything. I give you my word."

His word. For some reason, that doesn't comfort me as much as it should. I push doubts away and smile. "Fine, you're buying the beer."

We march our prisoners out of the alley and back into the chaos of the wharf. The crowd around Pope & Talbot's has dispersed, leaving only a few men working to clear the debris from the fallen log. No one pays us any mind as we make our way to 4th Street and then via cab to the police station on Battery Street. Loosh has a friend there and there will be no hard questions asked.

But I can't shake the feeling that I'm making a mistake. The visions from the dead hoppy keep circling through my head. The shadow figure with his vials of purple liquid.

Whatever's happening, it ain't finished. And Loosh knows more about it than he's letting on.

Chapter Three

WITH THE HOPPIES LOCKED away and Loosh safely loaded on the ferry to Sausalito, I head to Calpurnia's, which is conveniently just a few blocks away from the police station. The walk gives me time to think, and I don't like where my thoughts are leading me. Loosh lied to me. Those hopheads knew him by name, had been watching him. And whatever they'd been dosed with was something dark and magical.

If something new was making the rounds in the city, Abigail Colt would know. Information flowed through her bar like good whiskey, steady, reliable, and with just enough burn to make you pay attention. And with any luck, her son and my friend Edison will be there for a Saturday breakfast. Working at the local Bureau office, he might have the skinny on these hoppies. I'm killing the proverbial two birds.

The fog deepens as I head toward Pier 10. Sunshine is a fickle bitch at the best of times in this city by the bay, but in spring it's downright shy. A prickling sensation crawls up the back of my neck as I stride down the bustling waterfront, like someone's watching.

Slowing my pace, I drop back toward the water to scan the area. But no one seems interested in me except to throw a little stink eye my way for slowing the flow of traffic. I still feel like someone's watching. I sidle up to some crates at the edge of the quay, their bulk at my back, sheltering me while I get a good look at the crowd. No one looks out of place, or particularity suspicious, or suspiciously disinterested. The pulse at the base of my throat flutters.

Whirling at a splash to my right, my hand drops to the nonexistent holster at my hip. A shout dies in my throat. For a second, I thought a woman had fallen into the water, but on second look I recognize the shining dark head of a seal. Its eyes flash before sinking into the murky water. Jesus, Mary, and Joseph. I chuckle. I'm an idiot. A few passersby give me a wide berth. Paranoid woman with a hook for a hand laughing to herself, not the strangest thing at the Port of San Francisco but worth keeping your distance. Squaring my shoulders, I continue on.

Calpurnia's is a squat little shack squeezed between a warehouse and a sailmaker's shop. There is no sign identifying it from the outside. I step down into the low-ceilinged sanctuary. Sunlight fights through grimy windows facing the wharf, casting the entire room in soft dimness. Calpurnia's is Abigail Colt's thriving dockside bar, catering especially to English sailors. Abby inherited the bar from old Mother Johnson, who got her start slinging rotgut to the 49ers. Not long after Abby took over, her then-paramour, a navigator in Her Majesty's Navy, started calling the bar Calpurnia's because Abby's grog was beyond reproach. A portrait of a young Vicky hangs by the front door, its frame inscribed "The Queen—God bless her."

Even this early in the day, a handful of sailors huddle over battered mugs of beer at the rickety tables. They don't even glance my way. Serving beer and grog from old-fashioned pewter mugs keeps glassware costs low. Abby looks up from wiping down the bar, her pale blue eyes crinkling in a welcoming smile.

"Well, look what the tide washed in! Good to see you, Mick." Her welcome a balm after the morning's start.

"Good to see you too, Abby." I slide onto one of the only stools, taking in the familiar smells of stale beer, brine, and tobacco. Across the narrow room, Abby's daughter, Emma, is washing tankards, her auburn hair a few shades darker than her mother's blond curls.

Feels like I've known Abby forever, but it's only been six months since I'd first set foot in this place. When me and my sister, Julianna, and her companion, Gudrun, decided to make a fresh start in San Francisco, Edison had regaled me with stories of his mother's legendary toughness and the rowdy waterfront bar she ran with an iron fist. I'd been expecting a grizzled old harpy with a voice like a foghorn and a face like a bulldog chewing a wasp.

Instead, I'd found Abby, with her keen blue eyes and sharp mind. Our first meeting had been a bit prickly, the two of us sizing each other up like alley cats in a territory dispute. But after I'd told her the story of my meeting a hero-worshiping Edison, she'd about fallen off her chair with laughter.

Ever since, we'd bonded over our shared exasperation with Edison's youthful misadventures and our own challenges of the fairer sex.

"Everything all right, love? You look like you've seen a ghost." Abby sets a steaming mug of tea in front of me, the chipped ceramic handle turned toward my right hand.

"No new ones." I wrap my fingers around the mug, letting the warmth seep into my bones. "A rough morning. Poor fool got crushed down at Pope & Talbot's. A giant redwood came loose when they were unloading, squashed him flat."

"The old gods count their due given the opportunity." Abigail clucks her tongue sympathetically. "Poor bastard."

I sip my tea, the bitter tannin an echo of the taste of that hophead's death.

"Is Edison around?" I ask. "Haven't seen that rascal in a few days." He'd have heard the official reports on what's been happening down at the waterfront.

She sighs, elbows on the scarred bar. "That boy's as elusive as a bucket of steam these days."

Damn. There went half my reason for coming here.

Abby continues, "He's out all hours, drinking and gambling like he's got a money tree out back. Emma tells me he's seeing some floozy from one of the dance halls. Spanish Kitty, they call her."

I raise an eyebrow. "Spanish Kitty? Sounds like trouble." Great. Now Edison's running with a questionable crowd.

"Aye, that she does." Abigail snorts. "Not that I'm one to judge how a girl makes a living. Lord knows I've done my share of things best left in the dark."

I smirk at her; she's shared a story or two. Abby unashamedly has no idea who Edison's father is and Edison's mystical ability doesn't come from her side of the family.

"But this Kitty, she's got a reputation. A little older, more worldly; she's hard in a way Edison isn't."

"Abby, Edison's nearly a man grown," I remonstrate, shaking my head.

Abby purses her lips and glares. "I know." She snatches up a rag and starts polishing the bar. Slumping her shoulders, she sighs. "I know. But I don't want to see him get his heart broken, or worse. He's naive for all his tough talk and swagger."

"At least Edison always shows up for Sunday supper, right? That counts for something."

Abby laughs, the lines around her eyes crinkling. "True enough. That boy would walk through fire for a taste of my roast beef and Yorkshire pudding. At least I know he's eating one decent meal a week."

"Speaking of trouble." I nod, tracing a finger over the rough grain of the bar. "You hear anything about a new kind of drug making the rounds? Something a little more energizing than opium, a mite nastier than cocaine?"

Abby's expression sharpens. "Why? You thinking of taking up the pipe?"

"God, no." I hold my palm up and grimace. "Ran into some hopheads this morning, but they were...different. Stronger. Meaner. They'd been dosing something that wasn't just poppy."

"Funny you should mention that." Abby cocks her head, studying me. "I've been hearing whispers. Rumors of strange things lurking in the shadows. Sailors coming off the night watch, swearing they've seen things that shouldn't be walking around, if you catch my drift. But drugs?" She shakes her head. "Nothing new that I've heard."

"Dead men walking, maybe?"

"Probably just drunk fools seeing shadows," Abby says, but her tone suggests she isn't entirely convinced. "But some of the fellows were spooked down to their boots. Men I thought were steady, and now you, asking about strange drugs...makes a body wonder."

Shit, yes, this body is wondering. Wondering if I really should risk my position as Special Agent for the BMI's Anti Death Magic Division by helping Loosh cover up this morning's events.

I should probably let Loosh handle his own mess. Warn my boss, Garret, about those empty eyes, the way the corruption had clung to those hoppies like a second skin.

The thought of telling Garret knots a band between my shoulder blades. Hell, Garrett will probably dismiss me as having a conniption and last thing I want is to put Loosh in deep water with our command. He's my partner, and real play, he and I are plenty qualified to investigate ourselves. If anything nefarious surfaces, we can bring Garrett in then. I exhale deeply. Yeah, Loosh and I can handle this just fine.

I drain my mug and set it down with a *thunk*. "Thanks for the tea and the talk. I'll keep an eye out for Edison."

"If you see that rapscallion son of mine, give him a good kick in the arse from his mother, would you?"

I laugh, the sound rusty but genuine. "Will do."

With a final wave to Emma, I step back out into the chaos of the docks to head home. The sensation of being watched prickles over my scalp again. As I stride down the boardwalk, the echoes of revenants and dark magic swirls at my heels, an ominous portent I can't quite bring myself to acknowledge.

Chapter Four

IT'S A SHORT WALK from the horse trolley stop to our house. The paved, bustling streets of San Francisco are welcome after the hardscrabble existence we'd eked out on that godforsaken pig farm in Trinidad. I keep what used to be my left hand tucked into the pocket of my skirt, the cool metal of the hook a constant reminder of all I've lost. And gained.

Our new home in the Mission District is a grand Italianate townhouse, elegant lines and cheerful yellow paint. A far cry from the cramped, dirt-floored cabin we'd shared in Colorado. It sits on a spacious corner lot, with a small stable out back.

As is my habit, I pause at the bottom of the front steps to scan the street, pretending to admire the lush ivy creeping along the façade. No sign of anyone or anything on my tail.

Letting myself through the wide front door, I sigh when it clicks shut behind me and I'm enveloped in the lively sounds of morning activity. Someone's enthusiastically banging on the piano in the front parlor and the staccato tap of a lady's boots hurries down the hall upstairs. No doubt one of our boarders preparing for her day. Julianna sweeps into the foyer from the back, resplendent in a crisp, narrow-skirted day suit and a jaunty hat. Jesus, are those feathers?

"Mary Catherine, thank goodness you're back. Ylva's impatient," she calls over her shoulder as she rifles through the coats hanging on the rack on the back of the door. "Have you seen my blue gloves? I'm going to be late for the charity luncheon."

In Trinidad, her biggest worry had been keeping the coyotes away from the chickens. Now, she's a regular society maven, all poise and polish, fretting about gloves. It exhausts me.

"Check the parlor, Jules. I think I saw them on the piano last night."

She flashes me a grateful smile as she turns to slide open the parlor's pocket door. A wave of discordant operatic singing rolls into the foyer. Frida, our newest boarder, is holding court among a gaggle of her theater friends. She recently landed a gig at the Grand Opera House, one of the newer upscale concert halls, but her bread is buttered working the more unsavory melodeons around Portsmouth Square. The buxom blonde gesticulates broadly as she belts out what could be German. Billed as the Singing Cow, her popularity has more to do with her impressive size at over six feet and her quick wit than her singing voice. Poor old Mozart must be laughing his head off in his grave.

I catch the eye of one of her companions, a slender redhead with kohl-rimmed eyes and a feminine cant to their hips. They give me a conspiratorial wink, and I nod back as Julianna slides the door closed, eyes rolling. Thankfully, the closed doors mute Frieda's caterwauling.

I shrug out of my coat and hang it on the rack by the door, careful not to snag the fabric with my hook.

"Auntie Mary Catherine, you're home!" Ylva, my nine-year-old niece, barrels down the stairs, her tangled white-blond hair flying behind her. I catch her up in a one-armed hug.

"Good morning, Little Wolf. You ready for our big adventure today?"

Her blue eyes sparkle with excitement. "Woodward's Gardens, and I'm going to ride the camel!"

Ylva has been downright obsessed with riding a camel ever since she saw an illustrated newspaper advert. We have been planning this outing for a week. No matter the hoppies on the wharf or Loosh's questionable behavior. I have plans with my niece.

I tweak her nose. "You shall be queen of the camels! But first, you'd best go put on a proper dress. You know how Mama Julianna feels about young ladies and decorum."

She huffs but trundles back upstairs.

Hoping for a bite to eat, I make my way down the main hall to the kitchen, following the pungent aroma of herbs and magic. Moist heat slaps me in the face As I push open the swinging door. Gudrun's working away on some potion or another. Her strawberry-blond hair has escaped its bun and is clinging to her sweating red face. She's athletically stirring the bubbling contents in a massive pot. I reckon I wouldn't be amiss to call it a cauldron. Rosemary-perfumed steam wreaths her head.

Julianna's already there, lips pursed in disapproval. She must have come through the dining room. "Really, darling, must you do that in here? We have a perfectly serviceable workshop in the cellar for your concoctions."

Gudrun shoots her a good-natured smile, unperturbed. "The light's better up here, Jules. And the chickens can't wait. Widow Hartley's been without eggs for a week now."

Julianna sighs, but her eyes glow with affection. She reaches out to tuck a stray curl behind Gudrun's ear, her fingers lingering on the other woman's cheek. "What would the neighbors do without you, my love?"

Gudrun's grown her knack for animal husbandry, and by combining minor spells, and potions has turned it into a regular commercial enterprise selling worming tonics, egg laying spells, and whatnot. She and some of the other neighborhood hedge witches meet every month to compare notes, share recipes, and for all I know dance naked under the full moon. But between Gudrun's tonic sales, our six boarders, and renting the extra horse stalls, we haven't had to touch our nest egg. Even if my boss, Garrett, revokes my contract, we'll be fine.

"Auntie MC, I'm ready!" Ylva's voice echoes in the hall. She bounds into the kitchen, a vision in a crisp white pinafore and shiny black boots. Her hair is wrangled into a pair of haphazard plaits tied with blue ribbons.

Pushing worries of Garret and contracts to the back of my mind, I smile. "You look properly attired for our excursion, Wolf Cub. Give your mamas a kiss, and we'll be off."

Ylva dutifully pecks Julianna and Gudrun on the cheek, then slips her small hand into my right one. "Do you think they'll let me feed the monkeys, Auntie MC?"

"I don't know, kid. But I reckon we'll have an adventure either way."

She grins up at me, gap-toothed and trusting, and something eases in my chest. Like Julianna and Gudrun, Ylva's happy here too.

I squeeze her hand, letting her chatter wash over me as we head out into the fleeting San Francisco sunshine to make our way to the trolly. Merchants hawk their wares, children play marbles on the sidewalks, and ladies in colorful bustles stroll arm in arm, parasols bobbing. No sign of hoppies, thugs, or bad actors of any stripe.

Once we climb aboard the horse car and settle into our seats, I let myself relax into the moment. The clop of the horses' hooves, the chatter of the other passengers, Ylva's lighthearted humming beside me.

The ghosts will keep, for now. Today, I have a date with a camel and a little girl who thinks I hang the moon. Plenty of time to find my place.

Chapter Five

THE CLATTER OF THE horsecar fades behind us as Ylva and I join the throng to approach the multistory arched gateway marking the entrance to Woodward's Gardens, the largest amusement park in the city. The place is bustling with families and couples streaming through the gates. I dig in my chatelaine for the admission fee, the coins clinking against the various sundries Julianna insists a proper lady should never be without. Like a thimble. Even when I had two good hands, I had no use for a thimble.

"Thirty-five cents, please," the attendant says, his eyes flicking curiously to my hook before his professional smile snaps back into place.

I drop the coins into his palm, accepting the souvenir map he shoves into my hand. I ignore the persistent twist of self-consciousness. My left hand was victim of a bad man's crazy ritual almost a year ago, during the job that brought Edison into my orbit. The hook came about only a few months ago. Turns out, this city boasts a robust prosthetics industry. Whaling, shipbuilding, large scale slaughterhouses, mechanized textile manufacturing, and all other manner of paying jobs that sometimes cost life and limb have created a commercial opportunity to replace those limbs. The competition keeps the prices low.

Ylva bounces impatiently at my side, her blue eyes wide as she takes in the wonders beyond the gate. "Come on!" She grabs my hand, practically vibrating with excitement. "We have to see everything!"

"Keep your pinafore on. We've got all afternoon." I laugh at her.

We pass through the gate, into a world that could be a thousand miles away from the brick and dust of the city. Towering trees and lush gardens stretch out before us, dotted with strange, enticing buildings. Paths lined with crushed seashell connect the buildings.

"Oh, wow!" Ylva points to a beautiful castle just ahead, its façade a mix of gleaming glass and intricate ironwork. "What's that?"

I consult the little map the attendant handed me. "Says here it's the Conservatory. Want to take a gander?"

Her face scrunches. "Like plants and stuff?"

"Yeah, but weird and exotic from all over the world. Have you ever seen a blue Mongolian poppy?"

"No..." She scuffs her shoe, her nose wrinkled up, lips pushed out. "Let's see something fun."

"Don't come cryin' to me if your face gets stuck like that."

Ylva crosses her arms and huffs.

Off to our right is a low-sprawling building surrounded by taxidermied animals, its daub and wattle façade adorned with curiosities including animal skulls, strange totems, and maybe Nordic runes.

Consulting the map again, I suggest, "What about the museum?" I nod toward the structure. "Says here it includes the Anthropological Museum of Oddities."

"What kind of oddities?" Interest replaces her scowl.

I tweak her braid. "The kind that will put your mama Jules's nose out of joint when she finds out I let you see."

Ylva's face lights up, and she bounces ahead, dragging me in her wake. We stumble up to the shadowed front of the museum. Unlike the conservatory, there isn't another visitor in sight. Even Ylva pauses for a second, confronted with the massive, dark, wood-carved doors flanked by a pair of stuffed Tasmanian Devils. They don't look nearly as fierce as their name. I yank one door open by its iron handle, and we step through, blinking as our eyes adjust to the dim light.

The museum sprawls labyrinthine before us. We skip past cases filled with shimmering minerals that pulse in the flickering light, their hues shifting from deep emerald to blood-red.

Ylva is captured by taxidermied displays of large cats: tigers frozen mid-snarl, lions standing on hind legs, felines I can't even name, with too many teeth and glittering marble eyes. The scent of old leather and preserving chemicals invades my nose.

Moving deeper into the museum, it gets darker. Outside windows are heavily covered or nonexistent. We pass a wall documenting various American scientific expeditions. One daguerreotype catches my eye, the silvered surface reflecting the gaslight as I tilt my head to see it clearly. Two young men in formal dress stand beside what look like ancient stone pyramids rising from dense jungle, their faces serious in that way folks got when posing for those old cameras. The caption reads: *"Yucatan Archaeological Expedition, 1842. Professor A. Temple and Dr. S. Sonderling documenting Mayan ruins."*

Could it be? I lean closer, studying the ghostly images trapped in silver. Hawkish nose, deep-set eyes... That's Loosh, all right. Forty years younger with an unforgiveable mustache, but unmistakable. And the man beside him must be Sonderling. They both look like earnest young adventurers, all stiff collars and determination.

Hell. Loosh's a legit scholar. Or was back in the day. Bet he could tell some tall tales. I'm gonna rib him to death about that mustache come Monday morning.

"Auntie MC!" Ylva's voice pulls me away from the daguerreotype.

An ache starts up behind my temples, New Mexico's parting gift again. Something in this museum besides Ylva wants my attention.

Ylva is blissfully unaware of my discomfort. Her pinafore practically glows in the lamplight as she flits among the displays.

"Look at those dolls!" She squeals, pointing at a row of small, hairy bulbs. To my eyes, they glow with the pinkish light of Animus Mortis. It should be released in death, but the men's souls must have been ritually bound. As I stare, the ache sharpens, grinding like broken glass behind my eyes. Bits of soul trapped, furious, demanding I set them free.

I read the placard below them. South American shrunken heads. They leer back from their shadowy alcoves. Anger pulses off them. Their desiccated features twist as I watch.

"Auntie MC." Ylva's pulling on my sleeve, like she's been trying to get my attention. "Hey! Aunt Mary Catherine, why'd someone shrink their heads?"

I glance down at her, at a loss for words. I swear the heads start laughing.

Nope, it's time for us to go.

"We've seen more than enough spooky to get me in trouble with your ma," I say firmly, taking her hand to lead her back the way we came. "How about we go find those camels you're so keen on?"

She casts one longing look at some unidentifiable medical curiosity bobbing in a murky jar, its pale form swaying in the still liquid, before nodding and racing me to the exit.

Chapter Six

THE HORRORS OF THE museum are blotted away by the laughter and chatter of the crowds that surround us as soon as we step outside. I take a deep breath. The aroma of popping corn and peanuts chases away the lingering tang of formaldehyde.

We beeline to the tunnel under 14th street that leads to the zoo area of the park. Carnival scents are replaced by the ammoniac, hay-rich scent of animals.

Apparently, Ylva isn't the only one with dreams of becoming a camel jockey. The camel paddock is ringed by a line of children waiting impatiently for their turn to mount the swaying, humped beasts. Ylva vibrates with excitement as we take our place in the queue. The little boy in front of us regales Ylva with stories of his camel expertise. He swears the faux Bedouin-garbed handlers are secret assassins with swords under their robes.

Ylva completely dismisses him with a wave of her hand as the line starts moving. I fish a penny from my purse and hand it over to the attendant, then help Ylva scramble up onto the kneeling camel's back.

She giggles with delight as the beast lurches to its feet, her small hands clutching the saddle horn. I hover nearby, ready to catch her if she slips.

As Ylva's camel starts its slow, swaying circuit of the enclosure, my shoulders finally unclench. Nothing scary out here except camel shit and bratty boys.

A voice catches my ear over the din of the crowd.

"Hey, Mick! Mick Kelly."

Edison Colt weaves through the crowd, his gangly frame narrowly avoiding a collision with a woman carrying a parasol. Even from here, I can see that eager-puppy grin splitting his freckled face. His round spectacles catch the afternoon light, and his brown suit, while pressed, hangs loose. Still looks like he raided his uncle's wardrobe, except for the ridiculous pink waistcoat peeking out from beneath the suit jacket. Oh me.

It's been a few weeks since I've seen the kid. At eighteen, he'd bristle at being called that. We'd partnered on that mess in New Mexico, back when he'd lied his way into the Bureau claiming he'd graduated from Boston Metaphysical Academy. His boss demoted him to desk duty when she discovered he was only seventeen and a dropout. From the bounce in his step, you'd never know it bothered him.

But it's the woman on his arm who draws my eye. A tall, striking beauty with dark hair, heavily lined eyes, and too much rouge. She's dressed to the nines in a figure-hugging gown of scarlet silk, cut scandalously low in the front.

My eyebrows climb toward my hairline, but I can't stop them. Why on earth would anyone wear red silk for a day at the amusement park? Her clothes and war paint mark her a dance hall girl from the less savory parts of town. This must be Edison's Spanish Kitty. I'll bet she's responsible for his waistcoat.

Edison doesn't seem to notice my shock or doesn't attribute it to his date. He bounds forward, practically dragging the poor girl with him in his eagerness to greet me.

"Mick, I want you to meet Kitty, uhm, Kate Lombard," he says, beaming like a kid on Christmas morning. "Kate, this is Mick Kelly, the best damn bounty hunter and all-around adventuress in the West."

I resist the urge to roll my eyes at his effusive introduction. "Pleased to meet you, Miss Lombard," I say politely, offering my hand.

Kate takes it gingerly, her nose wrinkling slightly as if she's just encountered something foul. "Charmed," she drawls, her voice a husky purr. "Eddie's told me so much about you."

I bristle slightly at "Eddie." His name is Edison, but I keep my smile firmly in place. "All good, I hope," I say lightly.

Edison laughs, slinging an arm around Kate's waist. She leans into him, her ample bosom pressing against his side in a way that makes me want to smack him upside the head.

"'Course it's all good," he says, giving me a wink. "You're a regular legend, Mick. Kate here has been dying to meet you."

I'm sure she's been frothing at the bit, judging by the bored expression on her pretty face. But I nod, not wanting to burst Edison's bubble.

"You'll have to regale us with some of your adventures sometime," Kate says, her tone making it clear that she'd rather have a tooth pulled than listen to my war stories. "But if you'll excuse me, I simply must powder my nose."

She extricates herself from Edison's grip and sashays off toward the nearby facilities, turning every male head in the vicinity as she goes.

"She seems...well...she's a looker," I say, trying to keep the sarcasm from my voice.

Edison, bless his oblivious heart, looks smitten. "Isn't she something? I met her at the Strausburg couple weeks back. She's a real firecracker."

I'll bet she is. But I hold my tongue, not wanting to lecture Edison on the perils of falling for a pretty face and an empty head.

"Listen, Edison—" I lower my voice, glancing around to make sure no one's near. "You heard any rumors or reports at the Bureau about hophead gangs getting violent?"

His expression shifts, the boyish grin fading. "Hopped-up hopheads? No. Why?"

"Loosh and I ran into some at the wharf this morning. They were strong, meaner than you'd think. And there was something else—" I hesitate, not wanting to reveal too much about my recent sensitivity to residual death. "They felt wrong. Corrupted somehow."

Edison's eyes sharpen behind his spectacles. That eager puppy look he gets when something piques his professional interest, same one he got when we were working together last year. The same look when his knack kicks in, showing magical signatures. "Corrupted? Like foul Animus?"

"Not exactly. More like..." I struggle for words to describe the mystical miasma around Toothless. "Like they'd been dosed with something beyond regular opium. Something that left a stain."

"Fascinating." He pushes his spectacles up his nose. "We've been chasing some reports of strange sightings near the docks coming from regular coppers. Boss chalked it up to crimps, shanghaiing shenanigans. Nothing magical. Did you report it?"

I'm caught flat-footed. No, I didn't report it. I'm covering for my partner. Edison would understand the importance of partners. "Uhm—"

"No matter." He cuts me off before a lie can form. Puffing out his chest, he brags, "Workings are gonna leave fingerprints. I can smell 'em in a crowded room." He's cocky enough to make me want to slap him, again. "One of the local coppers reported a sighting near the club Kitty and I are headed to tonight. I'll see what's what."

Something cold touches the back of my neck, but I shake it off. Edison's experienced even if he is stuck on desk duty. He can handle a few hopheads.

At that moment, Ylva rushes up, cheeks flushed with excitement. "Did you see me? I rode the camel!"

I bend down to scoop her up, ignoring the twinge in my lower back. "I did see, Little Wolf. You looked mighty sharp up there."

Edison grins, reaching out to tug one of Ylva's braids affectionately. "Well, if it isn't the prettiest camel jockey in all of San Francisco," he teases.

Ylva laughs at him, her arms looping around my neck. Dear God, this child has grown. "It was the most fun ever! Can we do it again, Auntie MC?"

Before I can answer, a young woman approaches us, a bulky dry plate camera in her hands, large canvas bag across her back. She's dressed sensibly in a plain blouse and skirt, her dark hair pulled back in a no-nonsense bun.

"Pardon me." Her voice is crisp and businesslike. "I couldn't help but overhear. Would you like a photograph to commemorate the young lady's first camel ride?"

Ylva lights up at the offer, bouncing eagerly in my arms. "Oh, can we? Pretty please?"

I hesitate, my hand crushing the nearly empty coin purse at my waist. "Thank you so much, Miss..." I trail off. I don't know the photographer's name.

"Rambound," she supplies, extending a hand for me to shake. "Harriet Rambound. And you won't pay anything today. I'll develop the plate and bring the finished photograph 'round to your residence in a few days, if that suits?"

"All right," I say, setting Ylva down. I imagine Jules would fancy a picture.

Ylva claps her hands in delight. Miss Rambound directs us to a reclining camel, apparently a set piece for her photos. She helps Ylva gain the camel's saddle and positions me beside her.

"All right, that's terrific, we've got the whole park behind you. Smile big now," she instructs, ducking beneath the black hood of her camera. "And hold very still...there!"

There's a burst of bright light as the flash powder ignites, leaving spots dancing in my vision. Ylva blinks owlishly, then dissolves into giggles.

"Thank you," Harriet says. "I'll bring the developed plate round in a few days. Could I have your address?"

I scribble it on her clipboard. She smiles and nods, tips the camel handler a coin, and is gone into the crowd. Edison stares after her admiringly.

"Hey." I nudge him with my elbow, interrupting his ogling. "I was at Calpurnia's this morning. Your ma's been asking after you. Told me to give you a swift kick if I saw you."

Edison has the grace to look sheepish. "I know, I know. I've been meaning to drop by, but I've been busy with...well, you know." He shrugs.

"Women?" I snark, shaking my head.

"It's not like that." He laughs, then sobers. "I'll go to Ma's for dinner tomorrow. I promise. Maybe even drag Kate along, if she's not too hungover."

I grin at the thought of Spanish Kitty swanning into Calpurnia's in that red dress. "You do that," I say neutrally. "I'm sure your ma will be thrilled to meet her."

Edison opens his mouth to reply, but the return of Kate interrupts him, who links her arm through his possessively.

"What did I miss?" she asks, her eyes flicking over me and Ylva as if we're something she's scraped off the bottom of her shoe.

"Auntie Mary Catherine and I got our picture taken!" Ylva pipes up, oblivious to the swirling tensions.

Kate raises a perfectly arched eyebrow. "How quaint," she drawls. Then, turning to Edison, "Eddie, love, I'm parched. Let's go find some refreshment, shall we?"

Edison, ever the gentleman, nods agreeably. "Sure thing, sugar." He tips his hat to me and Ylva. "Mick, we'll catch up. I'll let you know if I find that signature."

"Of course," I say, forcing a smile. "And don't be a stranger."

He gives me a jaunty salute, then allows Kate to lead him away, who shoots me a smug look over her shoulder as they walk to the lemonade stand.

I sigh, shaking my head. "That boy's going to be the death of me," I mutter under my breath.

Chapter Seven

THE APPLAUSE DIES AWAY as we file out of the Grand Theatre Sunday night. There must be 2,000 people packed into this velvet-and-silk palace.

I trail behind Julianna and Gudrun as they walk arm-in-arm, Ylva's small, warm hand clasped in mine. In lieu of this week's rent, Frida had scored tickets for the family for the Sunday performance. The show had been a genuine delight—comedy sketches that made even Julianna laugh, dancing that stayed on the right side of respectable, and music that didn't sound like cats being strangled. A far cry from her usual bawdy performances at the Storybook.

"I liked the lady with the accordion," Ylva announces, skipping a little as we creep toward the exit. "She was funny."

"She was indeed," I agree, adjusting my grip on her hand as the crowd is pinched like cattle at a chute, vying for the exit.

Gudrun's hair glints in the electric light. The Grand is on one of the first electrified blocks of the city. "Such a lovely evening," she says contentedly. "Frida should do more family shows."

Julianna nods, though she looks tired. The charity work she's thrown herself into since we arrived in San Francisco is taking its toll. "Perhaps we can convince her—"

Her words cut off as we finally push through the heavy doors onto Mission Street.

All horse and trolly traffic is blocked, the roadway packed with people. Hundreds of them, packed together in a roiling mass under the harsh glare of the new electric streetlights. A makeshift platform has been erected in the middle, occupied by a man in an expensive suit, his voice carrying over the bystanders through a speaking trumpet.

"—foreign pestilence that breeds in the very heart of our city!" he bellows. "While honest American workers struggle to feed their families, these Oriental invaders spread their filth and disease through our neighborhoods!"

"Oh, hell," Julianna mutters under her breath, her hand finding Gudrun's arm. "It's Kollach."

Isaac Kollach. I've heard the name plenty, usually followed by Julianna's creative cursing. The would-be mayor who's been making life difficult for her charity work, particularly anything that helps Chinese families. But this is my first time seeing him in person.

He's a handsome devil. Tall and broad-shouldered, with the kind of commanding presence that draws attention. His dark hair is perfectly styled, his suit tailored to show off his frame. His stance is pure arrogance.

"We should go," Gudrun says, her usual good humor nowhere to be found.

She's right. The blue-collar crowd suddenly swelled by the swanks exiting the theater is agitated. The faces nearest us appear to be a mix of genuine working folks and hired muscle. The kind of men who get paid to be bully boys—show up at rallies and create noise. Get violent, if needed.

"We're being invaded?" Ylva asks, pressing closer to my side.

Before I can answer, a small figure darts through the crowd toward us. A boy, maybe ten years old, his clothes marking him as one of the street kids who run messages for anyone with a penny. He weaves between the adults seamlessly, his eyes fixed on me.

"Ma'am," he says, bobbing his head. I reluctantly release Ylva's hand to accept the paper he shoves into my hand and melts back into the crowd without even asking for a tip. Weird.

I pocket the note without looking at it, my attention focused on getting my family clear of this mess. We were planning on riding the horse trolly back down Mission, but with traffic blocked, that ain't gonna happen. Kollach's voice booms again, and as the crowd rushes forward, we're getting forced into the fray. Between the people on the street in front of us and the theater patrons pushing for exit behind, we're in danger of being trapped.

"The time for half-measures has passed!" he shouts. "We must cleanse our city of this Oriental contagion before it spreads to our wives and children!"

A roar issues from the throng, and the mood shifts from ugly to dangerous. Someone near the front hurls a brick at one of the electric streetlamps. The glass explodes in a shower of sparks and fragments, plunging the south section of the street into darkness.

"Move," I tell my family, pulling Ylva closer. "Stay together and move northeast toward Third."

But people ain't cooperating. Bodies press against us from all sides as his supporters surge toward the platform. With the theater to my left and Mission Street on my right, I lose sight of Julianna and Gudrun for a heart-stopping moment before spotting Gudrun's pale hair a few yards in front of Ylva and me.

Another lamp goes out. Glass crunches under hundreds of feet, and the entire city block becomes a patchwork of bright light and deep shadow. Some asshole lights a torch. The bully boys came prepared, casting the entire tableau into nightmarish flickering light.

A figure coming from my right stumbles into our path, blocking our progress toward Third Street. At first glance, he looks like any other hoppy—hollow-eyed, gaunt, clothes hanging loose on his frame. But he's not moving like a man lost in poppy dreams. He's moving with purpose, his attention locked on Ylva.

"Clear out," I growl, menacing him with my hook.

Not even sparing me a glance, he reaches toward my niece with pale, claw-like hands.

I grab his wrist to push him back, and ice shoots up my arm. He stumbles back and falls against one of the toughs, who shoves him again.

Shit, it takes me a second to understand what I felt. No pulse. No warmth. No animus. No life at all.

It's a walking corpse, a bona fide revenant. Damn. I hate zombies and the necromancers who animate them.

The thing's head ratchets around toward us, and he starts regaining his feet.

"Auntie MC?" Ylva's voice is small and scared.

Around us, the crowd continues to push and shout, oblivious to the supernatural threat in their midst. A torch near Kollach flares to life, revealing two more pale figures seemingly materializing near his pulpit.

Three of them. Not an army, but enough to cause real trouble.

The first revenant takes a shambling step forward, its dead eyes fixed on Ylva. I could end this thing right here, blast the bejesus out of it with a little Gleaner juice. But not with my family watching. Not with hundreds of witnesses. It seems to be a frail thing. I reckon we're in more danger from the crush than the dead.

"Oye!" Julianna shouts over the chaos. I spot her through the shifting crowd ahead. She's made it to the corner, one arm raised high. "Driver! Please!"

A hackney pulls up, the horse dancing nervously at the rally's energy. The driver looks like he'd rather be anywhere else, but he waits.

Choosing discretion over valor, I scoop Ylva up in my arms and bolt for the vehicle, pushing through bystanders as another brick sails through the air.

The revenants try to follow, but they can't navigate the mob. They're terrible sad sacks for walking dead. Either their maker is lackadaisical or a weakling. But still, zombies inside the city are gonna be a problem.

We pile into the cab in a tangle of skirts and limbs. "Mission District," I tell the driver, pressing coins into his sweating palm.

As we pull away from the square, I catch one last glimpse of Kollach on his platform. He's still speaking, but he's scanning the square. Looking for something.

Or someone.

The note the boy gave me crinkles in my pocket as I settle Ylva on my lap. I unfold and try to read it despite the intermittent light.

Meet me at Calpurnia's 3:00, tomorrow. Else see Phalanx—A

Relief washes through me. Loosh's back from Sausalito, safe and sound. Whatever he's mixed up in, we can sort it out tomorrow.

Who the hell or what the hell is Phalanx? Racking my brain, I can't come up with an answer. I sigh heavily. Just like Loosh to be cryptic even in a simple note. I'll ask him about his musty, old Greek riddles when I see him Monday.

As the cab rattles through the darkened streets, I can't shake the image of the revenant's pale hands reaching for my niece. Three revenants in a crowd of hundreds. We got a necromancer inside the city, however unimpressive. I don't care what Loosh says. His attack at the wharf, now zombies at a crowded political rally. It's time to bring in the Anti Death Mage Division.

Chapter Eight

MY SKULL POUNDS AS I shuffle down the hall toward the kitchen. Sleep came grudging and brief, same as it had for months now. I'd always been prone to restless nights and peculiar dreams, but since that business last year, proper rest felt like chasing smoke. Loosh liked to joke that Morpheus had marked me as one of his special projects. Between last night's revenant mess and whatever the hell had been lurking at the wharf, I'd spent more time staring at the ceiling than sleeping.

The smell of bacon grease hits me first, then, thank all that's holy, coffee. Hallelujah. I'm gonna need both before facing my boss, Garret, at the office.

The kitchen already feels crowded. Julianna's at the stove. Gudrun and Ylva are tucked into their usual spots at the big oak table by the window.

"Morning, Auntie MC!" Ylva chirps, waving a piece of toast at me.

"Morning, Cub." I snitch a piece of bacon off her plate before dropping into an empty chair. My knees creak like old hinges. "Frida make it home all right?"

"Still dead to the world." Julianna nods without turning from the stove. "Didn't get in until near dawn."

Gudrun pushes the coffee pot my way, barely looking up. Newspapers and magazines are scattered in front of her. She loves to keep up on the news. "You look terrible," she mumbles around a mouthful of toast.

"Feel worse." I pour myself a cup of the black oily elixir.

Three revenants in a crowded square. Not exactly unprece-
dented—I've seen necromancers get sloppy before, let their
pets wander. But inside city limits? That takes brass. Or incom-
petence. Either way, it means we've got a death mage operating
in San Francisco, and that's gonna require paperwork I don't
want to fill out.

Odette, one of our boarders, breezes into the kitchen, a
vision in a smart green walking suit and a cunning little hat. Her
dress is perfectly tailored, gently sweeping a curve from bust to
hip. She pauses to press a quick kiss to Julianna's cheek and flash
me a shy smile.

"Morning, Mary Catherine. Love the skirt. That color suits
you."

I glance down at the deep blue fabric, fighting the urge to
tug it straight. "Thanks, Odette. You're looking right fashionable
yourself. New hat?"

She beams, reaching up to pat the jaunty feather adorn-
ment. "Just finished it last night. I'm hoping to show it to
Madame Renault today, see if she'll let me put a few in the shop
window."

"Odette," Ylva interrupts, bouncing a little in her seat. "Last
night was SO FUN! There was a lady with an accordion and
afterward there was the group of bad men outside. They had
torches! And this scary-looking man bumped into us—Aunt
Mary Catherine beat him up!"

Odette's eyes go wide. "Your aunt beat someone up?"

"Well...mostly," Ylva confirms, eyes bright with the thrill of
it all. "Aunt Mary Catherine shoved him with her hook. You
should've seen it!"

I catch Julianna's warning glance and change the subject
quickly. "Just a hoppy, probably. Streets are full of them these
days."

Odette nods, accepting the explanation. She works for a
modiste on Market Street and often trades Julianna clothes and
hats for rent. She gets the most beautiful fabrics. "Frida told

me about the riot when she got home. She said she was so late because Mission Street was closed for blocks."

"Sure, that's why she was so late." I wink, and she giggles.

Gudrun unfolds the morning paper with a disgusted snort. "Speaking of chaos—listen to this horseshit." She reads aloud, "'Chinese Agitators Incite Violence Grand Opera House.' Says here that 'foreign elements attacked peaceful American workers gathering to discuss employment concerns.'"

"That's a damn lie!" Julianna spins around, spatula in hand like a weapon. "There were no Chinese. Just Kollach's thugs raising a rumpus!"

"How'd they even get this to press? It must have been eleven thirty by the time we left?" Gudrun's frown deepens. "The ink's barely dry on what happened."

The pieces click together in my sleep-deprived brain. "Because they knew. Whole thing was planned, and the publisher was in on it."

"It fits Kollach's playbook." Julianna growls. "He's got his grubby hands in the media, too. It's bad enough his thugs are all over the streets, but if he controls the media, he controls public opinion."

Odette's gone pale. "Madame Renault reads that paper religiously. If she thinks the Chinese started it..." She trails off, swallowing hard. "Half of our fabric comes from Chinatown."

"Kollach's got a very long arm." I drain my coffee in one burning gulp. "Which means I need to get to the Bureau, tell them what really happened before—"

Three sharp raps on the front door cut me off. We all freeze.

"Bit early for visitors," The color drains from Julianna's face.

The knocking comes again, harder. Authoritative.

I'm already on my feet, hand drifting toward where my gun would be if I had one. "Stay here."

Before I'm halfway down the hall, a voice booms through the door, "Open up, BMI. We're here for Mary Catherine McClellan!"

Shit. So much for getting there first.

The two BMI agents don't say a word on the walk to Market Street, except I'm wanted by Captain Garret immediately. I don't know either one of them. Field agents at the main office, I guess. Their badges were real enough. I bite my tongue, though questions burn in my throat. I'd planned to march into Garrett's office and let him know about Kollach's thugs and the walking dead. Instead, I'm being escorted like a criminal. The irony isn't lost. Whatever this is about, it ain't good.

The Anti Death Magic Division office squats above Schultz's German Bakery, the smell of fresh bread and cinnamon a cruel contrast to the dingy stairwell we climb. Paint peels from the walls like dead skin. The wooden steps groan under our weight, threatening to give way.

The two-room office itself ain't much better. Two battered desks drowning in dusty files, one clerk who looks like she hasn't seen sunlight since the Grant administration, and a single grimy window overlooking Market Street.

The far wall is festooned with wanted posters. Sketches of necromancers, rogue Gleaners, and worse make a rogue's gallery. One catches my attention.

Hoodoo Jones glares back, gaunt face captured in careful pen strokes. Five-hundred-dollar reward. Last seen Las Vegas, New Mexico.

I flip him the bird. That son of a bitch murdered my best friend and cost me my hand. I'd gladly pay five hundred to be the one who brings him in.

But he's a thousand miles away, and I've got more immediate problems than old grudges.

Supposedly, this office is responsible for defending the United States from all foreign and domestic hostile death magic. Politicians liked to spout about threats from China, Russia, the

Sandwich Islands. You'd never guess from this underfunded, understaffed, and underappreciated shithole. It's the red-headed stepchild to the Bureau headquarters office on Kearney.

My escorts shove me into Captain Garrett's office. He's hunched over some paperwork, face sour as week-old milk. Garrett never much cared for me, resented my presence. I'm a burden foisted on him by Commander Elizabeth Van Lew. I still haven't figured out if this contract was intended as punishment or reward for my service in New Mexico. But Garret resents my connection with Van Lew almost as much as he resents having a woman operative.

"Sit," he barks, not looking up from whatever paperwork he's pretending to read.

I drop into the rickety chair across from him. The agents who brought me stand by the door like gargoyles.

"You attract trouble, McClellan." Garrett finally raises his head, his expression cold above luxurious muttonchops, almost long enough to brush his shoulder. "Like flies to shit."

"Nice to see you too, Captain."

He leans back, the chair creaking dangerously. "Where were you last night?"

"I need to talk to you about that. Took my family to 'Bertha, the Sewing Machine Girl' at the Grand Opera House. We got caught—"

"Can anyone verify that?" He cut me off.

"About two thousand theatergoers." I lean forward. "But listen, Captain, this is important. There were revenants in the crowd afterward. During Kollach's rally. Walking dead, right here in the city—"

"I don't give a damn about Kollach's rallies." He waves me off like I'm a buzzing fly. "That's city police business."

My jaw drops. "Did you hear me? There were undead in the crowd." My voice rises. "Three revenants, Captain. I felt no pulse, no warmth, no life. Someone's raising the dead."

Rolling his eyes, he leans back and sighs. "You saw some drunks stumbling around and your imagination ran wild. Mrs. McClellan—"

I snort at the ridiculous statement. "Come on, sir, you think I don't know a revenant from a drunk?" Almost without thought, I tap the Gleaner. I don't care to be dismissed by this mutton-chopped idiot. "Van Lew assigned me to your division because I know a thing or two about death magics. Do you understand what a Gleaner is—"

Here's the thing about Gleaning; I drink all that delicious power when I ride a death, then I get to decide how to use it. It's energy and energy can do work, move things. Sometimes really big things, and sometimes—I push a flicker of power at the iron match safe on his desk—small things. It rattles before tipping to the floor with a clatter.

Garrett jerks back in his chair, and fear wipes away his disdain. He's scared. Of me. He has no idea what a Gleaner is, but my power threatens him. Here's a man who relies on authority to keep his little kingdom intact, and I'm a wild card in a deck he thought he had stacked. No wonder he acts the prick.

He inhales sharply. "McClellan—"

"Sir, this morning's newspaper lied about what happened. There weren't any Chinese agitators. Kollach planted thugs in that crowd. Maybe he's responsible for the undead too—"

"Enough!" Garrett slams his hand on the desk. "I don't care what you think you saw last night. I brought you in this morning to discuss Agent Temple."

My stomach clenches. Loosh's in trouble. Maybe Garret found whatever Loosh is trying to hide. "What about Loosh?" I ask cautiously.

Garrett's lips curl into something that ain't quite a smile. "Found him floating in the bay this morning. Off Meiggs Wharf. Very dead."

My heart stutters, the blood draining from my face. "What?"

"You heard me. Dead."

"That's..." I swallow hard, trying to process. Loosh. Gone. My chest constricts, cutting off breath. Loosh, who'd treated me like a partner when everyone else saw a dangerous freak. Who'd shared his terrible Latin puns and worse whiskey. Gone. My only ally in this cesspool of bureaucracy. Just...gone. "How?" The question seems to echo in my skull. There has to be a mistake.

"Throat cut." His tone sharpens. "Funny thing is, you were the last person seen with him. Saturday morning, down at the wharf." His eyes narrow, not in grief, not concern. Calculation. Is he looking for guilt? Christ.

"You know we were following up on possible revenant sightings." How much should I tell him? "We were attacked. These dosed hopheads jumped Loosh in an alley—"

"And you didn't report it?" His voice rises. "An attack on a federal agent and you didn't think to inform me?"

"Loosh asked me not to. He wanted to handle it himself." I feel like I'm floating above my body. This can't be real. "I'm investigating, figuring out what happened."

"I don't care what Temple was mixed up with. Probably another antiquities scam. He never could resist. It's what got him fired from the University."

My memory flickers to that photograph at Woodwards, Loosh and that Sonderling fellow grinning beside Mayan ruins. But the thought slides past, drowned under the heat building in my chest at Garrett's words.

"...he was a bad seed. You two were a perfect mach." He dismisses me with a wave of his beefy hand. "We're done here."

My temper rises, my cheeks burning. "Are you wool-headed?" I slam my hands on his desk. "We have an actual necromancer in the city. I saw revenants, touched one. There have been reports from the docks for weeks. An agent was attacked and then murdered. It's all connected. I'm your best agent for this kind of investigation."

"McClellan, you're unreliable and overly imaginative. I can't use you in my department." He rises, looming over the desk. "Consider yourself suspended."

"Who got to you?" I accuse, leaning forward. "Someone's paying you to look the other way."

"Get out." His voice drops to a dangerous whisper. "Before I have you arrested on suspicion of murder."

"You think I'm just a bitch with a knack for trouble?" I stand on shaky legs, fighting the urge to smash his face in. Upend the desk, vent my grief and rage on his stupid muttonchops. "I'm more dangerous than you realize, Garrett. I don't toe the line. I erase it."

The agents who brought me in take my arms and pull me toward the exit. Garrett's practically quivering, his whiskers shaking. "Don't leave town."

⁂

I push through the outer door into the hallway, my hand still shaking. Loosh's dead. Garrett's a compromised idiot. I straighten my spine. Screw them. Ain't my problem anymore.

"Mick?"

Leona Freeman. The Bureau's star agent, lioness shapeshifter, and once upon a time, one of my closest friends. Her golden eyes, the ones I haven't seen in over a year, pin me in place.

"Leona!" Unbidden warmth blooms in my chest, quieting the rage for a moment. I throw my arms around her before I think better of it.

She hugs me back, tight and fierce. "God, I've missed you."

"You can't even imagine." I pull back, drinking in the sight of her. She looks good. Damn good. Expensive tailored jacket, her dark skin glowing with health and success. "Look at you, all fancy and official."

Her head tilts, reading me like she always could. "You look terrible."

"Thanks." The warmth drains away as reality crashes back. I fight the urge to grind my teeth. "Got some sad news."

"I heard shouting." Her brow furrows as she glances at the closed door behind me. Her hand still on my good arm. "Are you all right?"

"Not so much." The words come out bitter. Leona goes still. "What are you doing here? I thought you were assigned to the Portland office?"

"Leading a task force." Her whole face lights with pride. "We're after a Russian smuggling ring. Got a fellow on the inside. Looks like they're using whalers to distribute mystical contraband. And since all roads lead to San Fran, here I am."

"Sounds important. Good for you. Really."

"I could use your help." She brightens, energy sharpening her voice. "Your experience with magical artifacts. Word is they got hold of something major. Your expertise could tip the balance."

"Leona—"

"No, listen. It's not like the small potatoes you've been stuck with here. Thatcher loosened the purse strings. Real resources, real backing. I'm gonna poach Edison for my unit." Her smile turns conspiratorial. "Can you imagine? The three of us back together? Like old times, but official."

My chest tightens. Edison, Leona, and me. "I can't."

"Why not? Whatever Garrett said—"

"It's not about Garrett." It's a bit about Garrett. But I'm sick of being supplicant on the Bureau's altar. I pull free from her grip. "I'm done with the Bureau." I adjust the straps of my hook with sharp, angry movements.

"Mick, that's ridiculous. You're one of the best..." She sighs, pulling a card out of her reticule. "I'm staying at the Palace Hotel. When you change your mind—I know you will—come find me."

I take the card, fingering the heavy card stock.

"I mean it. This city's about to explode, and we're desperately understaffed. But more than that…" She chucks my shoulder gently. "I need someone I can trust at my back."

I shake my head. "Trust me. After this morning, my name's mud around here. You don't want that stink on you."

"You're wrong about that." She straightens her jacket. "You've always been your own worst enemy, Mick Kelly."

"Everyone calls me 'McClellan' now. Kelly's off the record."

"Fine, whatever, Mick. But—"

Behind us, the department's door opens, cutting her off.

"Agent Freeman? Captain Garrett's ready for you now."

Leona's mouth twists. "Duty calls. But think about what I said." She grasps my hand. The three of us, together again. Doing what we do best."

She stalks into Garrett's office, her head high. Garrett ain't gonna know what hit him.

Starting down the stairs, my mind is churning. Loosh's dead. My job's gone. And my best friend is offering me a lifeline I want no part of.

I need a drink. Hell, I need several.

Chapter Nine

I HEAD STRAIGHT FOR Calpurnia's, Loosh's note burning a hole in my pocket. The walk from Market Street to Pier 10 passes in a blur of anger and grief. Loosh's dead. The words keep repeating in my head like a phonograph. Dead. Floating in the bay. Throat cut.

He was alive yesterday. Alive when he sent that note asking me to meet him. Alive and scared and needing help.

And I was at the goddamn theater.

The clock above Schultz's Bakery reads half past two. I'm early for an appointment with a dead man.

Dock workers haul cargo, oblivious to my turmoil. Life goes on. It always does.

I slam through Calpurnia's door. A few faces turn my way, but most ignore me. The familiar smell of sawdust and stale beer envelops me. The usual afternoon crowd's quiet, huddled in worried knots. A few regulars are bellied up to the bar. But no one at darts, no cards or dominoes in sight, just hushed whispers.

"Mick!" Abby's behind the counter, but the moment I appear, she rushes around it. Her face is drawn tight with worry. "I was just going to send a boy to get you."

"What's wrong?" Besides my partner murdered and me being suspended, that is.

"Have you seen Edison?" Her voice cracks. "He didn't come for dinner last night."

For Christ's sake. He's eighteen in the most corrupt city on the coast. "Maybe he's just—"

"No." She cuts me off with a hand on my arm. "Emma went to his office. He didn't show up for work today, so she checked his rooming house. His landlady said his bed wasn't slept in. No one's seen him since Saturday." Her fingers tighten on my forearm.

When I saw him at Woodward's Gardens with that woman. Kate. Spanish Kitty.

"Did Emma ask around? Maybe he stayed with...a friend?"

Abby sighs and puts her hands on her hips. "Mary Catherine, don't go and try to shield my sensibilities." She clicks her tongue. "His 'friend' came asking after him earlier. Kitty ain't seen him either and she was pissed. Says he was supposed to meet her at the Bella Union last night. She scored him a seat at a high-stakes poker game. He never showed."

I lean on the end of the bar. Loosh's note feels heavier in my pocket. Two men connected to me, both missing or murdered within hours of each other.

Abby wrings her hands. "Emma spent the morning asking at all his usual haunts. The gambling halls, the boxing gym, even that awful place on Dupont Street where they fight roosters. Nothing."

"Could be sleeping off a bender somewhere."

She shakes her head violently. "I put the word out on the docks. Every sailor, longshoreman, and frog catcher I know. Nobody's seen hide nor hair of him." Her voice drops. "But there have been more sightings."

"Sightings?"

"Revenants, weird hoppies. Whatever they are." She leans closer, lowering her voice further. "Down near Meiggs Wharf."

Where Loosh's body was found. I press my palm to my forehead. "I need to ask. Loosh sent me a note. Said to meet him here today. You know anything about that?"

She looks confused. "Agent Temple? No, haven't heard from him in weeks. Why would he want to meet here?"

"Don't know." My head drops before I roll my shoulders and continue. "He's dead." The back of my throat aches. "They found him in the bay this morning."

Her hand flies to her mouth. "Oh. Hell."

"He sent me a message last night. Said meet him here 'Else Phalanx,'" I say, gauging her reaction. "Do you know what it means? Someone or something called Phalanx?"

Her brow furrows, confusion replacing the worry. "Phalanx? Never heard of it."

A grizzled sailor, hunched over his mug at the bar, looks around and manages to focus in our general direction. He's bleary-eyed, and his beard's a tangled mess, like seaweed or worse. "Phalanx?" he slurs. "Ain't that how them old Spartans fought? Shoulder to shoulder, spears pointing out like a forest o' death."

I turn to him. "What?"

"Phalanx," he repeats, shrugging. "Old battle line, y'know. Damn near unbeatable, them Spartans were."

He returns to his beer, muttering into the froth. I don't know about no Spartans, but I file it away. Typical Loosh. Even facing death, he's gotta be clever with his classical references.

"Okay." I lean against the scarred wood, suddenly exhausted. "Listen, about Edison—"

"You'll find him?" Desperation edges her words. "Maybe with your Bureau contacts?"

"I don't have any Bureau contacts, Abby." Might as well tell her. "I'm suspended. As of this morning."

"Your boss is a saphead." She doesn't even blink. "Please, Mary Catherine."

"You think'n he's been nabbed, shanghaied?"

"No." Her tone rises. "He's a federal agent. Folks around here know that. And everyone knows he's my son. There's not a crimp house in the city that would touch him."

She's probably right. No one with a lick of sense would go to war with her, even so, "Can your uncle have a look-see, just to be sure?"

Uncle Nico is revered on the wharf. He is one of three men who walked away from the Farnsworth disaster in '76. Surviving the worst Arctic whaling catastrophe in living memory made him something of a legend. Along these docks, word reaches him before the tide turns. Nothing happens here without Nico knowing it.

"Aye, he's already out there. Gonna swing back by later if he finds anything." She looks at me pleadingly. "Please."

I bite my lower lip, then nod. "Jesus, Abby. Of course I'll look into it." Edison is one of my best living friends. And what else am I gonna do? Sit at home, join Julianna's charity work? "Do you know where Kate lives?"

"Damn. I didn't think to ask." Then she brightens. "But she hustles pool at The Strausburg most nights."

Loosh and I worked a case there a few months ago. Concert saloon, gambling den, and brothel all rolled into one. Disreputable but pure "normie" establishment, no magic except what floats in with the clientele.

"I'll go tonight." I straighten up. "We'll both go. You know the docks better than me."

"You think he's alive?" Fear sharpens her voice.

"Of course he's alive." I hold her gaze. "BUT Loosh's dead and hopped-up hopheads and revenants are wandering the streets. We'll err on the side of caution."

"The new drugs," she says suddenly. "You asked about them last time you were here. What if Edison stumbled onto something?"

Possible. It would be just like him to willy-nilly stick his nose where it don't belong. Idiot.

"We'll start with Kate tonight," I say. "Eight o'clock? Meet here?"

"Yes." She grabs my hand, and squeezes tightly. "Thank you, Mick. Edison is...well, Edison...he's my boy."

"We'll find him," I promise, hoping it's not a lie. Turning to leave, I say. "Eight o'clock. Be ready for trouble."

"Aren't I always?" she calls after me.

Outside, the afternoon sun reflects off the bay like shattered glass. Somewhere out there, Edison might be floating like Loosh.

The faint burn of past deaths hums at the edge of my senses, calling from every shadow. A year ago, I was as unaware as the next mage about magical residue left by a soul's passing. No remnants buzzing in my brain from some random Joe's murder.

Now there's almost constant noise when I pass through places where someone died. A low hum. A pull. I catch glimpses of the ghosts of folk I've never met. Hoodoo's Equinox ritual in New Mexico took Morgan, cost me a hand and turned me into some kind of crooked death-compass. I don't know what it means, I don't love it, but I'll use it if I can.

Tonight, Spanish Kitty and I are gonna have a chat about Edison. And if she knows more than she's telling, well, I've got ways of making people talk that don't require Bureau authority.

The thought should disturb me more than it does.

I find Julianna and Gudrun in the front parlor, heads bent over the household ledger. The moment I enter, the ledger snaps shut.

"What's happened?" Julianna's on her feet, crossing to me in three quick strides.

"Loosh's dead. Edison's missing." The words rush from my mouth. If I talk fast enough maybe they won't ask too many questions. "I need to go into the Barbary Coast tonight. Find him."

Gudrun sets down her teacup with a careful clink. "The dead are walking, aren't they? I can smell it on you."

Leave it to Gudrun to cut straight to the bone. "Yeah. Revenants in the city. And I'm suspended from the Bureau, so I've got no backing."

"Suspended?" Julianna's voice climbs. "Mary Catherine—"

"Edison's been missing since Saturday night. Maybe longer." I sink into the wing-back chair, exhausted. "I promised Abby I would help."

Julianna paces to the window, arms crossed tight, and stands there, frozen. She turns and spears me with a glare. "You're talking about going into the Coast without backup, without authority, while someone's murdering federal agents."

"You're just repeating what I said."

Her voice sharpens. "Where I stand, you're talking about robbing Ylva of her aunt. Leaving us without—" Her chin wobbles. "Things were supposed to be different in San Francisco."

Gudrun rises, moves to Julianna's side, and puts an arm around her shoulder. "I threw the bones last night," her arm tightens. "There's something dark in the city."

"All the more reason to find Edison before—" I can't finish the thought.

Julianna's shoulders slump. "You're going regardless of what we say."

I nod once.

She sighs. "What do you need?"

"Your blessing would be nice."

She crosses to me and cups my face in her hands. "You have it. But you come back, with all your limbs? This house, Ylva, our life here—none of it works without you."

My throat tightens. "I'll be careful."

"No," Gudrun says firmly. "You'll be smart. That world doesn't respect careful. It respects dangerous."

She's right. I push myself up from the chair. "I need to change. Can't go prowling the Coast dressed like a respectable landlady."

Upstairs, Mary Catherine McClellan hangs in the wardrobe. Respectable skirts. Pressed blouses. I reach past them for canvas and gun leather. The weight of the Colt is an old, ugly comfort. I strap the holster tight, checking the cylinder out of habit. Five rounds. The knife goes in my boot, handle positioned for a quick draw.

By the time I'm done dressing, the woman in the mirror isn't a landlady. A year ago, I'd have seen a monster. The Gleaner in me, always hungry, always reaching for the next death. I'd believed power made me like Lafayette Baker. Like Hoodoo Jones. Took a long time for the visions of my last encounter with those two to fade... How they killed my best friend Morgan, took his heart for their foul ritual.

Now I see the real Mick Kelly. Who survived the war. Who rides death for justified power. Who does what needs doing. I touch the glass, staring at my own reflection. "Let's go find Edison."

Downstairs, Julianna's breath catches. "I forgot," she whispers. "I forgot what you looked like before."

"Not before," I correct her, checking the knife in my boot. "Just...underneath."

Gudrun squeezes my hand, a quick, fierce grip. "Give 'em hell, Mick."

"I'll be back before dawn."

"You better be," Julianna says fiercely. "We've got a lunch date tomorrow. If you don't return, I'll come looking for you myself."

The thought of my proper sister storming the Barbary Coast almost makes me smile. Almost.

I pause at the door and take one last look at my family. Then I step out into the darkening night, leaving Mary Catherine McClellan behind.

Time to see what Mick Kelly can find in the dark.

Chapter Ten

THE WHARF AT NIGHT is a different creature than its daylight self. An uneasy quiet replaces shouting stevedores and clanging cargo hooks. Fog rolls in thick as cotton batting, muffling everything down to whispers and water slaps. Occasional oil lamps glimmer through the gray mist. Somewhere in the murk, riggings creak.

I'd had months to grow accustomed to the humming death sense, but still hadn't. Sometimes it's faint, like a kettle simmering on the edge of hearing. Other times it rattles my teeth. Tonight, the wharf thrums with it, old violence soaked into the timbers. I pull my coat tighter and keep walking.

A new feeling starts between my shoulder blades, not magic. That prickle that says something's watching. I slow my pace. The fog swallows sound, but I catch low murmurs from somewhere ahead. Some crew's unloading in this soup.

A splash in the water stops me. I approach a small dock and see movement in the dark waves. At first, I figure it for a seal like the one this morning. But the movements are wrong. Pale arms wrap around the pilings, a head covered in long, tangled hair emerges. I start to run and help the poor soul, then skid to a stop as the woman gracefully pulls herself onto the dock. I fight a chill running over my scalp.

She raises an alabaster hand, fingers beckon me. Oh, for Christ's sake. I don't have time for another dead thing with a sob story. But curiosity tugs me a few reluctant steps closer, keeping out of reach of those long, white arms.

Up close, I glimpse her face behind the dark curtain of hair. Her features are sharp, eyes huge and dark.

She's crooning, not quite words, not quite song, focused on the wharf at my back. The hair on my neck stands to attention. No vitae. Not a flicker of living warmth anywhere in her. Where a person would pulse with the yellow glow of life, she's hollow. But she's not empty. Animus crackles across her form like heat lightning, bright and fierce and entirely her own. No fading remnant clinging to the world out of spite. Whatever she was before death, the dying made her into something else. Something with roots in the bay itself, fed by the water, shadow and whatever violence put her there.

I've seen this before. Human once. Not human anymore.

Her eyes pin me in place, bright and sharp, and she smiles, revealing small, predatory teeth. "He speaks so pretty, makes such promises. But his hands are cold, cold, cold," she whispers, her voice like the murmur of water in lungs.

"You talking about someone specific?" I move closer, curious.

"The sweet-talking man." She tilts her head. "The one who walks with shadows. The one who makes the dead dance."

I sigh, here's another creature trying to lure me into her twisted web of intrigue. Seems like my new sensitivity is gonna drag up every murdered soul in the bay. "All right then. Thanks, I'll keep that in mind."

"I must tell you. He'll promise you things." She twirls a matted strand of hair while studying me. "Don't listen."

"Okay." I shrug, not sure what to make of any of this. "Why do you need to tell me?"

She resumes her soft crooning, her focus drifting across the bay. I think she's forgotten I'm here. She slips back into the water, but before sinking beneath the surface, she answers, "Because you'll help Phalanx."

"Wait!" I rush to the edge of the pier and drop to my knees on the wet planks. "What do you know about Phalanx? Who—"

But she's gone. Not even ripples to mark where she went under. Just black depths.

I stay there a moment, staring into the darkness, my mind racing. How the hell does this thing know about Loosh's message? Unless...unless Phalanx isn't a thing. It's a person. Someone Loosh knew. Someone this creature thinks needs protecting. Maybe from the sweet-talking man?

How'd she know I'd be here?

I push myself to my feet. There are more things in heaven and earth, I remind myself, adjusting my coat before pressing on to Calpurnia's. The world abounds with creatures and it's more than I'm worth to try to fathom their wants. But this one knowing about Phalanx? That ain't coincidence. That's a warning.

Chapter Eleven

LIGHT SPILLS WARM FROM the windows of Calpurnia's, cutting through the fog like a lighthouse beacon. The rumble of conversation and clink of pewter mugs reaches me before I touch the door. I push through into warmth, tobacco smoke, and the yeasty smell of good beer. The usual crowd of sailors pack the tables, hunched over their mugs, arguing and laughing in half a dozen languages. Queen Vicky gazes down serenely from her portrait by the door.

Abby's ready to go, decked out in trousers and a knit sailor's cap. She's leaning against the bar beside her Uncle Nico, a barrel-chested Norwegian with a handshake like a bear trap. He nurses a beer, surveying the room the way seamen read the weather. Nico survived the Arctic ice, walked home when his ship went down. Half the captains in the bay still buy him drinks on the strength of that feat alone.

Taking in my canvas pants, gun belt, and pale face, Abby frowns. "You look like you've seen a ghost."

"It wasn't a ghost." I tell them both about my encounter with the water spirit. The Phalanx reference, though I keep to myself.

"That'd be the rusalka." Nico sounds matter of fact. He wipes beer foam from his mustache with his sleeve. "She's been haunting the bay since before the Rush. Some say she's a ghost. Some say she's worse."

My money's on worse. A creature with that much Animus dancing under her skin is definitely worse.

Abby nods along. "I've never seen her myself. Legend has it she only appears to those acquainted with death." Her attention flicks to Nico, then back to me. "That's you right down to the ground, Mick."

"She likes to watch the ferry come in from Sausalito, when she's not luring pretty sailors to their deaths." Nico takes a long pull of his beer. "I don't believe the tales of her dragging men to the depths. But I've heard her singing, once or twice. On still nights." He sets the mug down carefully. "You don't forget it."

While Abby drains her glass and gives Nico instructions to close up, I consider the encounter. She didn't lure me; she warned me about a sweet-talking man. Could the rusalka know something of Loosh's death?

Abby pats Nico's shoulder before turning to me. "Ready?"

I nod once. "Let's go find out what Spanish Kitty knows."

We step into the chill night, heading for the Strausburg Music Hall. The fog has thickened, swallowing our footsteps.

⁂

Pacific Street thrums with vice and violence. Every other doorway spills light and laughter, piano music competing with fiddles, accordions, and the occasional shriek of delight or fury. Abby and I shoulder through crowds of sailors, miners, and swells slumming for a thrill. The Barbary Coast don't sleep, and even on a Monday night, it's just getting warmed up.

The Strausburg Music Hall squats between a deadfall and a faro palace, trying hard to look respectable with its painted sign and doorman in a threadbare uniform. Inside, it's all mahogany woodwork and burgundy wallpaper, crystal chandeliers throwing rainbow sparks over the crowd. Pretty waiter girls in low-cut gowns work the room, leaning close to whisper in men's ears, laughing at jokes that ain't funny.

The clientele's a mix: dock workers with their week's pay burning holes in their pockets, clerks in cheap suits pretending they belong, and a few genuine swells who probably shouldn't be seen here.

"Pool tables are in back," Abby murmurs, nodding toward an archway draped in threadbare red velvet.

We push through the crowd. The room's hazy with cigar smoke, quieter except for the crack of balls and low-voiced wagers. Spanish Kitty holds court at the far end, bent over a shot that shows off her assets to the three men watching. She sinks the seven ball in the corner pocket, then straightens with a satisfied smile.

"Kate," I call out.

She turns, and her smile dies. "You. Edison's friend." Her dark eyes flick to Abby. "And his mother. I already told you, I haven't seen him."

"Tell us again," I say, moving closer.

Kitty's jaw tightens. She lays the cue down and waves off her companions. "Fine." She scoffs. "Saturday night, we were at the Lotus Club. Eddy's luck at craps had cooled off. Around ten, he said he had Bureau business to follow up on and he left." Her voice rises slightly. "Then he never showed for the poker game last night. You know how hard I worked to get him that seat? Jimmy Callahan's private table don't open to just anyone."

"Bureau business?" I press. "What kind?"

"How should I know?" She fluffs her bangs, and scowls. "He got that look, you know the one. Like a dog with a scent. Said he'd be back in an hour." Crossing her arms, her lips perse. "That was two nights ago."

Abby touches her arm. "You're concerned too."

Something flickers across Kitty's face. Vulnerability quickly masked. "I'm pissed is what I am. That seat cost me favors I can't afford to waste."

Abby's right, though. The tension in Kate's jaw, the way her fingers worry at the cheap bracelet on her wrist. She cares about Edison.

"Who might know something?" I ask. "Who runs information in this part of town?"

Kitty barks a laugh. "You're joking, right? You want me to point you at Gold Tooth Mary?"

Beside me, Abby goes still. Not scared exactly, but wary. "Mary Hunter," she says. "You sure about that, Mick?"

I turn to her. "You know this woman?"

"I know enough to know she doesn't do favors." Abby's voice is careful, measured. Not the brash woman who keeps drunken sailors in line with a truncheon. "She runs half the rackets south of Market. Information, theft, extortion. If she helps you, you owe her. And Mary always collects."

"Can you get me to her?" I ask Kitty.

"No." She picks up her cue and chalks the tip violently. "I don't know where she holes up, and even if I did, I wouldn't tell you. Mary don't take kindly to people bringing trouble to her door."

"Edison could be in real danger."

"Edison's always in danger. Comes with the territory." She lines up another shot. I pull just a tiny trickle of power, a nudge to the tip of her cue. She scratches. "Shit."

I pull out a ten-dollar bill and set it on the rail. "What if we make it interesting?"

Kitty eyes the money, then me. "What kind of interesting?"

I pick up a cue from the rack and test its weight. "You set up a shot. I make it, you arrange an introduction to Gold Tooth Mary."

"And if you miss?"

"The money's yours and we leave."

She considers, then starts arranging balls across the felt. Three stripes clustered tight against the far cushion, the eight ball kissing the short rail by the corner pocket, cue ball trapped behind a wall of solids. "Eight ball, corner pocket. But you have to bank it off two rails and jump the five."

The men who'd been watching drift closer, sensing blood in the water. One whistles low. "Can't be done, honey. Not even you could sink that."

Kitty smiles prettily at them. "That's the point."

I study the setup, calculating angles. Without help, she's right, it's impossible. But I've got help she doesn't know about. I lean in, bridging the cue on my hook, and let just a trickle of stored energy flow into my arm. Not enough for anyone to notice, just enough to give a little extra English.

The crack of contact echoes through the room. The cue ball leaps the five and kisses the first rail. I give it another tiny push, and it spins off the second rail, cutting the eight ball to drop into the corner pocket with a satisfying *thunk*.

Silence.

"Jesus Christ," one of the men breathes.

Kitty's face drains of color. "How did you—"

"I'm motivated." I set the cue down. "Now. Gold Tooth Mary."

She stares at me in shock for a long moment, then turns away. "Wait here."

Kitty weaves through the crowd to a young man in a tailored suit standing near the bar. His clothes are too fine for this place—pearl buttons, silk vest, shoes that actually shine. She whispers in his ear, gesturing at us. He looks our way, frowns, and says something that makes Kitty's shoulders tense. She argues, quiet but fierce. Finally, he nods and leaves.

She stalks back. "Fine. Mary will see you. Tonight."

"Good—"

"But not her." She jerks her chin at Abby. "You come alone or not at all."

"Like hell," Abby starts.

"It's fine," I cut in. "Where?"

"Now. Through the back." Kitty's already moving. "Take it or leave it."

I squeeze Abby's arm. "Go home. I'll come by when I'm done."

"Mick—"

"Go."

Abby studies me, jaw working. Her hand tightens on my shoulder. "You better come back." Then she nods and heads for the front door.

I follow Kitty wending her way toward a door marked "Private" in peeling gold letters.

"One more thing," Kitty says, hand on the knob. "Mary's got...security. Don't make any sudden moves."

She opens the it. The hallway beyond is narrow, lit by a single gas lamp. At the far end, filling the entire hall, lounges the biggest grizzly bear I've ever seen. A thick chain runs from its collar to an iron ring in the wall.

The bear lifts its massive head, nostrils flaring.

"You've got to be kidding me," I breathe.

"Mary likes to make an impression." Kitty starts forward. "Just stay calm. He can smell fear."

The bear rises to all fours. Its eyes track us as we approach, lips pulling back to show yellowed fangs the size of my fingers.

Kitty stops just out of reach of the chain. "Evening, Ephraim."

The bear huffs, sits back on its haunches, and dips its great head. Not a nod exactly. But not *not* a nod, either. Kitty approaches and he bumps her hand with his muzzle, gentle as a dog greeting its owner. She scratches the bear behind one ragged ear barely breaking stride.

"That's it?" I ask.

"What did you expect? A password?" She pushes the door open. "Welcome to Gold Tooth Mary's. Try not to die."

Chapter Twelve

THE DOOR OPENS INTO another world.

Where the Strausburg was cheap glamour and tobacco smoke, this place breathes money and menace. Persian rugs cover polished floors. Chinese silk screens divide the space into intimate alcoves. A crystal chandelier that belongs in a Nob Hill mansion throws rainbow light over what is probably stolen art from every corner of the globe: oil paintings, woodcuts, African masks, and what looks like a genuine Grecian urn.

Young men pack the space, but these boys ain't your average Barbary Coast muscle. Like the man out front, they're dressed to the nines in silk vests, gold watch chains, shoes polished to mirrors. They cluster around card tables and lounge on velvet settees, but attention shifts our way as Kitty leads me deeper into the lair.

And at the center of it all, presiding from a throne-like chair that might've been lifted from a French palace, sits Gold Tooth Mary.

I'd expected her to be rough, homespun, and weather-worn. But Mary's elegant. Maybe my age, give or take, with ramrod posture and a bearing associated with "good breeding" and finishing school. Her brunette hair's styled elaborately, framing her face, and her green silk dress sets off striking dark eyes. You'd take her for the governor's wife if you passed her on Market Street.

Until she smiles.

The gold tooth catches the light like a warning. Behind her, three maybe four shades hover at the edge of my perception. Not threatening. More like...attendants. Guards. Perhaps ghosts of those who served her in life and can't seem to stop in death?

"Mary Catherine Kelly," she says, her voice pure Dublin aristocracy with just a hint of street underneath. "Or McClellan now, I understand. The woman who killed Lafayette Baker."

Every tough in the room goes still.

"That's me."

Mary gestures to an empty chair across from her. "Please, sit. Kate, thank you for the introduction. You may go."

Kitty hesitates. "About Edison—"

"We'll discuss young Mr. Colt momentarily." Mary's tone brooks no argument. "Privacy, if you please."

Kitty shoots me a look, part warning, part apology, then disappears back the way we came.

Settling into the gilt chair, I note how the young men have arranged themselves. Not randomly. Strategic. Every exit covered just in case things go sideways. They might dress like peacocks, but they know their business.

"Nice bear you got guarding the door," I say, keeping my tone casual as I lean back and cross my legs. "Don't see many grizzlies working security."

Mary's laugh ripples through the room like music. She's charming. Half her crew gazes at her calf-eyed. "Ah, yes, poor Ephraim. Only one of his natural forms, you understand. He's a shifter, though not by choice at the moment."

"Ephraim?"

"Ephraim Whitmore. Perhaps you know the name? His father owns half the shipping contracts in the bay." Mary sips from a crystal glass of what looks like sherry. "Young Ephraim developed quite the gambling habit. Terrible at cards, I'm afraid, but convinced he'd inherited his father's business acumen."

The ghosts behind her shift and seem to whisper amongst themselves. Agitated, though Mary doesn't seem to notice. Or maybe she's used to it.

"So now he's your guard dog?"

"Guard bear," she corrects, gold tooth flashing in a hard smile. "And only temporarily. He lost heavily, poor dear, bit of a self-control issue when it comes to cards. Ephraim works off his debt in a form that suits me and ensures he can't access the family lawyers. Quite elegant, really."

"How long's temporary?"

"At the rate I've set... Another six months should clear the ledger. Less if he proves particularly useful." Mary sets down her drink with a delicate clink. "I'm not cruel, despite what you may have heard. Everyone who enters my service does so by choice. Poor choices, perhaps, but their choices nonetheless."

One of the toughs flanking her fusses with his waistcoat, and I catch the glint of knives under his vest. Mary reads my attention.

"You're wondering if you could take them," she says. Not a question. "The answer is yes, probably. You did kill Baker, after all. But then you might never find young Edison. T'would be a great tragedy."

My shoulders tighten at the innuendo. "You know where he is?"

"I know many things. Information is my true currency, Ms. Kelly. Or do you prefer Mick?" Her head tilts, regarding me. "Yes, I think Mick suits you better. Mary Catherine is the woman who lives in that lovely Italianate townhouse in the Mission with her sister's unconventional family. The woman dismissed by the cowardly Captain Garrett. But Mick, Mick is the one who walks into my parlor carrying death on her shoulders like an old friend."

Now she's just showing off. "Edison's been missing since Saturday. His mother wants him back."

"Abigail Colt." Something shifts in Mary's expression. Respect, maybe. "It's unlikely anyone would put that boy on a ship, knowing whose son he is. Ms. Colt earned her bones on the docks. Even the worst crimps know better than to cross her. I doubt he's been shanghaied, so..."

"Look, Mary, I'm tired of this game. You know all my business. Good on you." I roll my shoulders, working at the knots building there. "Can you help me find him or not?"

Mary settles back on her throne, eyes glittering as she studies me. How could I have thought she resembles a governor's wife? Half lying there, indolently swathed in emerald silk, she's more a barbarian queen, a regular Morrigan, ready to command me thrown from the sea cliffs. Damn criminal masterminds always love the drama.

"Perhaps we can help each other? Your particular...talents could be of use to me."

The hum in my bones, little pricks of old death. The shades flicker more brightly, roused by her power or by my Gleaner. Finally, we're getting to the nut. "Uhm, how so?"

"I represent a consortium interested in acquiring a rare Chinese antiquity that was being offered for sale. Unfortunately, the item has been...withdrawn."

Fingering the gilt arm of my chair, I frown. "I don't really understand—you mean someone nicked it?"

That gold tooth winks. "Such a crude term. Let's say it's been misplaced. My clients would still very much like to acquire this item."

"Okay, what exactly is this antiquity your clients find so interesting?" I uncross my legs. Garrett said Loosh had been tangled up in the antiquities market. Maybe there's a connection? Or maybe something to do with Leona's Russian smuggling ring?

"The Nü Gua Jade." Mary rolls the phrase out with a theatrical lilt, the barest hint of a smirk threading her tone. "Named for the goddess who saved the world from chaos."

She rises from her throne and moves to a lacquered sideboard. Her ghosts trail her.

"Supposedly, it's carved from a single large piece of imperial jade." She pours herself another sherry and offers me one with a raised eyebrow. I shake my head.

She returns to her seat, cradling the crystal glass.

"Mystical?" I ask, brow quirked.

"Some say it holds the power of creation itself." Mary sips the sherry. "Though that seems rather grandiose, doesn't it? What matters is that it vanished hundreds of years ago until it resurfaced in India a mere forty years past. Seems some East India Company nabob 'liberated it.' But when he came to a tragic end it was lost again." Leaning forward her voice falls to a faux whisper. "Three weeks ago, word spread through certain circles that the Nü Gua would be offered at a private auction, right here in San Francisco."

Enchanted artifacts. Of course it's enchanted. Because my life isn't complicated enough. The last thing I want is to get tangled up with some ancient goddess's token. But anything for Edison. One of Mary's ghost attendants drifts closer, drawn by something in the jade's story. Or maybe just by me.

"But," I say, "it never made it to auction."

"No." She swirls her drink, studying the amber liquid. "The broker arranging the sale went quiet. Someone known as Professor T."

Professor T as in Aloysious Temple, maybe? Dead would be incommunicado in most circumstances. "How did you get in touch with this Professor T?"

"It was all very clever and anonymous. He initiated contact through a messenger. Then via a series of epistles passed through rotating drop locations. But Professor T never retrieved my last communication." Mary slams back the rest of her drink, her knuckles white around the cut glass.

"Mary, I don't believe that you didn't make it your business to know who you're dealing with." Women like her don't stay on top by trusting anonymous letters and shadow games. Maybe Loosh's friend Sol has a bead on this jade. If Loosh was mixed up in it, Sol might know something.

"The point is, Miss Kelly, I need to find the jade and get it into responsible hands." The delicate crystal threatens to shatter in her grip. "There are those who'd use the Nü Gua for less...constructive purposes." The crystal chimes as she plonks it onto the side table. "Someone less high-minded could corrupt its protective properties. Turn it into something quite nasty indeed."

I use my hook to carefully scratch behind my ear while I think. I need to tread carefully. Last thing I want is to put myself under her thumb, but I would do worse for Edison. "You said you deal in information. Seems you're better equipped than me to find the jade." Shifting forward, I prop my elbow on my knee and and fix her with a direct stare. "What do you want me for?"

Mary reaches out and touches my hand. "Join me for dinner. We'll discuss details more privately." Then standing she waves and the room clears, her toughs file out. "My cook is excellent. She's Creole, from New Orleans."

My stomach chooses that moment to growl. I haven't eaten since breakfast. No harm in breaking bread. "Fine. But remember I'm here on account of Edison."

"Of course." She flutters her fingers dismissively.

We're soon seated together by a softly glowing fire, alone except for Mary's hovering shades and a silent serving woman. The woman brings course after course—soup, fish, beef that melts on the tongue. Mary pours wine that probably costs more than I make in a month.

"So," I say, cutting into beef dressed with crab and some kind of buttery sauce. It's a tad awkward skewering the steak with a fork wedged into my hook, but I need my hand to work the knife. "What do you want from me?"

"Protection."

I pause mid-bite, my eyes widening. Mary's got a whole crew of well-trained men at her beck and call. "From what?"

"Revenants." Mary says it casually, like mentioning rats in the cellar, but the way her hand tightens on the linen napkin hints at fear. "Or something like. They've been lurking around my townhouse, my places of business. They're always watching." Her voice creeps up in pitch.

"Describe them," I say. "These revenants."

Mary's brow furrows. "Pale. Gaunt. But they're quick. Why?"

"Because what you're describing sounds like the spiffed-up hoppies I ran into the other day. They're rough, but they've got a heartbeat." I think about the attack on Loosh. "True revenants are walking corpses."

"Does it matter what we call them?" Mary snaps. "They're following me. Watching me."

Mighty Mary's got a weak spot, bingo. "You know any necromancers in the city?" I pop food in my mouth. I'd seen zombies my own self, felt their coldness at the Kollach rally. Someone is raising the dead, and Mary might know something.

"None capable of animating humans. And none who would dare move against me." But uncertainty flickers across her features. "I suspect the Celestials. They have their own magics."

I snort and drop my knife. "Why in heaven would the Chinese sic zombies on you?"

Mary's eyes flash dangerously. "Those heathens aren't above intimidating an innocent businesswoman to get what they want."

The casual hatred in her words makes my stomach roil. I've seen enough blood spilled over that kind of thinking, watched good men die in ditches while rich folks spouted poison about preserving their way of life.

Her accent thickens with anger. "Ah Toy wants the jade and she knows I stand in her way. I'm aligned with true Americans, Mick. It cannot fall into yellow hands."

"That's enough." I push my half-eaten plate away in disgust. Whoever this Ah Toy is, I don't need to get scooped up into whatever business Mary is conducting, Edison or no.

"Mick, please." She takes a breath, composing herself. Reaching across the table, she touches my wrist. A spark—static?—jumps between us, so brief I can't be sure it happened. My pulse stutters. "Forgive me, Mick. Respect is...precarious for women like us. We can't afford to show weakness. You understand, don't you?"

"Women like us?" The room tilts slightly. I blink, refocusing on her smile.

"Those who refuse to be what they tell us we should be." She pats my wrist, then refills my wineglass. "Tell me, do you regret killing Lafayette Baker?"

The question catches me off guard. Where were we? The jade. Edison. Something about— "No," I say , uncertainly.

"Good. Regret is useless weight." She leans forward. "I've heard other stories too. Billy Lee Wonder. The vampire nest in Nevada. You've lived more in your years than most do in a lifetime."

A blush warms my cheeks. "You're well-informed."

She sips her wine. "I admire you, Mick. You take what you need to survive and don't apologize for it. That's rare in a woman."

There's something in her tone, not exactly flirtation, but interest. Recognition. Like I'm looking in a dark mirror. Something warms in my chest.

Mary drums her fingers on the table. "I have concerns that something is siphoning my vitality. I believe it's related to these special hopheads or revenants or whatever is following me."

Checking through my Gleaner sight, I examine her vitae, her life force, looking for anything mystical affecting her. No sign of corruption, but I realize she's a good bit older than she looks. The careful makeup, the coiffed hair, it's armor against time. "It's just age, Mary."

Her expression chills. The ghosts behind her fade, and I think I've gone too far. Then she throws her head back, and throaty, genuine laughter erupts.

"Christ, you've got balls." She pours herself a shot of whiskey from a crystal decanter and downs it neat. "Maybe you're right. Maybe I'm just old and scared."

"Didn't say scared."

"No, you didn't." She smiles. "Will you take the job? Be my bodyguard, help my people secure the jade?"

"What about Edison?"

"I'll put the call out tonight. Every eye at my command will be looking for him. If he's in the city, we'll find him."

I consider. I don't trust her. Hell, I'd be an idiot to trust her. But she's got resources I need, and something about her calls to me. Her refusal to apologize for what she is, maybe.

"All right. But I work my way, and I don't hurt innocents."

"Agreed." She stands, extending her hand. "We start tonight. You come with me to the Night Market."

Our hands clasp. Her grip is cool and dry.

For the first time since Garrett suspended me, I feel hopeful. I've got a job, a purpose, and maybe a way to find Edison.

Even if it means working for the most dangerous woman in San Francisco.

Chapter Thirteen

I FOLLOW MARY INTO the alley, the dim glow of the gas lamps dissipating into the shadows behind us. Our footsteps echo in the narrow passage as we approach a heavy wooden door.

"Ready?" Mary shoots me a bored look, her expression devoid of even a hint of the thrill pulsating through my chest.

"Ready as I'll ever be," I mutter, adjusting my coat.

Three of Mary's boys flank us. Tommy, a lanky Irish kid with quick hands and knives tucked in his garters. Brass's fancy suit strains around his arms and shoulders. He's built like a prizefighter, with a permanent scowl. Connor's cherubic face is pink beneath a stylish bowler.

As we reach the end of the alley, I clock two figures huddled in a doorway across the street. Hollow-eyed, hunched, the telltale waxy pallor of hop addicts.

"Friends of yours?" I murmur to Connor.

He barely acknowledges them. "Mary's shadows. They've been trailing her for a week now. Better the ones you can see than the ones you can't."

Funny. Mary hadn't sounded like she thought they were harmless when she'd asked me to protect her from them.

"And you let them?"

Connor adjusts his bowler. "Boss doesn't want us starting fights with every hophead who looks her way. Bad for business."

Mary raps on the door with the head of her walking stick, three quick knocks, pause, two more. A slot I hadn't noticed slides open at eye level, revealing nothing but darkness beyond.

"Fortuna's wheel turns," Mary chants, her cultured voice carrying just enough to reach whoever lurks inside.

"And fools ride with it," comes the response, gravelly and suspicious.

The slot snaps shut. Bolts scrape and tumble, then the door swings inward on well-oiled hinges. A hunched figure steps into the shadow, gesturing us through.

We descend a narrow staircase, the air growing warmer with each step. The smell of incense and ozone, herbs I can't name hits me first, and underneath it all, an electric tang that makes my fillings ache.

Then we reach the bottom, and the Night Market opens before us like a fever dream.

Electric lights blaze high overhead, strung between rough-hewn support beams holding up what I assume is the Palace Hotel above us. The illumination is harsh, unlike the flickering glow of gas lamps.

"Christ," I breathe. "How—"

"That charming little Jesuit, Father Neri has been quite generous with his new technology. For the right price." Mary sweeps forward like she owns the place. Seems her fingers are in all the pies. The light shines off the navy silk of her coat. "I contributed to the new roof on St. Ignatius."

A warren of stalls and makeshift shops stretches deep into the hotel's cavernous basement. The air is thick with the hum of conversation. I trail Mary through the crowd. Folks clear out of her way, stepping aside automatically.

Vendors hawk their wares in seemingly every language known, creating a symphony of sound more diverse than even the wharf. Spanish, Italian, Portuguese, and what sounds like Russian flit through the air, whispers of secrets shared. An Ohlone man gestures animatedly, deep in conversation with a dark-skinned woman adorned in a colorful head wrap, offering bundles of herbs that promise remedies for all nature of malady.

But no Chinese. Not a single queue or silk robe in sight.

"Where are the—" I start.

"They have their own markets," Mary cuts me off, her tone making it clear the subject is closed. "Their own ways. Better for everyone."

I bite back a response. *Pick your battles, Mick.*

Every stall is crammed with the impossible. Bottles of liquids that glow without heat. Books bound in leather I hope isn't human.

I'm drawn to a display of songbirds. The proprietor is a young woman perched on a high stool, a raven clinging to her shoulder. One iron cage holds what looks like a regular canary until the small yellow bird sings three notes, bursts into flame, and falls to a pile of ash, only to reconstitute itself moments later. The vendor smiles at me, while her raven croaks out a price that would buy a coach and four. Jesus, Mary, and Joseph.

I quick step to catch up to Mary. Grabbing her arm, I pull her to a stop while her boys fan out to form a perimeter. "There is real magic here. Does the BMI know about this place?"

"Don't be fooled. It's not all real." Mary's laugh is musical, mocking. She slips her arms through mine companionably and continues walking. "Of course they know. Or some do. They choose to look away."

"That's impossible." I stumble over the words. "The Bureau keeps magic hidden, keeps normies safe."

"Mick, darling." She pats my arm like I'm a child. "How many federal agents do you think are stationed in San Francisco? Five? Maybe ten with that new task force? Now consider how many regular police patrol these streets. Perhaps three hundred on a good day, for a city of half a million if you count the transients?" Her gold tooth twinkles. "They can't be everywhere. They focus on the threats that matter, anything that might make the *newspapers*. A little market where desperate souls buy harmless charms and potions?" She shrugs. "That's just commerce."

I huff, cursed hypocrites. My last CO, goddammed Elizabeth Van Lew, threatened me with conscription for exposing normies to the supernatural. All those years hiding what I was, working to keep Bureau secrets, and here it is, thriving under electric lights and the goddamned noses of the local BMI.

Mary stops and nods toward a booth decorated with wooden cut-outs of geese. "I need to speak with Madame Auberjonois," she releases my arm. "Her dues are past due. Feel free to explore. No one will challenge you here, but stay close to Connor. And Mick?" Mary's expression hardens. "Don't cause trouble."

She glides away, Brass and Tommy in her wake. Dark-haired Connor stays near me, slouching picturesquely, thumbs hooked in his pockets.

I drift into the market's depths, past a German peddler hawking golem charms and a woman pressing "magic" Carolina rice into willing hands. The absence of Chinese faces nags at me, especially after Mary's pointed comment.

"Mary mentioned someone called Ah Toy earlier," I say, keeping my voice casual. "Thought all the big Chinatown players were men."

Connor lights a cigarette, cupping the match against a phantom breeze. "Most are. Miss Toy ain't most people." Smoke curls from his lips as he studies a stall claiming to sell "Genuine Atlantean Artifacts." More like cheap stoneware someone's dipped in Mission Creek.

"Mary don't cross her?"

"Hell no." He flicks ash onto the packed earth floor. "An associate of Mary's tried to open a crib on Jackson couple years back with Chinese girls. No wages, just beatings and opium. Thought hiding behind Mary's name would keep him safe."

We pause at a display of bottles filled with liquid labeled invisible ink. Connor studies them like he's interested, but his voice stays low and conversational.

"Ah Toy sent two old accountants around with ledgers and very polite questions. Week later, the house was empty, the girls were working for themselves up on Dupont, and the fella was on a ship to Hong Kong with a broken arm and no teeth."

He shivers, just a little, then moves us along toward a display of prosthetic devices. "Folks say Miss Toy doesn't raise her voice. She raises the bay. They got an understanding now. Mary stays out of Chinatown business, and Miss Toy don't interfere with hers."

I'm about to ask more when I hear the laughter. Mean and sharp.

A cluster of Paddy toughs have cornered an old man against a support post at the end of the basement. The guy's at least seventy if a day, gray as driftwood, with one leg ending in a wooden peg. Probably a retired sailor. A collection of small statues is arranged on a tattered blanket on the ground beside him.

"Greek artifacts, he says!" One of the toughs, a red-haired bruiser with a sprinkling of freckles and an accent thick as oatmeal, kicks at the statues. "More like shite."

"Please," the old man begs through a heavy white beard. "I'm just trying to make an honest living—"

"Honest!" Another tough, grabs the old man's collar. "You're peddling garbage to honest folk, you are. Ought to toss you and your rubbish in the bay—"

I never could countenance bullying. Assholes.

"Hey." I step into their circle, my voice flat. "Leave him be."

Red Hair turns, sizing me up. When he notices the hook, I see the calculation there. Woman. Crippled. Easy to ignore.

"This ain't your concern, love. Run along before you get hurt." He sneers.

I smile. It isn't a nice smile. "I don't run. And I don't ask twice."

The second boy moves toward me, hand dropping to his belt. I catch the glint of a knife handle. "Big words for a—"

I don't let him finish. I backhand him. The tough falls back, blood streaming from his cheek where the point of my hook tore his flesh. Red Hair lunges, but Connor sighs heavily and steps in with a knee to the ginger's gut and an elbow to the back of his head. Red hits the ground hard. Connor adjusts his suit coat with a blasé glance at my would-be attackers.

The third kid, younger and apparently smarter, recognizes Conner as one of Mary's crew. He retreats, with his hands up. "Sorry for the misunderstanding. Please give my best to Missus Mary."

"Smart kid." I watch him help his companions up as they disappear into the crowd, Red Hair stumbling and the other clutching his bleeding cheek.

"The boss told you to stay out of trouble," Connor scolds me halfheartedly before flipping a nail file out of his pocket. Rolling his eyes, he directs a disapproving sigh in my direction before slouching against a nearby support post and recommencing his manicure.

I turn to the old sailor. He's gathering his pieces with shaking hands, trying to wipe the dirt off them with his sleeve.

"You all right?" I ask, kneeling to help.

"Aye, thanks to you, miss." He clutches one of his statues to his chest. "I'm Jack. Jack Smith. Kind of you to come to my defense."

"These really Greek?" I ask, examining one of the figures. It's crude, but it almost glows in the harsh light, maybe carved from alabaster.

"Brought 'em back from Crete, I did. Forty years ago, when I still had both legs and a captain who didn't mind a bit of personal cargo." He smiles sadly. "Used to be a bit of a collector. Now I'm just a sad old beggar."

"Sounds like you've been around. Maybe you could help me?" I ask while I help him wrap his little figurines back into their protective rags.

He pauses, studying me. "Maybe. You lookin' for something in particular?"

I glance over my shoulder. Connor's still assiduously filing his nails out of ear shot. Jack seems like someone who might know a thing or two. Lowering my voice, I ask, "You hear anything about a fancy Chinese jade coming through town?"

Jack's face drains of any remaining color and he starts shoving his statues even faster into his bag. "No, no, ma'am, I don't know a thing about no jade." He avoids my eyes.

Bingo. Following a hunch, I ask, "Any chance you know my friend Agent Temple, Aloysius?" From what I've learned about Loosh in the last twenty-four hours, it seems likely that he and Jack might have crossed paths.

His lips purse, and he squints hard at me from under his shaggy white brows. "He really a friend of yours?"

I nod encouragingly.

Jack sighs. "Yeah, I know Loosh." He settles a little more comfortably. "He's a good man. A real scholar, not like most of these shysters." He gestures at the chaos of the market. "Comes down here sometimes, looking for genuine pieces." He taps one of his statues. "Bought a few from me over the years."

"Jack." I lean closer. "Loosh's dead. They pulled him out of the bay this morning."

His already stooped shoulders seem to collapse. His voice is barely a whisper. "Oh hell. Told him he was yanking the wrong tiger's tail." Jack dashes what could be tears away with the back of his hand.

"What do you mean?" I touch his shoulder. "What was he mixed up in?"

"Just…" Jack hesitates. His watery gray eyes brim with tears. "I don't know the particulars. You gotta go see Sol. Proprietor of Arachne's Castle. Sol will know what's what."

Sol Sonderling. The name from the museum, from Loosh's daguerreotype. Of course. I've been so focused on Edison, I missed it. Those two old villains have probably been up to no good for forty years.

"Thank you, Jack." I press a silver coin into his palm. "For the information and the statue." I pick up one of the crude figures, some ancient god with a trident.

Jack plucks it from my hand and rummages through his pockets. "Here, you need this one. It's special." He passes me what might be some kind of fish lady. "Protection from the deep."

I stand, tucking the statue in my coat pocket, I search for the rest of my party. I can just glimpse Mary finishing with Madame Auberjonois, who looks to be in tears. Brass and Tommy are each carrying heavy bags, I assume representing Mary's fee for protection. But my mind is racing ahead.

Sol Sonderling. Arachne's Castle is gonna be my first stop in the morning.

Connor materializes at my elbow. "Ms. Kelly? We're moving."

Saluting Jack, I follow Connor through the electric-lit warren, past the impossible and the improbable, past magic being bought and sold like produce at a farmer's market.

Chapter Fourteen

THE COOL AIR'S REFRESHING after the stifling warmth of the Night Market. Mary sweeps up the alley toward Market Street, her boys flanking her like well-trained dogs. I follow, my mind churning over what Jack told me. Sol Sonderling. Arachne's Castle keeps coming up.

"Per your request, The Lotus Club next," Mary announces as our coach rattles up, the driver tipping his hat. "Bit of a low-class den, but they pay on time. Usually."

The Lotus Club is the last place Edison was seen. Kitty said he slipped out Saturday night, mentioning Bureau business. Never came back.

Climbing in I settle next to her on the velvet seat. Tommy and Brass squeeze into the bench across from us. Connor joins the coachman in his box. The coach lurches forward, wheels clattering over cobblestones. Through the window, the city slides past alternating shadows and lamplight, the occasional burst of noise from a saloon.

Mary's watching me while Tommy and Brass debate which are the most admirable charms of someone named Siobhan. The conversation suggests the two of them are cousins and the lovely Siobhan won't give either the time of day. Pretending to ignore Mary's regard. I keep my mouth shut about what I learned from Jack. I wanna speak to Sol without Mary and her boys at my shoulder.

Within minutes, the carriage turns onto a side street, and Mary raps on the roof. The coach stops. Tommy jumps down first, then Brass. Mary gathers her skirt and, barely touching Tommy's hand, climbs down. I follow her out. We're near the mouth of an alley. Judging from the signs painted on the building, we're near the Lotus Club's kitchen entrance. My boots skid on slick stones, greasy from the gutter running into Pacific Avenue.

Brass, Tommy, and Connor form up around Mary without being told. The passage stretches into shadow, lit only by a single gas lamp halfway down. The coach rattles away.

That's when I see her.

A girl, maybe sixteen, is crouched against the wall a few yards past the kitchen door. Her blonde hair catches the streetlamp's light. Her dress is hiked over her knees. But it's the waistcoat she's wearing that freezes me, even in the dim light: bright pink silk, garish, and expensive.

Edison's waistcoat. The same ridiculous thing he'd been wearing at Woodward's Gardens.

"Hold on." I run into the alley before Mary can protest.

"Mick, we're on a schedule—"

Ignoring her, I drop to one knee beside the blonde. Up close, she's worse than I thought. Hollow-eyed, gaunt, with that waxy pallor I've come to recognize. Hoppy, for certain. She looks up at me with pupils dilated to the size of wagon wheels.

A couple yards farther in, I register three, maybe four figures lounging against the opposite wall. Unfocused stares, shoulders hunched, swaying slightly to internal music as they drag intently on cigarettes. More of Mary's shadows, I figure. Same vacant-eyed watchers Tommy shrugged off outside the Night Market.

"Hey," I say softly, beside her. "Where'd you get that fancy vest?"

She blinks at me slowly, like she's decoding my question. Then she grins. "Pretty, ain't it?" Her words slur as she strokes the silk covering her chest. "Traded for it. Man didn't need it no more."

My heart hammers against my ribs. "What man? Where is he?"

"Mick." Mary's voice carries, sharp with impatience. "We don't have time for this."

A glance shows Mary's tapping her foot at the alley mouth, irritation clear on her face. Brass and Tommy flank her. Connor's watching the street.

"Just a minute," I call, then turn to the girl. "Please. The man who gave you this." I poke at the waistcoat. "What did he look like?"

Her head lolls. "Same as all the rest, I suppose. Two legs, two arms..." She giggles, high and disconnected. "'Cept this one sees colors. Sees them dancing in the air, he does. Says they're pretty. Purple and gold and..." She trails off, head lolling back.

Someone who sees magical signatures dancing in the air...

"Edison," I breathe, grabbing her shoulder. "You're talking about Edison Colt. Where is he?"

The girl's head pops up, eyes going wide at something behind me. I turn, the loitering hoppies, the ones I'd dismissed as harmless, had stopped their swaying and watch us intently.

And there it is. That hum crawling up my spine, the same sick reverberation I'd felt on the men at the wharf. I'd been so focused on the girl I'd walked right past it.

"Oh shit." Her voice drops to a terrified whisper. "Was supposed to keep my yap shut. Wasn't supposed to—"

Ice slides down my spine. "Mary—" I scrabble to my feet.

The hoppies move. Fast.

Not the shambling shuffle of addicts. Nope, they're purposeful. Three shapes detach from the shadows, and two more emerge from deeper in the alley. Five total.

"Down!" I push the girl into the doorway as the first closes on me. But he barely looks at me as he shoves me into the wall, heading toward the girl. She scrambles backward, whimpering. The attacker grabs her ankle and starts dragging her out of the doorway. I regain my feet and jump on his back. My weight drives him face-first into the cobblestones.

Mary's boys are in motion. Brass catches one hoppy with a meaty fist, but the scrawny little shit doesn't fall. He takes the abuse and swings back. Tommy's got a blade out, dancing with two others.

"Protect Mary!" I shout at Connor, who's already put himself between his boss and the assailants. But they aren't even glancing in Mary's direction.

One of the hoppies waltzing with Tommy breaks away and charges in my direction, trailing blood from numerous slices from Tommy's knife. He runs straight for the doorway where the girl's cowering. I've got my hands full of the first hoppy's greasy hair as the man beneath me bucks and writhes.

What is happening? They aren't doing shit to protect themselves or to inflict much damage on me or the boys. But they seem determined to shut up one drugged-out woman.

Smashing my guy's face into the street, I try to scramble up—

The bastard grabs my ankle. I fall, chin cracking against stone.

Another set of tattered boots races past my face into the doorway. Damn it, the fifth guy.

Two of them now. On one terrified girl.

No time to think. No time to be circumspect.

Power I'd absorbed from Toothless Saturday still crackles under my skin. I've been hoarding it. But the girl's screaming, and I'm done being careful.

Visualizing a great wind, it grabs both the men swarming the girl and yanks. They fly backward, slamming against the opposite wall. One hits the ground and doesn't move.

Silence. Except for the girl's ragged breathing and the ringing in my ears. Mary stares at me, her mouth slightly open.

Connor mutters, "Bloody hell—"

The men fighting Tommy and Brass all stop and stare. Even Brass looks shocked, and I'd have thought nothing could surprise him.

Climbing off the man I've straddled I make for the girl. As I reach her, she makes a small, surprised sound and crumples. A knife protrudes from her chest. That fucking pink waistcoat is practically black now. Blood pools beneath her in the lamplight. I feel her death approaching.

The remaining attackers shake off Mary's boys and scatter like roaches, disappearing into the night.

I don't think. Just act. My hand finds the girl's chest as her last breath rattles out. "Please, please tell me where Edison is." I doubt there's enough of her conscious mind left to hear me. As I crouch in that damp, cold alley, my focus narrows to the pulsing knot of energy tethered to the ravaged husk of her body. The moment her heart stops, Animus Mortis is freed and breaks over me. Awash in her death, I drink it down, praying for answers.

Running through friendly darkness, chasing fireflies as a river chuckles to my left. Bare feet in soft earth. My lungs burn from exertion and laughter. The stars above spin and I'm falling down, down into darkness. Cold. A cellar. Stone walls slick with moisture. I'm holding a cup of water to a boy's mouth. Freckled face, cracked glasses. A hand on my shoulder pulling me away. Fetid breath in my ear. It spins away like water down a drain, fading to nothing but blackness.

I stumble backward, pulling my hand from the girl's motionless chest. The vision shatters. I'm back in the alley, gasping. The girl's animus burns in my veins, the Gleaner sated and thrumming with power.

Edison. Alive. Chained like an animal in the dark.

The relief hits first, loosening something tight in my chest that's been wound since learning of Edison's disappearance. Then the horror. Three days. He's shackled three days, bruised and broken, trading his ridiculous vest for water from a prostitute.

Then the shame hits with bile rising in my throat. I just rode an innocent girl's death. Fed on her like a goddamn vampire. And she'd been trying to help him. Keeping him alive. Goose flesh creeps up my arms as the shade of the girl appears across the alley, staring at me with accusing eyes.

⁓∞⁓

"Mick?" Mary's voice is uncertain.

I look up. Mary's staring at me, her boys beside her. Behind them, at the edge of the lamplight, the girl's shade watches. Pale. Accusing. Patient.

"I..." Swallowing hard, I taste blood. "Edison. He's alive."

Mary crouches beside me, heedless of the blood. "You're certain?"

"I saw him. She was bringing him water. He's chained in a cellar somewhere."

"Jaysus, Mary, and Joseph." Connor's crosses himself, his face gone pale. "Back at the market, when those toughs were closing in—you could've done that? Sent them flying like you did these boys?"

"Could've." I meet his eyes, seeing the fear there, the wonder. "But I can't go throwing folks around willy-nilly, can't draw attention to myself."

"So, at the market, if those boys hadn't backed down..." Connor trails off.

"You'd have been scraping me off the floor." I force a smile that feels stiff, like my face is gonna crack around it.

"Opportunistic parasite," Tommy whispers. He's crouched by the girl's body, wrapping her gently in his coat. He starts murmuring something into her ear, "...may your soul, through the mercy of God, rest in peace..."

He's praying for her soul. Past his shoulder, her shade stands motionless, watching him tend to what used to be her.

I could've let her bleed out without touching her, let her death pass me by. But I'd wanted the power. Wanted the answers.

Mary's watching me, calculating. "That was impressive, Mick. Truly. I'd heard stories about Gleaners, but seeing it..." She trails off, something almost like admiration in her voice. "You're more valuable than I realized."

I don't know how to respond to that. The girl's animus still hums in my veins, making everything sharp and clear. My Gleaner sated, at least for now.

I hate myself for loving the feeling.

Mary's silent for a moment, processing. Then standing, she turns to her men. "Brass, Tommy, clean this up. Make it look like hopheads killing hopheads. The usual story. We need to clear out."

Brass salutes. "I'll fetch the coach, ma'am."

"What about her?" Tommy nods at the girl's body.

"Take her to St. Ignatius. Get her buried right."

It's more than most would do. More than the girl probably expected from this city.

"Tell me about the vision," Mary says, turning back to me. "Everything you saw."

Closing my eyes, I reach for the fragments before they fade completely. "She knew whoever's holding Edison. She was..." I hesitate, then push forward. "She was servicing him. Prostitute, I think. He told her to bring Edison water, keep him alive. 'Not a word to anyone.'"

"Did you see his face?" Mary asks sharply. "The man giving orders?"

"Tall, thin. That's all I caught. Well-spoken. Sick, though. His breath...there's something wrong with him." I open my eyes. "The girl felt sorry for Edison."

"Where?" Connor leans forward. "Where's he being held?"

"Stone cellar. Damp, water seeping through the walls. He was chained by a collar around his neck." The memory churns my stomach. "He couldn't stand fully upright. Had to stay half-crouched."

"Our attackers, the hopheads," Mary says, her tone shifting. "They weren't here by accident."

"No." The choreography of the attack was deliberate. "Were probably watching when we went into the Night Market, followed us to the Lotus Club."

"But they didn't attack until we entered the alley," Connor points out.

"No, it was when I said Edison's name." I realize. "Not to attack Mary. To silence the girl."

Connor looks from me to Mary, understanding. "They didn't want her talking about Edison," he says.

And then the thing that's been nagging at me clicks into place. The one who grabbed my ankle. The ragged scar running down his jaw was red, still healing. Right where my hook had torn through Scarface's cheek at the wharf three days ago.

"It's one operation," I say, still thinking. "The ones who jumped Loosh and me at the wharf, the ones following you, and now this. All the same hand."

"Someone who wants the jade?" Mary asks.

"Has to be. Someone who thinks you'll lead them to it." The girl's vision flashes through my mind. "They're not trying to kill you. They're watching you. Hoping you'll find the jade for them."

"But why kill Loosh? Why take Edison?" Connor asks.

"Loosh knew something about the jade. Or they thought he did." Jack at the market and Garrett at the Bureau both said Loosh was neck deep in shady antiquities business. "Edison's different. He's a detector."

Mary's gaze sharpen. "Meaning?"

"Edison can see magical signatures. Enchantments, workings, residue. If he's seen a mage's handiwork once, he'll recognize it again anywhere. Like matching handwriting."

Connor sees it. "So, if the lad stumbled across magical workings he recognized Saturday night..."

"Then he can identify whoever's behind it." Edison leaving Kitty at the Lotus Club, saying he had Bureau business. At Woodward's he said he was interested in some copper's revenant sighting. Shit. "He didn't get grabbed because he's useful. He got grabbed because he's dangerous. He recognized someone."

The coach rattles up to the alley mouth. Brass holds the door open, his face grim. "We need to move, ma'am," he says. "Don't want to be here when the coppers arrive."

Mary nods, already gathering her skirts. I follow her into the coach, conscious of the blood drying on my hands.

Through the coach window, as we pull away, I catch one last glimpse of the alley. The shade stands where the body had been, alone under the gaslight. Still watching. Still waiting.

I look away first.

⁊⁊∾◑◐∾⁊⁊

The coach rattles over cobblestones. Beyond the glass, gaslights flicker against the dark.

Mary shifts restlessly. "Connor, send your feelers out. If Mr. Colt's being held in the area, someone's seen something."

"Aye, I'll have Seamus rally the magpies."

"Magpies?" I ask. "Like birds?"

"Naw. Magpies are the young'uns, the up-and-comers. Kids from Irish Hill looking to earn a way out." Connor pulls a cigarette from his vest and rolls it between his fingers without lighting it. "Little blighters can slip in places my men would get noticed."

"We need to make good on our promise to Miss Kelly to locate Mr. Colt. Tell them the first one to find Colt earns my personal gratitude and a position at the club." Mary says, "But remind them of the importance of discretion."

"Aye, ma'am." Connor nods.

Something nags at me. Scarface. Three days ago I hooked him hard enough to tear his jaw open. That kind of wound doesn't heal in three days. It festers, swells, puts a man on his back. But tonight he was fast. Strong. And the others, those wasted bodies, cloaked in the same malaise, hitting like men twice their size, shrugging off Tommy's blade like it was a bee sting.

That takes serious resources.

I stare at the blood on my hands. "Who has this kind of reach?" I ask. "Money, magic, a network of hopped-up thugs spread across the city?"

Mary's thoughtful, her expression unreadable in the dim coach light. When she speaks, her genteel accent is replaced by a harsher tone. "It's most likely the Chinese, that old bit of laced mutton, Ah Toy."

"Mary." I lean forward. "Who hired you?"

"Several local businessmen pooled resources. Steel investors, mostly." She sighs, a delicate sound of resignation. "But the primary backer is Isaac Kollach."

"Kollach?" The memory of his rally surges back, his poisonous words, the mob howling for Chinese blood, the revenants lurking in the crowd. The man who hired Mary to find the jade. "You're working for him?"

"I'm working *with* him, darling. There's a difference." Mary fiddles with the lace on her sleeve. "Mr. Kollach is a respected civic leader with deep pockets and an interest in acquiring valuable antiquities."

"He's also stirring up race riots and getting people killed." My voice hardens. "And if he wants the jade badly enough to hire you, what's to stop him from running his own operation on the side? Using hoppies as his spies to track your progress, maybe trying to cut you out entirely?"

"That's absurd—"

"Is it?" I press. "He has the money. He has the connections. Politicians hire all sorts of people to do their dirty work. What if he brought in a necromancer? Someone to rough up competition, silence witnesses, keep tabs on you?"

"You're wrong about him." Mary's voice takes on an edge, sharp enough to cut. "His concerns about immigration are shared by many honest working people."

I stare at her, disbelief warring with anger.

"He's protecting American interests." Her eyes flash, and her voice shifts, becoming smooth, honeyed, almost musical. "Think about it, darling. Someone has to stand for what's right."

The anger burning in my chest...slips away. Like trying to hold water in my hands, the fury drains out of me, leaving confusion in its wake. What was I angry about?

I open my mouth to argue. "I... I suppose..." The words feel thick on my tongue.

Kollach. The thought was about Kollach and the Chinese. But the it's indistinct now, dissipating like smoke.

Mary's watching me with calm green eyes, and when she speaks again, her voice washes over me like warm water. "In any case, darling, we needn't worry about politics. Our concern is finding Edison and recovering the jade, yes? Let's not make this more complicated than it needs to be."

"Yeah." I agree, shaking my head, trying to clear the fog that's settling over my thoughts. "Yeah, you're right."

She smiles, and warmth spreads through my chest. Safe. Everything's going to work out fine as long as I trust Mary.

The coach turns a corner and the feeling fades slightly, leaving me vaguely unsettled. What the hell just happened? My skull throbs, and my mouth tastes like copper pennies.

Chapter Fifteen

THE MORNING SUN STABS through my bedroom window like a vindictive bastard. Groaning I pull the pillow over my face, but it's no use. My skull feels like someone's using it for a bass drum, and my mouth tastes like something died in it.

Mary's whiskey. Christ, how much did I drink?

Fragments of last night drift back. The Night Market's electric glare. The girl in Edison's waistcoat, bleeding out in the alley. The way Mary's voice had gone smooth and honeyed when we'd argued about Kollach, and then...nothing. Like trying to remember what I was angry about after the anger's gone.

Something about a gala. Kollach's fundraiser, day after tomorrow. Mary wants me there as her bodyguard. I'd agreed, I think. Agreed to wear a gown. When had I agreed to that?

A knock at my door makes me wince. "Mary Catherine?" Julianna's voice, bright and cheerful. "Are you awake?"

"No," I croak.

The door opens anyway. She sweeps in, already dressed in one of her charity-work outfits—a sensible navy walking suit that still manages elegance. Her hair's pinned up neat, not a strand out of place. The sight of her makes me acutely aware that I'm still wearing yesterday's clothes and probably smell like a distillery.

"You look dreadful," she says, setting a cup of coffee on my nightstand. The smell alone makes my stomach lurch.

"Feel worse." I struggle upright, wincing as the room spins. "What time is it?"

"Half past nine. Which means we need to leave in an hour."

Staring at her blankly, I ask. "Leave for what?"

Her expression shifts from concern to exasperation. "The luncheon, Mick. The Ladies Benevolent Aid Society? I told you about it three days ago. You promised you'd come."

The memory surfaces through the hangover. Right. Some charity thing in Chinatown. I'd agreed because Julianna had been so excited about it, and I'd been trying to be supportive of her new civic engagement.

"Jules, I can't. I've got—"

"No." Her voice goes flat in that way that means she's done negotiating. "You promised. Besides, the hostess specifically requested your presence."

That pulls me up short. "What?"

"Miss Ah Toy." Julianna settles on the edge of my bed, smoothing her skirt with careful movements. "She's one of the most influential women in Chinatown. Quite fascinating, really. Former courtesan who became a successful businesswoman. She heard about you—your work with the Bureau, I imagine—and asked if I'd bring you along."

I reach for the coffee. Ah Toy. Connor's voice from last night surfaces unbidden, the little shiver when he'd described accountants doing the work most people need thugs for. And Mary, dismissing her as "laced mutton" while her knuckles went white around her sherry glass.

Now this woman wants to meet me. The morning after I signed on with her rival.

That's a summons dressed up as a tea party.

"How'd she hear about me?"

"I may have mentioned you." Julianna fidgets with her sleeve. "When I was helping organize supplies for the working girls' refuge, Miss Ah Toy contributed generously. We got to talking, and..." She trails off, looking almost sheepish. "I suppose I bragged a bit. About my sister who works for the Bureau, who helped solve that terrible business in New Mexico."

Great. Just what I need, my reputation preceding me while I'm trying to keep a low profile. If Ah Toy wants to meet me, I'd bet a shiny nickel it's not about charity work.

"Jules."

"Please, Mary Catherine." She takes my hand and squeezes tightly. "This work means something to me. These women we're helping, they're desperate. Ah Toy's support could make a real difference. And if she wants to meet you, well... it's a small thing to ask."

The hope in her eyes makes my chest tighten. I'd been so wrapped up trying to find a place to fit, and then Loosh's death, Edison's disappearance, Mary's schemes, that I'd missed my own sister's loneliness.

"All right." Sighing, I sip the coffee"But you owe me."

Her smile could light up the whole city. "Thank you. Now get cleaned up. We can't be late."

⁓∽∿⌇∿∽⁓

An hour later, I'm marginally more presentable. Toast and a shot of Gudrun's special tea has helped ease the pounding in my head. Ylva helped me pick out a "proper lady dress," as she called it, a burgundy day dress that Odette had altered to fit me. It's a far cry from my trousers, but at least the sleeves are wide enough to accommodate my hook.

I follow the sound of laughter to find Gudrun in the front parlor giggling over the latest society pages from the Examiner with Mrs. Chen from two blocks over. They're in the armchairs by the window, a plate of almond cookies between them. Ylva's gone off to play, and Julianna's fussing with her hat in the hallway.

"Morning, Mrs. Chen, Gudrun." I interrupt their hen fest.

"Morning, Mick. You look like ten miles of bad road." Mrs. Chen's flat Oklahoma drawl always makes me grin. Born and raised in Guthrie, she sounds more like a cowhand than the herbalist and small-magic practitioner she is. She peers at me over the glasses perched at the end of her nose. "Gudrun's tea help any?"

"Saved my life." Dropping into the chair across from them, I lower my voice, glancing toward the hallway where Julianna's still occupied. "I need to pick both your brains, actually. Can you think of something that could enhance a person? Make them stronger, faster, more aggressive? Mixed with opium or cocaine, maybe."

The two women exchange a glance. Mrs. Chen lays the newspaper on her lap.

"Funny you should ask," she says. "I was just telling Gudrun about poor Mrs. Wagner. She came to me last week about rhinoceros horn." She tsks, shaking her head. "For her husband's personal vitality, if you take my meaning."

"And?"

"And I told her what I tell everyone. It's just horn, same as hooves or fingernails. Won't do a blessed thing for your marriage."

Gudrun snorts and the ladies exchange a wink. I roll my eyes.

Mrs. Chen picks up a cookie, snaps it in half. "Magically inert. Complete nonsense as an aphrodisiac. I recommended ginseng and honest conversation."

Gudrun pauses with a cookie half way to her mount.. "But tell her the rest, Li."

Mrs. Chen's expression sobers. "Raw horn is inert, that's true. But it has a peculiar property. It absorbs enchantment. Soaks it up like a sponge." She brushes crumbs from her fingers. "In the old practice, the kind my grandmother learned in Guangdong, there are warnings about it. The right binding spell, the right herbs, and powdered horn becomes something else entirely. You could pour vitality into a dying man. Make a wasted body strong again. Heal wounds that shouldn't heal."

My pulse quickens. Scarface's jaw. Three days from torn open to nearly closed.

"At what price?" I ask.

"Devastating." Mrs. Chen scowls. "The body wasn't meant to burn like that. Wasting, organ damage, madness. And the binding..." She glances at Gudrun.

"Would do terrible things to their soul," Gudrun finishes. "The kind of binding you'd need is dark work. Big Magic. Death magic, most like."

"Could either of you make something like that?"

They both look at me like I've suggested eating the cat.

"Lord, no," Mrs. Chen says. "Neither the skill nor the inclination. You'd need someone who works with animus. Twists it. Binds spirits. Someone with access to Big Magic."

"A death mage," Gudrun sounds anxious. "Or a necromancer."

Someone who already animated corpses and bound spirits. Adding alchemical enhancement to living bodies wouldn't be much of a stretch.

"Where would someone get the raw horn?" I ask.

"Any apothecary in Chinatown carries it. A few places south of Market too." Mrs. Chen shrugs. "It's not rare, just expensive. The horn itself isn't the dangerous part. It's what you do with it that matters."

"Mary Catherine?" Julianna calls from the hallway. "The carriage will be here any minute!"

"Coming!" Standing, I squeeze Gudrun's shoulder, then nod to Mrs. Chen. "Thank you both. This helps."

"Be careful," Gudrun says quietly.

Mrs. Chen gives me a look over her glasses. "If someone's really making what I think you're describing, careful might not cut it."

Chapter Sixteen

THE CARRIAGE JULIANNA HIRED rattles through the city, heading west toward Chinatown. She chatters about the Aid Society's latest project, a refuge for girls escaping brothels, a program to teach English and practical skills, fundraising for a community clinic.

Nodding along, half-listening, I watch the city transform outside our window. The streets narrow as we cross into Chinatown, brick and clapboard giving way to colorful painted wood and tile. Signs in Chinese characters hang from every building. The smell shifts to ginger and star anise, incense and roasting meat, unfamiliar spices that make my nose tingle pleasantly.

The carriage slows, then stops. Outside, a high wall of whitewashed brick stretches along the street, broken by an ornate gate painted red and gold. Dragons coil up the posts, their scales glinting with what might be real gilt.

"We're here," Julianna says, gathering her things.

The gate swings open as we approach, revealing a large rectangular courtyard. It's a piece of another world dropped in the middle of the city. White, crushed shell paths meander between trees in massive ceramic pots, a small pond where koi flash orange and gold. The building itself is elegant, all curved rooflines and carved wooden posts, decorated with more of those coiling dragons.

A young Chinese woman in an exquisite dress the color of spring rain greets us at the door, bowing slightly. "Mrs. Swenson, Mrs. McClellan. Welcome."

She leads us through a wide hall, decorated to display the owner's wealth. Scrolls of calligraphy hang on the walls. Porcelain vases sit on carved stands. Jade figurines of all shapes gleam in glass cases: horses and scholars, phoenixes and flowers, all carved with breathtaking detail.

My hangover recedes, pushed aside by wariness. This much wealth, this much art means Ah Toy's more than a neighborhood matriarch. I don't believe for a second that she requested my presence just because she was curious. She wants something.

We're led to a long, narrow sitting room with high ceilings. Actually, it's more the size of a ballroom, broken into smaller seating areas, spaces for viewing art and intimate conversations. The windows are heavily curtained, creating a dim, slightly solemn atmosphere. At the far end, a few steps lead up to huge double mahogany doors carved with clouds and ocean waves.

In the center of the room, several women are already gathered around a long dark wood table, seated on horseshoe-back chairs. They're all dressed in their finest and include familiar faces from Julianna's charity circles. Mrs. Henderson, who runs the refuge; Miss Washington, a schoolteacher; and a striking blond woman I don't know.

Before Julianna and I can join the group at the table, the far doors swing open as if on cue, revealing who I assume is Ah Toy. Perhaps fifty, her skin is smooth as porcelain with the depth of ivory. There's barely a hint of gray at her perfect part.

"Ladies, welcome. A pleasure to make your acquaintance." Ah Toy surveys her guests, pausing at Julianna and me. She flows down the stairs and into the space, her voice smooth, wrapping around us. The silk of her trousers and tunic swish pleasantly as she comes to greet us.

She nods at the seated women before bowing slightly to Julianna. "Miss Swenson," she says in perfect English, with barely a hint of an accent. "How delightful. And this must be your sister, the formidable Mrs. McClellan."

"Just Mick," I say, extending my right hand.

She tilts her head, and a small crease appears on her smooth brow, but she takes my hand, her grip firm. No shrinking violet.

"Mrs. Swenson, please, sit. Lunch will be served shortly." She gestures to the women at the table. "But allow me a moment with Mrs. McClellan, if the ladies will please indulge me." Turning to me, she continues, "I would appreciate your thoughts on a new acquisition. I understand you are considered an expert on horses?" Her eyebrow cocks slightly.

"Uhm.." Blinking I work to decipher her intent. "No more experienced than most."

She glances deliberately toward the hallway's end.

Of course, she wants to speak privately. The hangover must be slowing me down. "Happy to assist, ma'am," I say quickly.

Julianna settles in with the other ladies as Ah Toy takes my arm and leads me back through the mahogany doors into what I can only describe as a solarium. The ceiling is iron work set in glass, bathing the space in spring sunlight. There is very little furniture, but one entire wall showcases a sword collection. Or is this space intended as a gymnasium? Maybe those are practice swords?

Releasing my arm, Ah Toy gestures around us. "Swords are considered old-fashioned weaponry, but I find the practice soothes my mind and spirit."

"Everyone needs a hobby, I suppose." Shifting slightly I berate myself. When am I going to learn not to underestimate people just because they're female? You'd think I would know better. The swords and her talk of 'a practice' cast her gracefully assured movement in a different light, less barn swallow, more barn owl.

Watching me study the sword wall, she runs her fingers along the nearest hilt. "When I first came here, there was only one kind of Chinese woman on Dupont Street," she says. "The ones men paid to forget their names."

I snort. "Seems to be the way of most cities."

"The tongs brought girls in like cargo," she goes on, mild as tea. "Most had no idea about the life waiting them here. I could do nothing to stem the flow of the flesh trade. But I could choose what kind of house I ran once they stepped through my door."

Her gaze finds mine, steady. "They earned wages. They kept some. No man laid a hand on them without my permission. And when their contracts were paid, they walked out with money in their pockets and all their teeth. That was my sin." Her mouth curves. "And my line in the sand."

She's not confessing. She's laying out terms. I've known madams who'd sell their girls' bones if there was a market for them. Ah Toy's still running in the gutter, but she wants me to know she keeps it swept. There's a code here, same as Mary's, just written in a different language.

"Come." Ah Toy leads me around the perimeter, to a strongbox case at the far end. It takes a few moments for her to open the complex latching mechanism to reveal a carved jade horse, maybe a foot tall, rearing on its hind legs. My eyes immediately catch bits of soul dust clinging to it. It's essentially soul dander, this horse has been in contact with many a death.

"Tang Dynasty," Ah Toy says proudly. "Eighth century. It used to be part of a pair used in burial rites, meant to carry the deceased's soul to the afterlife. Beautiful, isn't it?"

"It's something." I lean closer, examining hints of animus remnants. It is beautiful, every muscle defined, the mane flowing like water frozen in stone.

"I collect these pieces not just for their beauty, but for their history. Their power." She glances at me sideways. "You can feel it, can't you? The magic worked into the jade."

Straightening I meet her eyes. "What makes you think I'd know anything about that?"

Her smile hints of danger. "Because you are a Gleaner, able to command the energies of death... And because you've enlisted into Gold Tooth Mary's service."

The room seems to shrink. My fingers twitch. I catch myself. Jiminy, even if I were armed, it's not like I'm gonna draw on this woman in her own parlor. The last few days have brought out the worst in me.

"I've survived in this city for thirty years. One of my strategies is to know how powerful people are aligning themselves." She turns back to the jade horse. "Mary is searching for the Nü Gua Jade. And she's hired you to protect her while she does so. Am I correct?"

No point in lying. "Maybe."

"Then you should know who you're protecting. And what you're looking for."

She reaches into the cabinet and retrieves a small wooden box, lacquered black with gold designs. Opening it reveals a piece of jade about the size of my palm, carved in the shape of a lotus flower. It vibrates with power. My senses pick up traces of old rituals, blood and prayers, animus worked into stone over centuries.

"This is a true treasure," Ah Toy says. "Made during the Ming Dynasty, and owned by a Taoist sorcerer. It offers protection from earthquakes, calms Earth's fiery veins and prevents disaster."

She sets it carefully back on the shelf.

"The Nü Gua Jade is similar but far more powerful. It was crafted to stabilize the very foundations of the earth, to prevent catastrophe. San Francisco sits on unstable ground. Surely even for the short time you have spent here, you have felt the ground tremble? There is a great disaster coming, one that could destroy everything we've built."

My mouth goes dry. "How do you know that?"

"I can feel it." She touches her chest. "In my bones, in my blood. Old beings beneath the city stir. And when they wake" She shakes her head. "The Nü Gua could prevent that. Or at least mitigate the destruction. That is why it must stay in San Francisco. That is why it must not fall into the wrong hands."

"And Mary's hands are wrong?"

"Gold Tooth Mary cares only for herself and her power." Ah Toy's voice sharpens. "She would use the jade to consolidate her control or sell it to the highest bidder without thought for the consequences. She certainly doesn't care about protecting Chinese lives."

The memory of Mary's casual bigotry surfaces—her dismissive comments about "Celestials," her alliance with Kollach. My stomach turns.

"There's something else you should know about Mary Hunter." Ah Toy leans forward, her dark eyes intense. "The blood of sirens runs in her veins."

Barking a laugh I scoff. "That's ridiculous. Sirens are myth."

"Are they? You're a Gleaner who rides death for power. Your friend Edison sees magical signatures. Your own bureau monitors mystical activity. A rusalka lives in the bay." She arches an eyebrow. "Why not sirens?"

Because I hadn't thought about it. Because Mary seemed so...normal. Cultured. Human.

Ah Toy continues, "Haven't you noticed how persuasive she can be? Her words slide past your defenses. Have you found yourself agreeing with things you would normally question?"

Arguing with Mary about Kollach, feeling my anger drain away, thoughts going fuzzy. That strange warmth, the certainty that she was right even when every instinct screamed otherwise.

"Sirens charm with their voices," Ah Toy says. "They compel agreement, loyalty, even love. It's subtle, especially in someone of mixed blood like Mary. You might not even realize it's happening. You just find yourself...compliant."

My hand trembles. I press it flat against my thigh. "How long have you known?"

"Long enough." Ah Toy softens. "I do not suggest you're under her control. Siren daughters cannot force you to act against your core nature. But they can guide. Coax. Bend your will to match theirs."

Christ. Christ. Christ.

How much of my decision to work for Mary had been mine? How much had been her words, smoothing over doubts, making everything seem reasonable?

I think about the way Mary had watched me ride the death of the girl without flinching. How she'd smiled when I'd agreed to keep working for her.

"Why are you telling me this?" The words scrape my throat.

"Because I require your help." Ah Toy closes the wooden box and sets it aside. "And because you deserve to know what you're dealing with. Mary is dangerous, Mrs. McClellan. Not just to me, but to this entire city. If she gets the jade—"

"You want it for yourself."

"I want it for San Francisco. Where it can protect this city from calamity." She faces me unflinchingly. "I want you to ensure it goes to someone who will use it properly."

"And that's you."

"My life is woven into the fabric here. I built my fortune here, made my home here. My family is here." Something fierce crosses her face. "I will not see it destroyed because a half-siren crime boss wants to play with forces she does not understand."

It's too hot. My head throbs, hangover reasserting itself. "I'll not work against her."

"I'm asking you to think for yourself. To question, remember that you have a choice." Ah Toy's tone drops. "Mary may have your loyalty now, but is it truly yours to give? Or has she stolen it with her voice?"

The door to the sitting room opens, and the young woman who greeted us appears. "Miss Ah Toy? Lunch is being served."

"Thank you, Soo-wai." Ah Toy turns back to me, her expression unreadable. "Think about what I've said, Mrs. McClellan."

She glides past me with a gracious smile. Standing there, staring at the jade horse in its case, my mind races.

Mary's voice, honeyed and persuasive. Arguments melting away.

Had any of it been real?

⁂

Lunch is an elaborate affair. Courses of delicate dumplings, pillowy buns, steamed fish, and vegetables I don't recognize arrive on painted platters. Everyone has been provided with chopsticks, but forks are tucked discreetly into napkins. The women eat and enthusiastically discuss their work, talking about fundraising and logistics.

I pick at my food. My meeting with Ah Toy killed my appetite. Julianna's engaged, passionate, laughing at something Mrs. Henderson says. When had this happened? When had my sister stopped being the woman who worried about propriety and started being someone who fought for the powerless?

"Your sister is remarkable," Ah Toy observes, from her seat beside me. "She has a gift for organization. And compassion."

"She's always been good at seeing what needs doing."

"As are you, I think. Though your methods are different." Ah Toy sips tea from a porcelain cup so thin it's practically translucent. "Are you close? You and Mrs. Swenson?"

"She's my baby sister. We've been through a lot together."

"Family is precious." Something sad flickers across her face. "Worth protecting."

I set down my chopsticks.

"Mrs. Swenson and her companion have built something admirable," Ah Toy continues, her voice still conversational, still light. "Their work with the Aid Society. Their home together." She selects a dumpling and adds it to my plate. "Mary has interesting political connections. The sort of men who win elections by promising to clean up moral degradation. Who make examples of women who step outside their proper sphere."

The room narrows. I grip the edge of the low table with my good hand.

"Your sister's happiness is her own concern," Ah Toy says. "But Mary is not known for her sentimentality when leverage is required."

She pours tea into my barely touched cup. "Mr. Swenson died, is that correct?" She fills her own, unhurried. "Widows are afforded more latitude. But even they can be accused of unnatural affections. Particularly when they share a household with another woman and agitate men in power."

That's all it takes. No threats. No ultimatums. Just a clean sketch of how easily everything Julianna has built could be torn apart by the wrong word in the wrong ear. And the unspoken truth that I handed Mary that leverage the moment I signed on with her.

"Get to the point," I say through my teeth.

"The point is simple. If you help me secure the Nü Gua Jade, ensure it stays in hands that will protect this city, my influence shields your family. If you remain entangled with Mary..." Ah Toy shrugs, one delicate shoulder rising and falling. "I cannot speak for what she might do."

The carrot and the stick, presented with tea and dumplings.

"I'll consider your offer," I say.

"Of course." Ah Toy smiles, gracious as a hostess should be. "But don't wait too long. The jade will surface soon."

She turns her attention to Mrs. Henderson on her right. I sit, food untouched, watching Julianna laugh at something Ah Toy said. My sister, glowing with purpose and belonging, completely unaware that two of the most powerful women in San Francisco are using her as a chess piece.

The lunch drags on. More courses, more polite conversation. Finally, mercifully, it ends. We make our goodbyes at the gate. Ah Toy clasps my hand.

"Pay attention to your own mind when you are with Mary," she murmurs, too quiet for anyone else. "Ask yourself which thoughts are truly your own."

She releases me and bows. "Please come again, Mrs. Mc-Clellan."

In the carriage, Julianna chatters about the food, the other ladies, Ah Toy's generosity. I nod in the right places.

"Mary Catherine?" Her hand finds my arm. "Are you all right? You've been quiet."

"Just tired. Rough night."

"Did you find anything? About Edison?"

The girl's death flashes through my mind. The basement. The chains. "Maybe. I've got a lead."

"Good." Julianna squeezes my arm. "Abigail must be beside herself."

"Yeah." I watch the city slide past the window. Mary wants me at her heel. Ah Toy wants me at hers. Both of them so certain they know what's best for everyone.

"Julianna, can you stop the coach?"

Her brow knits. "What? Now?"

"We're closer to Meiggs Wharf here than if I go all the way home. I need to see a man about some spiders."

She calls to the driver. The carriage slows. I'm out the door before it fully stops, boots hitting cobblestones, the salt air off the bay cutting through perfume and incense and the lingering taste of other people's plans.

"I'll catch up with you later!" I call back.

Julianna waves, bemused. The carriage pulls away.

The afternoon is mine. No Mary. No Ah Toy. No one telling me what to think.

Chapter Seventeen

THE HORSE TROLLEY LURCHES to a stop at the wharf, and I step down into the salt-thick air. The wind off the bay cuts through my coat, but I barely feel it.

Looking around with interest I head toward the line of buildings near the water. I hadn't yet had occasion to visit the combination lumber wharf and tourist carnival that is Meiggs and I'm curious. Arachne's Castle is at the foot of the wharf, highlighted in the fading afternoon light. Outside the two-story clapboard, a handful of tourists huddle at small tables, cracking crabs and pretending the wind isn't freezing their backsides off. Large commercial windows face the dock on the north side.

Pushing through the door I'm stopped in my tracks, eyes drawn up. It's like stepping into an arachnophobe's nightmare. Decades' worth of cobwebs festoon the high ceiling, thick as lace curtains. They drape over mounted fish, across trophy antlers, between the rafters. Yup, Arachne's Castle it is. Wonder if the name or the webs came first?

A macaw the color of sunset preens on a perch to my left, eyeing me with one bright, suspicious eye. It ruffles its feathers and lets out a squawk that sounds almost like a greeting. Some-where deeper in the room, a monkey chatters in response—no, two monkeys, their voices overlapping.

Turning slowly, I try to take it all in. The walls are crammed with scrimshaw showcasing whaling scenes. Monkeys scurry up totem poles looming from the back corner. Japanese masks hang beside brutish war clubs.

"Welcome, welcome!" A warm voice, infused with a professional cheerfulness. "What'll it be?"

I finally register the long mahogany bar stretched across the back wall. Behind it stands a man who I recognize from the daguerreotype with Loosh at Woodward's as Sol Sonderling. Older, but the same pale eyes, the same neat beard. He's dapper in a waistcoat and starched collar, drying glassware with a dingy towel. His white hair and full beard are neatly trimmed. An old-fashioned stovepipe topper completes his look. A gray parrot is performing acrobatics on an iron perch mounted to the counter.

"Navy Grog's the specialty. I make a fine one." He smiles, smoothing the bird's feathers as I pick my way between an assortment of wooden tables and a variety of chairs and benches to the bar. As I reach the bar, he picks up a crystal decanter and shakes it enticingly. "Finest Barbados rum with cloves and lime, guaranteed to set you right!"

The gray squawks. "Gimme a rum and gum!"

Sol reaches up to scratch its head. The bird leans into his touch.

Shelves cover the entire back wall to the ceiling. Treasures sit cheek-by-jowl with pure junk amidst a huge collection of high-end brandies and liquors.

"You've got quite a menagerie," I say, nodding toward the chattering monkeys. One of them is missing part of its tail, and the other has a club leg.

"My sweet little orphans." He leans over the bar, eyes twinkling, "Each of them has a story. Most are rejects. Sailors pick 'em up thinking to make a buck selling them as a fancy pet, but it doesn't always work out." Sol pulls a peanut from his pocket and tosses it to one of the monkeys waddling across the floor toward us. The capuchin catches it and retreats back to its perch. "I've always fancied myself a guardian of the lost and forgotten. Plus, the tourists like it."

"How long have you been doing this?" I ask, spying what looks like a small kangaroo or a large rabbit watching me from the floor at the end of the bar.

"Almost thirty years since I set up shop on Meiggs." He sets down the towel. "Started with Werner here." He gestures at the gray. "Poor little man had about plucked himself bald, and was destined for the big drink, too ugly to sell." He strokes the parrot. "I offered his captor a penny to take 'im off his hands. After that...well, the critters just keep finding their way here."

Sighing I remind myself I am not going to be seduced by this old charlatan with stories about kindness to animals. Nope, I am here to learn about the jade.

"You're Sol Sonderling, right?"

"The very same." He casts the towel over his shoulder before sticking his hand out to shake. "And you are?"

"Mick Kelly." Surprise and something else flicker across his face. Not quite fear. Not quite guilt. But close enough. His offered hand drops. I plow ahead. "I'm a friend of Loosh's. Aloysius Temple."

"Ah, yes. Temple." He starts shifting clean glasses down the bar, avoiding my eyes. His exuberance gone. "I know him. An acquaintance, really. Comes in now and again for a drink."

"Dead. But you know that, don't you?"

He pulls the towel off his shoulder and starts folding it very precisely. "I heard about... I'm very sorry for your loss."

I scan the shelves behind Sol. Between a bottle of French brandy and a stuffed armadillo, the same daguerreotype as the museum. Two young men grinning like fools in front of a stone ruin. Barely knew him. Right.

"Sol, you knew he was dead before I walked in here. And you two were a damn sight closer than you're letting on." Leaning against the bar, I tap my hook against the wood. "Loosh sent me a note before he died. 'See Phalanx.'"

Sol's face pales beneath the beard. Werner screams, Sol reaches up to calm him. But his hand is shaking.

"Mean anything to you?" I press.

He swallows hard. "It's...it's from mythology. Arachne's brother in some versions of the tale. But I don't see what—"

Looking at the cobwebs draping the ceiling I feel like a rube. Phalanx. Arachne's brother. Damn it, Loosh. "All right, *Phalanx*, what were you and Loosh mixed up in?"

Sol's grip tightens on the bar. "I really can't—"

"Can't or won't? Because from where I'm standing, it looks like you know why he sent me that note telling me to see *you*. And it looks like you're scared."

"Of course I'm scared!" The words burst out of him. "Loosh's dead. Murdered. And you come in here asking questions about—" He cuts himself off, jaw clenching.

"About what?" I ask. "About the Nü Gua Jade?"

His face goes from pale to white. One of the monkeys shrieks, picking up on the tension.

"I don't know anything about that."

I walk around the end of the bar, joining him behind the counter. Examining the tall shelves, I crowd him just a little and pick up a golden clock. I turn it over, and run my thumb across the face. Take my time with it, make him wait before continuing. "I think Loosh was trying to sell it. And you were helping him fence it, weren't you? All these artifacts, wealthy collectors coming through. You were the perfect partner."

Sol's back hits the shelves as he tries to distance himself from me. Bottles rattle. "You don't understand the position I'm in."

"Then explain it."

He reaches for a glass with trembling hands and pours himself whiskey. "I'm in debt. This place is mortgaged to the rafters. If I can't make good by the end of the month..." He gestures helplessly at the animals around us. "What happens to them?"

Sympathy flickers in my chest. But I push it down. "So Loosh came to you with a way out. A big score."

Sol nods slowly, taking a long drink. "He said it was authenticated. Sixteenth century. Worth a fortune to the right buyer. We could both solve our problems. His health was failing. Doc said his heart was giving out. He couldn't keep working for the Bureau much longer, but he needed money for treatment..." His voice cracks. "I thought we could both save ourselves."

"What happened?"

Sol's glass clatters against the mahogany. "We started putting out feelers. In my business you gotta have a network of specialized buyers. Lots of powerful folks from all over the country were interested. Then Loosh found a buyer willing to pay more than top dollar. He went to meet them Saturday night. In Sausalito, to see if they were legit."

My grip tightens on the clock. "Who was the buyer?"

"I don't know." His hands shake as he pours more whiskey. "But when he came back Sunday morning... Christ, he lost his nerve. I've never seen him like that. Said we had to call it off and lay low."

"Why? What happened at the meeting?"

"He recognized the buyer." His voice drops. "Someone dangerous. He wouldn't give me a name, just kept saying, 'If he knows I'm in San Francisco, if he knows about you...'" Sol drains the glass. "Kept looking over his shoulder. Said he had to warn someone at the Bureau. That he was going to meet Agent McClellan."

The pieces click together. Loosh was trying to reach me. Bet he went to my house Sunday night and I wasn't there. The note left with the street boy when I wasn't home.

I set the clock back on the shelf. "I'm McClellan. Kelly's my maiden name. I use it for work outside the Bureau."

Sol's expression shifts to surprise, then something like relief, then fear all over again. "You're... Christ. He said you were the only one who could..." He stops, jaw working. "But if you're here, and Loosh's dead, then—"

"Then whoever killed him is still out there." I shove a loose pin back into my hair. "Which is why I need to know everything, Sol. Everything Loosh told you."

But instead of opening up, Sol's expression shutters. Shit, now he's gonna think whatever he tells me could put him in deeper water than he's already in. He reaches for his glass and pours himself another drink and tosses it back

Tugging at my collar I try again. " C'mon, Sol. What else did he say about this buyer? Anything at all?"

Sol hesitates, then, "He said...he said it was a necromancer." His knuckles are white around the empty glass. "Loosh was BMI. He'd faced down vampires, ghouls, all manner of dark magic. I'd never seen him scared before. Not like that."

A necromancer who scared Loosh. Who showed up in Sausalito looking to buy powerful artifacts. Dollars to doughnuts, it's my guy running the hopheads, the one responsible for those revenants at Kollach's rally.

"Where's the jade now?" I demand.

Chapter Eighteen

Sol's eyes dart away. Just for a second. But it's enough.

"Loosh took it with him when he left Sunday," he says. "I assumed he hid it somewhere. To keep it safe."

Every instinct I have screams "lie." The way his gaze won't meet mine. The tremor in his voice. The way his hand moves toward his vest pocket, then stops.

"Bullshit, Sol." My voice hardens. "Loosh is dead. A young agent is missing. I've got two of the most powerful people in the city dogging me to find it. And you're standing there lying to my face."

"Please. You don't understand the position I'm in."

I grab his collar with my good hand. Pull him forward. Not hard. Just enough so he can't look away. "Did Loosh leave it with you?"

His mouth opens. Closes. "I can't. If she finds out—"

"Who?"

Sol's eyes go wide. Not at me. Past me.

"Let him be."

The voice rolls through the room like water over stones. Every animal goes still. The monkeys stop chattering. Werner's acrobatics freeze mid-swing.

The rusalka stands just inside the doorway, water pooling beneath her bare feet. Her hair drifts in an invisible current, dark tendrils reaching like curious fingers.

I don't release Sol. My grip tightens instead.

"Let him be, let him be," she croons, gliding forward. Her too-large, too-bright eyes fix on me. "You come with your anger. Breaking things. Always breaking."

"I'm not breaking anything." I struggle to keep my tone level. "Just asking questions."

"Asking?" Her head tilts, and water drips from her hair onto the floorboards. "You hold him. Shake him like a rat. That is not asking."

She's closer now. Close enough that I catch the scent of something that's been at the bottom of the bay for a very long time.

I assess her, looking for a weakness. The rusalka blazes in pure animus. No vitae, no life. No heartbeat to still. No death to ride. Just endless, patient hunger.

And shit, she studies me the same way.

"Death-touched," she murmurs, circling us. Her hair reaches forward, testing the air between us. "You see. You *see*."

The temperature drops. I feel it on my skin, in my lungs. The water spreading across the floor creeps toward my boots.

Her expression shifts. Something like curiosity crosses her face. "I see the one who walks with shades trailing like children. One who feeds on endings."

My jaw tightens. That's uncomfortably accurate.

"I see the one," she continues, drifting closer, "who would hurt my Sol."

"I'm not hurting him."

"No?" Her hair caresses Sol's wrist, his shoulder. "You grab. You threaten. You make him tremble."

"I'm all right. She's just asking questions." He's surprisingly steady.

The rusalka turns her bright gaze on him, glowing with affection. The way you might look at a faithful dog. "My Sol," she murmurs. "My sweet Sol who sees me. Who remembers."

She cups his face with one dripping hand. Water runs down his beard. He holds still, patient, while her attention drifts past him. Back to me.

Could I fight her? My Gleaner is charged with enough power from the girl's death in the alley. Maybe I could sever her connection to this world. Send her back to whatever depth she crawled from.

But that would cost me everything I have left. And I'd still need to find Edison.

And, God help me, I understand. She's protecting what's hers.

"Sol's good," the rusalka says, stroking his beard absently, the way you'd pet a cat. "He feeds me. Brings me pretty things from the ships. Talks to me when the loneliness comes." She releases him, drifting away, and his hand drops to his side. "He's mine."

His fingers curl where her hair had been, as if to hold on.

"I'm not here to hurt him," I say, and mean it. I release Sol's collar, then step back. Not retreating, just giving space. "I'm here to find out who killed Aloysious Temple."

The rusalka pauses. The water stops spreading. The temperature levels off.

"The frightened one," she says softly. "Silver-hair, sad eyes. Sol's friend. Used kind words."

My chest tightens. "You knew Loosh?"

"Knew, knew. Many years. He and my Sol always talking, laughing. Making their schemes." Her expression shifts. Something predatory slides behind her eyes. "Then he came running. Brought his burden here. So frightened."

"When?" I press. "Sunday?"

She nods, hair swaying like kelp in the current. "Sunday morning. Bright sun, but he brought shadows."

"Did you see who killed him?"

"Saw him after. At night, in the water where he didn't be-long." Grief crosses her face. "I pulled him to shore. Sang to him. But he wasn't there, already gone."

The image hits me hard. Loosh floating in the bay. This strange creature trying to comfort his corpse.

"But I saw the sweet-talking man on the dock," she contin-ues, voice dropping to a whisper. "Pretty words, pretty smile. But cold, cold, cold underneath." She tilts her head. "Winter wrapped in velvet. Makes the dead dance."

The sweet-talking man. Same warning she'd given me at the wharf Monday night. I'd brushed her off then. Stupid.

"He hunts the same tale you do," the rusalka says, almost contemplative. "So much anger. So much fear. All over rocks and stories."

She drifts toward the back of the bar, Sol's collection, trail-ing one hand along the shelves. Chinese porcelain. Scrimshaw. War clubs. Her fingers ghost over them without understanding.

"Real, not real. I never see the difference," she murmurs, fingers skimming a porcelain vase. "All just things he loves. But you breathe-and-bleed ones fight and kill for the stories you wrap around them. The sweet-talking man seeks the same dreams. Killing for smoke and shadows."

No help there. To her, it's all rocks and the trouble men make over them. I look at Sol. He's watching the rusalka, guilt carved in the lines of his face.

"I didn't want Loosh to get hurt." Sadness colours his voice. "I swear it. I wish to God I knew who murdered him."

The rusalka glances back at him. "I know, *Mily moy*. I know." The Russian endearment is casual, thoughtless. The way you'd call any small creature "sweetling" or "pet."

The grieving man and his inhuman guardian. He's still hold-ing something back. The jade, maybe. Or what Loosh told him. Or what he's planning to do. Or everything.

Pushing harder won't help. Not with the rusalka ready to drown me if I threaten him.

I look around the room one more time. Hundreds of artifacts. Any one of them could hide the jade. Or it could be in the bay with Loosh's blood. Or hidden somewhere between here and Sausalito.

My Gleaning sight is no use, there's nothing. Just the background hum of death that clings to the waterfront. Old drownings. Sailors lost. The rusalka's blazing animus. Nothing that points to carved stone and ancient power.

I turn to leave, then pause. "If you remember anything, anything at all about who Loosh met or what scared him, leave a message for me at Calpurnia's bar. You know it?"

He nods. "I will. I promise."

The rusalka watches me, her expression unreadable. As I step out into the wind off the bay, I hear her singing softly, sounds like a lullaby.

Meant to comfort a man who loves something that will never love him back.

The tourists are gone. Just old newspapers and crab shells rattling in the wind.

Sol knows where that jade is. I'd bet my good hand on it. But getting past his guardian to prove it is another matter.

I pull my coat tight and head for the trolley. I'm due at Mary's for a dress fitting in two hours. Hunting a necromancer and a missing agent, and I've got to stop for a ball gown. The things I do for this job.

Chapter Nineteen

THE SEAMSTRESS'S PARLOR SMELLS of lavender sachets and sizing starch. I stand on a low platform in my chemise and drawers while two women circle me with measuring tapes and pins, murmuring to each other in Portuguese. Mary lounges on a velvet settee by the window, watching with the lazy attention of a cat at a mousehole.

"Arms up, please," the older seamstress says, her English thick with a Lisbon accent.

Raising my arm, I'm conscious of how the afternoon light catches every scar. The bullet graze above my hip. The puckered burn on my arm from Gettysburg. The ragged mess where my left hand used to be.

"Such interesting skin," the younger seamstress lies politely, stretching the tape across my scarred shoulders.

Mary sips tea from a delicate cup. "How was your luncheon?"

My jaw tightens. Of course she knows. "It was for Julianna's charity work. Benevolent Aid Society luncheon."

"How lovely." She sets down her cup with a click. "And what did you ladies discuss? Fundraising? Refugee operations?"

The older seamstress tugs the tape tighter around my ribs. I exhale slowly. "The usual charity talk. Nothing interesting."

"Hmm." Her tone suggests she doesn't believe me. "Ah Toy specifically requested your presence, I'm told. Surely she had some purpose beyond polite conversation?"

How the hell does she know that? Forcing my expression to remain neutral, I answer. "She wanted to meet me. Show off her collection. You know how collectors are—always eager to display their treasures."

Mary tilts her head. "And did she show you anything particularly... significant?"

The jade horse flashes through my memory, soul dust clinging to ancient stone. "Old things. Chinese antiquities. A jade horse, some kind of burial piece."

"Just a horse?" The question comes too sharp, too interested.

"Tang Dynasty, she said. Eighth century." I shrug, careful not to dislodge the pins the younger seamstress is setting in the muslin draped over my shoulder. "Beautiful work, but nothing like what you're looking for. She doesn't have the Nü Gua Jade, if that's what you're worried about."

"You're certain?"

I nod. "She made it clear she's looking for it. Thinks it needs to stay in San Francisco, protect the city from earthquakes or some such."

Her laugh is sharp. "Of course she does. Ah Toy's always wrapping her ambitions in civic virtue." She waves a dismissive hand. "The woman's been trying to consolidate power in Chinatown for thirty years. The jade would be quite the prize for her."

"She said the same about you."

A chill skitters across my bare shoulders, not magic, just Mary's wintery glare. The seamstresses exchange glances, suddenly very focused on their pins.

"Did she now?" Mary's voice is silky. "And what exactly did she say about me?"

Something pulls at me. An urge to soften this, smooth it over.

Pay attention to your own mind when you are with Mary.

Ah Toy's warning surfaces like a lifeline. I grab it, focusing on the discomfort of pins pricking through muslin, the ache in my shoulders from holding still. Anything to anchor myself against the tide of her honeyed words.

"She said I should question if my thoughts are my own when I'm with you." The words slip out before I can stop them. The seamstresses pause in their work.

Mary's eyes narrow fractionally. Then she laughs, the sound musical and genuinely amused. "Did she? How delightfully paranoid. Though I suppose I shouldn't be surprised. Ah Toy's made a career of planting seeds of doubt."

She gestures to the older seamstress. "Lower the neckline, Mrs. Silva. Not scandalous, but enough to show she's got a figure worth noticing."

Mrs. Silva nods, adjusting pins.

"A little birdy mentioned," Mary continues, her tone light, conversational, "that you spent some time at the waterfront yesterday afternoon, wandering around Meiggs Wharf."

My stomach drops. Shit. A little birdy. Or a little magpie?

"Needed some air after the luncheon," I say. "Walked around. Looked at the ships."

"Just walking?" The question hangs, weighted.

Meeting her gaze, I gamble. "Visited an oddity shop. Thought maybe one of the collectors might know something about Loosh or the jade."

"And did they?"

"Nothing useful. Just old men peddling junk to tourists." The lie is sour on my tongue, but I force a shrug. "Dead end."

"Old men peddling junk." Mary repeats the phrase like she's tasting it, then laughs. "The dealers at Meiggs are far too long of tooth to be involved in anything of interest to us. Hardly the sort to broker a deal worth a fortune. But I have associates in that area. Perhaps I'll have someone look into what's being peddled these days."

She rises, crosses to a side table, and pours herself more tea, meticulously adding sugar, fussing with the milk. "Meet me at the Strausburg at seven to dress. We'll take my carriage." Her gold tooth flashes. "First impressions matter, even for body-guards."

"A society party." Looking down at my scarred arms, my hook, "I'm not exactly the type they put on the guest list."

"You'll clean up nicely," Mary says. "Mrs. Silva is working miracles as we speak."

"If this gown has a corset, I'm out."

"No tight corseting," Mary agrees, amusement dancing in her eyes. "We need you able to breathe if you have to fight."

Mary's silent for a long moment, studying my face. The seamstresses work around us, their murmured Portuguese filling the quiet. Mrs. Silva pins the hem; her daughter adjusts the draping at my waist.

"You haven't been very forthcoming, darling." Mary's voice roughens, loses some of its cultured polish. "That worries me."

"I'm telling you what I learned, which is a big pile of noth-ing."

"Hmm." She circles behind me, and I fight the urge to turn, to keep her in sight. "It feels like you're keeping secrets. And we're supposed to be working together, aren't we? Partners?"

The word feels like a trap. "You hired me as a bodyguard, not a partner."

"Semantics." Her reflection appears in the mirror across the room, standing behind me. "The point is, I need to trust you. And trust requires honesty."

Warmth envelopes my thoughts like silk thread. Tell her. Tell her about Sol, about the jade, about everything. She de-serves to know. She's trying to help—

Digging my fingernails into my palm, I use the pain to cut the temptation. "I'm being honest. I spent the afternoon chasing dead ends. That's all."

In the mirror, her expression hardens. Just for a second, before smoothing back to elegant concern. "Mick. Whatever lies Ah Toy told you about me, whatever doubts she planted, remember who you're working for. Remember who's actually helping you."

My teeth clench.

"My boys are still looking." She steps around to face me again. "They'll find him. But that only works if you keep doing your part. If you stay focused on protecting me, not running around the city playing detective."

"I thought finding the jade was part of protecting you."

She smiles, but it doesn't touch her eyes. "You're new here, darling. You don't understand how things work. How dangerous it is to trust the wrong people."

The younger seamstress steps back, surveying her work. "I think we have what we need, Mrs. Hunter."

"Excellent." Mary's smile warms instantly. "The blue silk we discussed, elegant but practical."

"Of course." Mrs. Silva begins unpinning the muslin. "It will be ready by six, miss."

I step down from the platform, reaching for my shirt. My hand shakes as I button it.

Mary watches me dress with the same lazy attention as earlier, like I'm a gazelle and she's a lion. "Tonight is important, Mick."

"I'll keep you safe," I say flatly.

"I know you will." She touches my arm, and that electric spark jumps between us again. "We understand each other."

Do we? Or is that just what she wants me to think?

I nod and head for the door, desperate to escape the lavender-scented air, Mary's perfume, the weight of her attention.

"Mick?"

I pause at the threshold.

"Don't disappoint me," she says. "I'd hate to think I misjudged you."

Her words settle cold in my mind as I step out into the hallway, into blessed air that doesn't taste of flowers and manipulation.

As I leave I hear Mary delivering instructions to the seamstresses, warm and charming. Playing her role.

Just like she expects me to play mine.

Chapter Twenty

THE CARRIAGE ROLLS TO a stop outside a mansion that makes Mary's Strausburg look like a corner saloon. Gas lamps blaze from every window of the three-story Pacific Heights pile, and string music drifts through the open doors. Women in silk gowns and men in white tie cluster on the wide veranda, champagne flutes catching the light like tiny beacons of money.

I tug at the blue silk monstrosity Mrs. Silva delivered this afternoon. It fits like a second skin, which means I can move if I try really hard. Worse, I feel naked without my Colt. Mary only allowed me a little derringer tucked into a garter holster and my knife in my boot. Might as well be protecting her with a hat pin and harsh language.

"Stop fidgeting," Mary murmurs as the footman opens the carriage door. "You look lovely."

I feel like a trained bear in a tutu.

Mary sweeps out first, emerald silk and borrowed confidence. I follow, conscious of how my hook catches the gaslight. A few guests glance our way, and I catch the whispers. *That's Gold Tooth Mary. What's Kollach thinking, inviting her sort?*

But Mary ignores them, gliding up the marble steps like she owns the place. I trail behind, scanning faces and exits out of habit. Twenty guests visible, maybe more inside. Two footmen at the door. Windows on three sides, balcony above. Tommy and Connor pick spots to lurk around the veranda.

Inside, the mansion drips wealth. Crystal chandeliers, Persian rugs so thick you sink into them, paintings in gilt frames covering damask walls. The string quartet plays from an alcove while white-gloved servants, many of them Chinese, circulate with champagne and canapés.

The guests seem to be railroad men and their wives, shipping magnates, mine owners. The kind of people who winter on the Riviera and summer in San Francisco, who've never set foot south of Market Street. Their kind built empires on land grants and broken promises, then built mansions to celebrate it.

"Tragedy, what's happening to this city," a silver-haired man with muttonchops booms near the fireplace. "Those Celestials, filling our streets. Mark my words, it'll be our ruin if we don't put a stop to it."

His wife, dripping diamonds that could fund a small army, titters behind her fan. "Oh, Charles, don't be dramatic. Though I do wish they'd stay in their own quarter. The smell of their cooking, honestly."

Same people who built their fortunes on Chinese labor, complaining about the smell of food. Assholes.

I accept champagne from a passing servant, more to have something to do with my hand than any desire to drink it. The young man's face is blank as he moves through the crowd, invisible except when someone needs their glass refilled.

Too many people, too much perfume and cigar smoke rattles me. It's not mystical; there's not enough history pressed into these floors to set off my extra senses. Good. Last thing I need is my death-sense acting up at a society party.

Mary's already working the room, holding court near the fireplace, surrounded by men who lean in like she's sharing state secrets instead of gossip. Her gold tooth flashes as she laughs at something one of them says, and they drink in her charm. They look harmless, but there's something brittle about her tonight. She's working harder, smiling a little too bright, laughing a little too shrilly.

Then the crowd parts, and I see him.

Isaac Kollach.

He's smaller than I expected. At the rally, surrounded by his muscle and backed by torchlight, he'd seemed larger. Dangerous. Up close, he's slight, almost delicate, with a neatly trimmed beard and cold blue eyes. His black suit is tailored to within an inch of its life, and he moves through his guests with the easy confidence of a man who's never been told no.

A man who's never had to wonder if the floor would hold.

"Mrs. Hunter," he says.

The confident crime boss doesn't vanish entirely, but she softens. Her shoulders angle slightly away from him, chin dipping just a fraction. It's gotta be an act, making him feel like he holds the reins.

"Mr. Kollach." Her voice carries that honeyed warmth, but there's a careful edge to it now. "Thank you so much for the invitation."

"Of course, Mary." He takes her hand, pulling her a half-step closer than most would consider comfortable. I move to cover her back, not like I think he's gonna attack her in a crowded ballroom, but I don't trust him. His expression doesn't soften at her smile. Doesn't warm at her tone. "Though I was beginning to wonder if you'd forgotten our arrangement. It's been three days, and I've heard nothing about progress on our little project."

She doesn't pull her hand away, though her jaw clenches. "These things take time, Mr. Kollach. Delicate work requires—"

"I'm well aware of the timeline." His eyes are flat, unaffected by whatever charm she's trying to work. "My associates are growing impatient. They were promised results."

"And they'll have them." Mary's smile never wavers, but her voice climbs half an octave. "I have several promising leads. In fact, I believe we're very close—"

"Leads aren't results, Mary." He releases her hand finally, his gaze sliding past her to me. "And who's this?"

"My bodyguard," Mary says, and there's the faintest relief in her voice at the subject change. "Mick Kelly. She's very skilled—

"Ah, yes. The Gleaner." His eyes sweep over me with the casual assessment of a man evaluating livestock at auction. "I've heard the stories. Quite the colorful résumé."

"Just doing my job, sir."

"I'm sure." He turns back to Mary "I trust she's competent. You've had some... difficulties lately, I understand. Dead men in alleys. Very messy."

"She's very competent," Mary assures him, and I tighten my jaw.

"Good." He touches Mary's shoulder proprietorially, adjusting the strap of her gown like a painting that's gotten crooked. "Come. There are some donors I want you to meet. They're very interested in your perspective on the Irish question."

Mary follows without hesitation, and I trail behind like a faithful hound. Maybe her deference isn't an act? Maybe that's how it is. Mary doesn't work *with* Kollach. She works *for* him.

People make room as they glide from group to group. I'm ignored in their wake.. Kollach introduces her to various donors, and she performs: charming, knowledgeable, offering just enough insider information about working-man politics to make these wealthy bigots feel informed. But she chooses her words carefully. She never pushes back when Kollach interrupts, never quite meets his eyes for too long.

"Fascinating," a portly man with a gold watch chain responds to something she said. "But you think they'd riot if we pushed through the property restrictions?"

"Undoubtedly. Which is why Mr. Kollach's measured approach is so brilliant. Apply pressure gradually, let them feel the noose tightening..." She glances at Kollach, almost seeking approval.

He nods, satisfied. "Mrs. Hunter understands the necessity of strategy. Don't you, my dear?"

"Of course, Mr. Kollach."

I want to vomit. Or drink. Both, in succession.

The next hour is more of the same. Mary works the room and I trail behind, bumping chairs and bankers to stay in her orbit. Every conversation is a variation on the same theme: the Chinese are ruining everything, Kollach will fix it, aren't we all terribly brave for saying so. I smile when smiled at and keep my mouth shut.

I'm considering whether drowning myself in the punch bowl would cause a sufficient scandal when a young man, obviously in his cups, sways up to Kollach's shoulder.

"Speaking of strategy, Kollach, when's your mystic doing another séance? My wife keeps blabbering on about the last one."

My ears prick. Kollach's got a mystic?

Kollach's expression lightens immediately, Mary apparently forgotten. "Ah, yes, Doctor Nightingale. He's become quite popular with the ladies, hasn't he? Such theater! Communing with the spirits, revealing the future." He lowers his voice conspiratorially. "Between us, it's mostly parlor tricks and showmanship, but the constituents eat it up. Makes them feel they're part of something magical."

Silly name, 'Doctor Nightingale.' Sounds like a two-cent carnival act.

I try to catch Mary's eye, but she's focused on Kollach, her smile plastered on like paint.

The conversation shifts again, voices blending into a dull roar of self-congratulation. I stand there in my blue silk prison, playing statue while they discuss their plans to squeeze every drop of profit from this city, regardless of who gets crushed in the process.

I need air. Need to move. Need to be anywhere but here, playing dress-up while Mary performs and Kollach threatens and these parasites plan their next venture in human misery.

Tommy and Connor are at the front door. They've got the main covered. I should check the perimeter anyway. Do my job.

Make sure there aren't any other ways someone could get to Mary while she's busy selling her soul in installments.

I slip into a side hallway, blessedly cooler and quieter. A few couples murmur in alcoves, but mostly it's empty. I press my hand against the silk wallpaper and try to breathe.

I should feel sorry for her.

Instead, I feel tired. And angry. And trapped in this god-damn dress.

I head deeper into the building, away from the noise and light and casual cruelty dressed up as civilized conversation.

The door to the service hallway dulls the party noise. Gas sconces flicker every ten feet, casting pools of yellow light that don't quite touch.

I follow the corridor deeper into the house.

Should check the back entrances anyway. A familiar ache settles behind my eyes. Death. Close and violent. Shit. It pulls me forward. Despite promises to Mary to behave, I can't ignore this.

The hallway veers left, and I spot what looks like a service door at the far end. Probably leads to the kitchen or—

Footsteps.

Heavy. Purposeful.

I turn.

Brass stands at the corridor's bend.

Mary's prize fighter enforcer, the one who'd flanked her at the Night Market and the Lotus Club. He's still wearing his fancy suit, but something's wrong. His eyes are glassy, unfocused. His skin's the color of tallow. And the way he moves—

My Gleaner sense screams.

Revenant.

"Brass?" I take a step forward, not wanting to believe what I'm seeing. "What happened to you?"

He doesn't answer. Just starts walking toward me in a horrible, purposeful shuffle. The click and wheeze of air moving through dead lungs emerges from his open mouth.

Then he charges.

I throw myself sideways as he crashes past, his momentum carrying him into the wall hard enough to crack the plaster and send a framed painting crashing to the floor. In life, Brass was strong. In death, he's a battering ram animated by necromantic will.

Brass spins, grabbing the skirt of my dress. The fabric tears at the seam as I twist away.

My hand closes on the derringer. I fire point-blank into his chest.

The bullet punches through his sternum, dead center. He doesn't even flinch. Nothing. No blood. No pain response. No slowing.

Of course not. He's already dead.

Brass swings, and I duck, his fist whistling past my ear. My boot catches on my hem and I stumble toward him. His hand closes on my arm, the silk sleeve rips as I twist away backing down the hall.

Voices shout behind me. Guests fleeing, servants screaming. The string quartet's gone silent.

Brass lunges again, but this time I'm ready. I drop low and sweep his legs. He goes down hard, and I'm on him, my knee on his chest.

Then I see it.

Pinned to his waistcoat, under his jacket, right over his heart. A piece of paper. Scrawled in shaky handwriting:

Hi, Mick, want to play?

My blood runs cold.

Brass's hand closes around my throat, lifting me off the ground as he stands. My vision grays at the edges.

Can't fight him straight. He's too strong, doesn't feel pain, doesn't tire.

But I'm a Gleaner. And if he's a revenant, someone's necromantic threads are holding his corpse together like a puppet's strings.

The hallway's filling with voices. Footsteps. Witnesses.

Can't help that now.

I haven't done this since New Mexico. Since I freed Morgan's mortal remains from Hoodoo's control. Hopefully it's like riding a horse.

I reach for the hoarded power left from the girl in the alley. It surges up hot and eager. My hand slams against Brass's chest as I deepen my Gleaner sight.

The world shifts. His corpse is a tapestry of energies, sickly violet threads wrapped around the fading wisps of what used to be Brass. The necromantic bindings pulse with malevolent purpose.

I visualize my power as shears and reach for the nearest thread. It burns through my body like acid. Brass's grip tightens reflexively. Purple lightning shoots up my arm. I grit my teeth against the pain, focusing past it. The necromancer who made him put real craft into this construct.

My vision tunnels. Blood pounds in my ears.

I inhale and look deeper, searching for the knot of energy connecting Brass to the necromancer. The keystone holding the whole thrall together.

I cut it.

The connection snaps. It vibrates through my teeth, my bones, the base of my skull.

Brass's eyes clear long enough for recognition. For confusion. For the horror of understanding what's been done to him.

Then he crumples, and I fall with him, gasping. He's truly dead.

My shoulders tremble. My vision swims. The hallway tilts. Most of my hoarded power is spent. What's left sits in me like embers in a banked fire. Enough to warm my hands. Not enough to fight with.

Footsteps thunder toward me. Kollach appears first, flanked by two security guards with pistols drawn. His face red with fury.

"What the hell happened?"

I climb to my feet, swaying. "Revenant. Someone sent him."

"That's impossible. No one would dare—" Kollach catches sight of Brass's body. His expression shifts from fury to something closer to alarm. But not surprise. Not really. "Christ."

Mary pushes through the growing crowd of gawkers, her face pale. When she sees Brass crumpled on the floor, something breaks in her carefully maintained composure. "No. No, not Brass."

"Revenant," I say again, pulling the note from his jacket. My hands shake as I hold it out to her.

She takes it, and the color drains completely from her face as she reads. When she looks up, her eyes are wild with something I haven't seen in her before, genuine fear.

"How?" Her voice cracks. "How did they get to him?" She looks down at Brass's body, her lips quaver. "I sent him on an errand earlier today, just a simple collection. He was supposed to have been here by 10:00, but I thought—I thought he was sleeping off a drunk."

"Someone took him," I say. "Killed him. Turned him. Sent him here."

"No." The fear in her voice is raw, unguarded. Her usual polish stripped away. She's spiraling, her breath coming faster. "If they can get to him, they can get to anyone. Connor. Tommy. Me."

Kollach snatches the note from her shaking hands. "This is unacceptable. I won't have my guests endangered by your sordid business affairs, Mary."

Mary flinches like he's slapped her. "Isaac, this wasn't—I didn't—"

"I don't care whose fault it is." He crumples the note, unread. "You've brought violence into my home. Exposed my donors to...to whatever this is." He gestures at Brass's corpse. "That thing is one of yours, which means this is your problem."

"We'll handle it," Mary says quickly, desperately. "I swear, we'll find out who—"

"You'll do more than handle it. You'll finish the job I hired you for." Kollach's voice becomes dangerous, Mary actually takes a step back. "Find that jade, Mary. And do it fast. Because if you can't even protect your own people, I'm questioning whether our arrangement has any value at all."

The threat hangs heavy. Mary's hands clench at her sides.

"And Mary?" Kollach leans closer, his voice low enough that only we can hear. "When I terminate arrangements, I'm very thorough. Remember that."

He stalks away, barking orders to his staff. Clear the body. Calm the guests. Get the right police here quietly, the ones who won't ask inconvenient questions. Minimize the scandal.

Mary stands there, shoulders hunched, her haughty confidence stripped away. She looks smaller. Older. The carefully maintained illusion of power shattered like cheap glass.

"Ma'am?" One of Kollach's security guards hovers nearby. "We need to move the... the body."

"Yes." Mary's voice is barely audible. "Yes, of course."

She turns to me, and for a moment, I see past all her masks. See the woman who's been playing a losing game, pretending at power she maybe doesn't have.

"Mick." She touches my arm. "I need...can we..."

"Air," I finish. "Yeah. Me too."

⁂

We make our way through the chaos to a side door opening into the garden. The night air is cold and clean after the suffocating warmth inside. Fog's rolling in off the bay, turning the manicured hedges into ghost shapes.

Mary leans against a marble statue of some goddess, serene and untouchable, and covers her face with her hands. Her shoulders shake.

"Brass was with me for five years," she whispers. "Five years. Loyal as a dog." She drags her hands down her face, smearing her carefully applied cosmetics. "Someone killed him. Turned him into that *thing*."

I should comfort her. Should say something reassuring.

But all I can think about is how she deferred to Kollach inside. How she'd smiled and charmed while those bastards discussed burning down Chinatown. How she'd called him *Mr. Kollach* and angled her body in submission.

"You lied to me," my voice emotionless.

Mary's hands drop. "What?"

"About Kollach. You made it sound like you were partners. Equals." I shake my head. "But you work *for* him. He gives orders, you follow them. And whatever power you have"—I gesture back toward the mansion—"it doesn't work on him at all."

Her laugh is brittle. "You noticed."

"Hard to miss once I was looking for it."

"Isaac's clever. Had a charm made after he learned what I am." She touches her throat, as if feeling for a phantom chain. "Wards against mental influence, compulsion, charm. Cost him all of two dollars at some hack spiritualist's shop."

"And it works?"

"It wouldn't if—" She cuts herself off, jaw clenching. Then she meets my eyes, and I see calculation there. A choice being made. "I let him think I'm weaker than I am. It's useful, having him underestimate me."

"You *were* putting on an act in there," I say slowly.

"Some of it." Her smile is bitter. "But not all. That cheap charm shouldn't work on me at all. Five years ago, it wouldn't have. I could've sung Isaac Kollach into licking my boots if

I'd wanted." She touches her face, fingers unsteady. "Now? A two-dollar trinket is enough to slow me down."

"Ah Toy told me the truth," I say. "You're a siren."

Mary straightens, and for a moment, I think she'll deny it. Then her shoulders drop. "Half-blooded. But yes."

It's not a shock. I've suspected since the dress fitting, since I'd felt that strange pull in my chest when she spoke. But hearing her confirm it—

"How much of what I've felt around you is real?" My voice hoarse. "When I thought we understood each other, when I wanted to help you—was any of that mine? Or have you been working me since we met?"

"If I could compel you, do you think I'd have needed to *hire* you?" Mary's voice sharpens. "Do you think I'd be standing here *begging* for your help instead of simply ordering you to give it?"

She slumps back against the statue, and suddenly she looks older. Tired. Lines at her eyes, silver threading her dark hair.

"I was beautiful once, Mick. Not just pretty—*devastating*. I could walk into a room and every head would turn. I could make men love me, hate me, die for me, all with my voice." Her hands twist together. "I had *power*. Real power."

She laughs, broken and bitter.

"Now the mortal blood is pulling me down. Every year, the resonance gets weaker. Every year, I lose a little more." She meets my eyes, and I see fear. Raw, animal fear. "In another five years, I won't even need enemies. Time will do the job for them."

She's quiet for a moment. When she speaks again, her voice is stripped of performance.

"The Nü Gua Jade holds the power of creation. Not protection, not luck. Creation. The power to remake what's been broken." She meets my eyes. "You understand what that means for someone like me."

"You think it can restore what you've lost."

"I *know* it can." Her voice is fierce. "Make me young again. Strong again. Give me back what time's been stealing."

"At what cost?"

The question makes her flinch. We both know power doesn't come freely. I've paid enough to understand that.

"I don't care." She stamps her foot. "Whatever it costs, it's better than fading into nothing while my enemies circle."

I study her. The smeared cosmetics. The fear and rage warring behind her eyes. She's telling the truth, or at least, a version of it. But I can't shake the feeling that there's more she's not saying.

"Someone got to Brass," My words are slow as I find my way. "One of your own people gave him up. That's what scares you, isn't it? Not just that you're fading. But that they *know*."

Mary's face goes carefully blank. "What makes you say that?"

"Because Brass doesn't just disappear unless someone close knew where he'd be. When he'd be vulnerable." I lean against the statue opposite her. "Someone sold him to that necromancer."

The silence stretches.

Mary whispers finally. "You're right. Someone close." Her voice is barely audible. "That's why I needed you," she says. "You're outside it all. You don't know my people, don't owe them anything. You're the only person in this whole damn city I can be certain isn't trying to kill me."

Her desperation pulls at me. I don't see a manipulator. I see someone barely holding on. Clinging to power because without it, the world will eat her alive.

I know that feeling. Spent years washing it down with whiskey after the war.

"The note," I say. "On Brass. It was addressed to me."

Mary looks up, calculation flickering back. "What?"

"*'Hi, Mick, want to play?'*" I recite. "Whoever did this—they know I'm working for you. And they want me to know they know."

"Christ." Mary presses her hands to her face. "I'm sorry. I didn't think—I didn't mean to put you in danger."

If she'll lie to Kollach, why wouldn't she lie to me?

"You know something," I say. "About who's behind this."

"No." Too fast. "I told you, I don't know who—"

"Mary."

She meets my eyes, wavers, then looks away.

"I have suspicions," she says finally. "Names. Patterns. But nothing I can prove. And I can't start flinging accusations without proof. Not when I'm already losing ground to Kollach."

It's not the whole truth. I can feel that much. "You promised you'd find Edison."

"I'm trying—"

"Try harder," I order. "That's the only reason I'm still here. Not the jade. Not Kollach. *Edison.* I want that boy back breathing. If you can't deliver on that, we're done."

"I will." She straightens, chin tilting up. "I've got people looking. Contacts in places the Bureau can't touch. We'll find him."

"When?"

"Soon." Her hand finds my arm, and that static tingle runs through me. "I swear, Mick. We're close. One more day, maybe two, and we'll have leads on both Edison and the jade."

"Fine," I say, easing my arm out of her grip. "But I'm not waiting on your word. I've got my own leads to run."

Something flickers in her eyes. "What leads?"

"Nothing solid yet." I'm not ready to bring Sol and the rusalka into this. "You'll know if anything pans out."

Mary studies me for a long beat. Then she nods. "Just...be careful, Mick. Whoever's doing this—turning my people, sending messages—they're dangerous. And they clearly have an interest in you now."

"I can handle myself."

"I know you can." Her smile is tired. "That's why I hired you, remember? The legendary Mick Kelly who killed Lafayette

Baker and walked away from his death magic." She hesitates. "I only hope I haven't painted a target on your back by bringing you into this."

The concern in her voice sounds real. Or maybe I just want it to be.

"Come on," I say. "Let's get you home before Kollach decides to throw us out personally."

Mary wipes the worst of the smeared makeup from her face, then straightens her dress. The mask is mostly back in place. Cracked at the edges but holding.

We cross the garden toward the waiting carriage. Behind us, Kollach's mansion blazes with light and music. From out here, you'd never know a dead man had walked its halls tonight.

Chapter Twenty-One

With Mary safely tucked in at the Strausburg, Connor and Tommy are responsible for her, I can finally head home. I lean back against the carriage seat, closing my eyes. But the darkness behind my eyelids is full of images I can't shake.

Brass lurching down that hallway. The purple-black stain of corrupted animus crawling through his veins. The way he'd crumbled when I'd severed the necromancer's control, transforming him back into meat and bone.

And that note. *Hi, Mick, want to play?*

Someone's turning men into weapons. Someone who knows my name. Someone connected to the revenants stalking Mission Street, to the hoppies with their violet-stained eyes, to Edison's disappearance.

All the same necromancer. I'd pieced that together already. I don't know for sure who holds the strings, but I've got ideas.

The carriage stops.

I open my eyes, expecting to see my street. But we're nowhere near home, still in the better part of town. Two more carriages block the street ahead and behind. Men in dark coats standing nearby, hands in pockets.

"Driver?" I call.

No answer.

My hand moves toward the derringer.

The carriage door swings open.

Isaac Kollach leans in, all smiles and expensive cologne. "Ms. Kelly. What fortuitous timing."

I don't remove my hand from my gun. "I suppose it depends on your point of view."

He climbs in without invitation, settling onto the seat across from me. The door clicks shut behind him. Through the window, I see his men taking positions around the carriage. Blocking us in. Making sure I understand there's no running.

"Your driver's been compensated," Kollach says. "For his time and his discretion."

"Say what you came to say."

"Let's be plain, Ms. Kelly." He leans forward slightly. "You're looking for a boy. Agent Colt."

My chest tightens. "What do you know about Edison?"

"That he's alive. As of this evening." He pauses, watching me. "I have resources. When something is taken in my city, I can arrange its return."

Edison didn't wander off. He was grabbed. And Kollach knows who did it.

A violet buzz runs through my body, that same ugly stain I felt in Brass, in the hoppies on Mission Street. The revenants at Kollach's rally. The note pinned to Brass's chest in mocking invitation.

Want to play?

The necromancer who's been haunting this city, turning corpses into weapons and living men into addicts, is not some rogue operator. He's working for the man sitting across from me.

"Your Doctor Nightingale took him," I say. Not a question.

Something flickers across Kollach's face. Surprise that I've connected the dots. Then calculation. And underneath it all, something else.

Fear.

Just a flash, quickly buried, but I saw it.

"Doctor Nightingale is...overzealous in his methods," he seems to be searching for the right wrds. "I employed him for demonstrations. Séances for donors. Certain practical applications." He adjusts his cuffs, and I notice his hands aren't quite steady. "I did not authorize him to involve Bureau personnel."

"But you know he did it."

"I suspect." His tone sharpens. "Which is why I'm here. Nightingale has exceeded his brief. He's become indiscreet. Dangerous." He pauses. "Tonight's incident at my home made that abundantly clear."

The revenant. Brass, sent specifically to get my attention.

"Your mystic sent me a message tonight," I say. "Pinned to a dead man's jacket."

Kollach's jaw tightens. A muscle twitches near his temple. "That was ill-advised. Not at a social gathering. Not so publicly." He leans forward. "You see my problem, Ms. Kelly. I hired a consultant for controlled demonstrations. Instead, I have a necromancer who thinks he can act independently. Who takes liberties. Who makes threats."

There it is again. That flicker behind his eyes when he says "threats." He's not just annoyed with Nightingale. He's afraid of him.

"Who grabbed a BMI agent and is holding him hostage," I add.

"Allegedly." But he doesn't deny it. "Which brings us to our arrangement."

"What arrangement?" I ask.

"Deliver the Nü Gua Jade to me within forty-eight hours, and I will personally ensure Agent Colt is returned to the Bureau." He spreads his hands. "You'll be the hero who recovered both a missing agent and a dangerous artifact. Your suspension disappears. Your record gets cleaned. Everyone wins."

"Except your necromancer."

"Once the jade is secured—once the boy is returned—we can discuss Nightingale's... departure." His voice drops, and there's something careful in how he says it. Like he's testing me. "He needs to be handled. Delicately. By someone who understands the nature of his work."

"You mean killed."

"I mean managed." He straightens his cuffs again. Nervous habit. "The doctor has certain protections. Certain...abilities that make direct confrontation inadvisable. For my men, at least." His gaze flicks over me, assessing. "But you're different, aren't you? You killed Lafayette Baker. Tonight, you severed a revenant's bindings like cutting thread."

And there it is. The real reason he's here.

He's afraid to move against Nightingale himself. Afraid of what the necromancer might do if threatened. He's looking for someone expendable. Someone female, someone he can manipulate or discard.

Someone he thinks he can control.

"And if I refuse?" I ask.

"Then the boy's fate becomes...uncertain." He shrugs, but the gesture's too casual. Forced. "San Francisco is a dangerous city. Young men disappear all the time. Especially when they ask the wrong questions."

The threat hangs there, but I can taste the desperation underneath it. He needs me. Needs someone to clean up the monster he was arrogant enough to hire.

"Commander Garrett answers to people who answer to me," Kollach continues. "One word from me, and your suspension vanishes. You return to active duty with commendations. Transfer to a real division. Resources. The kind of position where your particular talents are appreciated. Respectability, Ms. Kelly. The thing every woman in your position wants but can never quite grasp. I can give you that."

He leans back, trying to look relaxed. In control.

I release my grip on the gun and lay my hand in my lap, demure-like. Why do men like him always think women like me want respectability from men like him?

"Mary Hunter is a liability, Ms. Kelly. Fading, unreliable, compromised. Work for me instead. Deliver the jade, help me tidy up Nightengale, and I'll ensure you never have to answer to someone like Garrett again." He pauses. "A woman of your abilities shouldn't be wasting herself as a bodyguard to a has-been criminal. You could have real power. Real influence."

His tone's so reasonable. So paternal. Like he's offering me a gift instead of asking me to kill the necromancer he's too scared to face himself.

"After all," he adds, and there's the faintest contempt in his smile now, "you're just a woman. Nightingale won't expect direct confrontation from you. Won't see you as a threat until it's too late. That's your advantage."

The anger builds slow and cold in my chest.

I've spent my whole life being used. By the Army. By Lafayette. By men who thought they could point me at their enemies and pull the trigger. Men who hired necromancers and then acted surprised when corpses started walking. Men who used Edison as a pawn, dangling him like bait.

Men who looked at me and saw "just a woman"—expendable, manipulable, less dangerous than the forces they'd already unleashed.

Through my Gleaner sight, Kollach's vitae pulses beneath his skin, vibrant, the steady rhythm of a healthy heart.

Lub-dub. Lub-dub. Steady. Confident.

People think my power's a battering ram. They've seen me throw men through walls, deflect bullets. What they don't realize is the same energy that flips a locomotive can squeeze one tiny muscle. A heart's just a fist-sized knot of flesh, opening and closing. All I have to do is hold it shut.

I push. Just a little. Just enough to make it skip. Once. Twice.

Kollach's eyes widen. His hand flies to his chest.

"What—what are you—"

His heart races now. *Lub-dub-lub-dub-lub-dub.* Too fast. Too hard. His breath's coming shorter, sweat beading on his forehead.

Right here. Right now. I could just squeeze. It would take so little to stop Isaac Kollach's heart in his chest. And then I could ride his death, take that tasty power and free San Francisco from this canker.

The thought is so tempting it scares me.

I lean forward, holding his gaze. Let him understand exactly what kind of "just a woman" he's trying to manipulate.

"You're afraid of your necromancer," I state. "Afraid of what he might do if you cross him."

His heart hammers against my invisible grip.

"But here's what you're missing, Mr. Kollach." I tighten my hold just a fraction. "I'm no less dangerous. And unlike your professor, I'm sitting right here."

I hold him there for one more breath. Two. Let the lesson sink in.

Then I release him.

Kollach gasps, fumbling inside his coat. The gun comes out shaking, pointed at my chest.

"Don't," he rasps, breath still coming too fast. "Don't you dare—"

"Fire Nightengale before he kills you," I say, reaching across to open the carriage door. My hand's steady even though that little display wrung me out.

Before he's clear of the steps, I slam the door shut and bang on the ceiling. "Driver! Move!"

The carriage lurches forward. Through the window, I see Kollach stumble back, his men tense, hands going to weapons.

But he waves them off. Trying to save face. Trying to look like he let me go.

The carriage pulls away, and I watch him through the rear window—a small man in an expensive coat, lost in the early dawn light. A man who hired monsters he couldn't control, then tried to manipulate a woman into cleaning up his mess.

I close my eyes. Exhausted. Furious. But the pieces are finally falling into place.

Kollach hired the necromancer. The same one who grabbed Edison, who animated Brass, who's been flooding the streets with enhanced hoppies. Doctor Nightingale, whoever he really is, has Edison chained somewhere, and Kollach's too afraid to stop him. He came looking for "just a woman" to do his dirty work.

Mary can't help me. She's barely holding on herself, and she's lying about something. I feel it in my bones. Ah Toy's got her own agenda. The BMI thinks I'm a liability.

I've got no allies. No power left. No leverage.

But I know who does.

Sol knows where the jade is. I'm certain of it. He's hiding something, and I'm done being gentle about it. Don't know how I'll get past his rusalka, but there's a way.

Everyone wants the jade. Mary, Kollach, Ah Toy. And apparently, Kollach's necromancer too, if he's willing to grab a BMI agent to force the issue.

But if I get it first then I'm the one with power. Power to make them all deal. Power to get Edison back.

I'll swing by home, get out of this dress, then head to Sol's.

And I'm not leaving until he tells me where that jade is. Even if I have to tear Arachne's Castle apart.

That note keeps echoing in my mind.

Personal. Mocking. Someone who knows me.

The thought should scare me. The violence of it. The desperation.

Instead, it steadies me.

I'm done playing by everyone else's rules.

Time to make my own.

Chapter Twenty-Two

THE CARRIAGE RATTLES TO a stop a block from home. I press a coin into the driver's palm and step down into the early morning fog, my borrowed evening gown whispering against the cobblestones.

"Keep the change," I tell him. "And forget you saw me."

He tips his hat and drives off without a word. Good man.

I wait in the shadow of the green grocer's, watching the empty street. No one followed me from Pacific Heights. I checked three times during the ride. But Brass's corpse shambling down that hallway has left me twitchy as a cat in a dog pound.

The street's waking up. The distant clang of a cable car starting its morning run, the iceman's wagon clattering past. A few early risers appear on the sidewalks.

Our townhouse glows pink in the early light. Through the parlor window, I catch movement. The house is already up. Of course, it's already seven. Ylva has school, and Gudrun's an early riser by nature.

Brass is dead. Mary's shaken but alive. Kollach showed his hand. And I walked out of that mansion with Mary's gratitude.

But right now, all I want is to see Jules and Gudrun. Maybe give Ylva a long hug before she leaves for school. Drink Gudrun's terrible coffee and listen to Jules fuss about the boarding house accounts.

Normal things. Safe things.

I let myself in through the front door as quietly as the hinges allow.

"Auntie MC!" Ylva barrels down the stairs in her nightgown, white-blond braids flying. "You're home! Did you go to a fancy party? Was there dancing?"

I catch her up in a one-armed hug, breathing in the soapy smell of her hair. She's safe. She's here.

"There was a party," I say, setting her down. "Very fancy. Very boring."

"Then why'd you go?"

"Work, Little Wolf." I tweak her nose. "Now scoot. Get dressed before your mama has a conniption."

She giggles and races back upstairs.

Voices drift from the parlor. Julianna's laugh, bright and warm. And someone else, I don't recognize—female, younger, enthusiastic.

I should check in. Let Jules know I'm home. But first I want out of this dress and into something mine.

I make it halfway up the stairs before Julianna appears in the parlor doorway.

"Mary Catherine? Thank goodness." She's already dressed in a crisp day suit, every hair in place despite the early hour. "Miss Rambound is here with the photographs from Woodward's Gardens. Come see. Ylva looks absolutely precious."

"In a minute, Jules. I need to change."

"It'll only take a moment." There's that note in her voice that says she won't take no for an answer. "Miss Rambound has another appointment at eight."

I glance down at the blue silk gown, torn and spotted with what might be blood at the hem. "I'm not exactly presentable."

"You're fine. Come." She's already turning back toward the parlor.

I sigh, muttering to myself about my bossy little sister, but I'm not going to be explaining my business in front of the photographer.

The parlor smells of fresh coffee and Gudrun's herb bundles drying by the window. Harriet Rambound, the photographer, stands beside the piano, laying out photographs on the polished surface.

"Mrs. McClellan." She smiles, warm and genuine. "I hope you don't mind the early hour. I have a sitting at eight and wanted to deliver these before I forgot."

"Not at all." I move closer, conscious of how I must look with my hair half-falling from its pins, and exhaustion carved into every single line of my face.

Julianna's already bent over the photographs, making pleased sounds. "Look at this one, Mary Catherine. Ylva's expression is perfect."

The first photograph shows Ylva perched on the reclining camel, her face split in a gap-toothed grin. Behind her, I'm visible in profile, one hand steadying her, the hook of my left arm reflecting the afternoon light.

Something in my chest loosens. She looks so happy. So safe.

"And this one," Harriet says, sliding another photograph forward. "It shows the whole garden behind you."

This one's taken from farther back. Ylva and I are centered, but the frame includes the wider scene showing other tourists clustered around the camel paddock, the elephant enclosures stretching into the background, the manicured paths winding through carefully tended greenery.

I lean closer, examining the background out of habit.

"It's lovely," Julianna says beside me, already reaching for her pocketbook. "We'll take all three."

I'm about to agree when something in the background catches my eye.

A family clusters near the elephants. A woman with a parasol. Children running with balloons.

And there. Partially obscured by a decorative palm. A tall figure in a dark coat.

My pulse skips.

"Miss Rambound," I hear myself say, voice strange and distant. "Do you have a magnifying glass?"

She blinks, surprised. "I—yes, actually. In my bag. One moment."

Julianna touches my arm. "Mary Catherine? What is it?"

"Probably nothing." But my hand is shaking. "Just think I recognize someone."

The photographer hands me a small magnifying glass, the kind she must use for examining negatives.

I position it over the figure.

The image swims into focus.

And my world stops.

Gaunt face. Cadaverous features. That fucking mustache.

No.

The photograph trembles in my hand. The magnifying glass slips, blurring the image. I force it steady, force myself to look again.

It's him.

The tilt of the head. The way he's standing with his hip cocked, lazy and confident. Not watching the camels or the other tourists.

Watching us.

Watching me. With Ylva in my arms.

The photograph slips from my fingers. Hits the piano with a soft sound that seems incredibly loud.

My hand spasms—not the flesh and bone hand, but the phantom. The hand that isn't there anymore. Phantom fingers curling into a fist so tight I can feel nails biting into a palm that doesn't exist.

The pain's white-hot.

The parlor tilts. I grab the piano's edge, my remaining hand white-knuckled against the polished wood.

"Mary Catherine?" Julianna's voice sounds distant, underwater. "Mick, what's wrong?"

I can't answer. Can't breathe. The walls are pressing in, the air too thick, too warm.

The phantom hand cramps again, so fierce I gasp. For a moment, I'm not in the parlor anymore. I'm in the cavern in New Mexico, Morgan's body lurching toward me with dead eyes and a slack jaw. The smell of death magic thick and sweet like rotting flowers.

"Mary Catherine!" Julianna shakes my shoulder. Hard. "You need to breathe. Breathe."

I gulp air. Force my vision to clear.

The parlor steadies. Julianna's frightened face swims into focus. Harriet Rambound stands by the door, clearly unsure whether to stay or go. Gudrun's appeared from somewhere, Ylva's school satchel in hand.

I reach for the photograph with a trembling hand. Pick it up.

Even without the magnifying glass, I can see him now. Can't believe I missed it the first time.

Hoodoo Jones. In Woodward's Gardens. Only a few days ago. Before Loosh was killed. Before Edison disappeared.

Watching me with my niece.

Sol said Loosh recognized the buyer in Sausalito. Said he'd never seen Loosh that scared. Of course he was scared.

"Who is that?" Harriet asks curious. "Do you know him?"

"Old acquaintance." My voice sounds dead. "From New Mexico."

Julianna goes very still beside me. She knows what New Mexico means.

She'd been the one who held me while I screamed myself awake night after night, convinced Morgan's corpse was coming through the door.

"Thank you, Miss Rambound," Julianna says, her hostess voice sliding into place despite the tremor underneath. "These are lovely. We'll take all of them. If you'll excuse us, we have a family matter to discuss."

The photographer glances between us, sensing the shift. "Of course. I'll just—"

She gathers her things and sees herself out.

The door clicks shut.

Silence.

Gudrun sets down the school satchel very carefully. "The man from New Mexico, the man who—" She cuts herself off, glancing toward the stairs where Ylva's footsteps thump overhead. "Is it him?"

I nod. Can't speak.

"You're certain?"

I hold up the photograph. My hand's steadier now, but only because I'm going numb. Shock, probably. Or maybe I don't have any more fear left in me.

"It's Hoodoo Jones," I say. Each word comes out flat, factual. "He's a necromancer. He murdered Morgan. He cost me this." I raise the hook. "And he was at Woodward's Gardens on Saturday. Watching me. With Ylva."

"We need to leave," Julianna says, her voice shaking. "Today. Take Ylva and go somewhere safe. Out of the city."

"No." Gudrun's voice cuts through the panic. "We don't need to run. My coven—Mrs. Chen's house is heavily warded. Old magic. Six bedrooms. Her husband knows how to handle trouble."

Julianna latches onto this. "Yes. Yes, that's better. Closer. We can—"

"Do it." I interrupt, my voice strange to my own ears. "Pack what you need. Go today. This morning. Take the horses."

Julianna starts to protest but Gudrun touches her arm. I stand in the middle of the parlor, the photograph still in my hand.

The note on Brass's chest. The violet corruption I'd sensed in the hopheads. The revenants at Kollach's rally. So much like New Mexico. But I can't tell one necromancer from another from their magic. It's all just purple smut.

But Edison can.

All of it. All of it was Hoodoo.

I hear myself say. "Edison, Edison must have spotted Hoodoo's magic on one of those hoppies and followed him. Stupid brave kid walked right into Hoodoo's hands. And Loosh... Loosh recognized him in Sausalito and Hoodoo cut his throat for it."

"But why?" Gudrun asks. "Why come here? Why now?"

I look down at the photograph again. At Hoodoo's stance. He's positioned deliberately in the frame. He wanted me to see this. Wanted me to know he'd been there. He was fifty feet away. Fifty feet from Ylva. And I didn't feel a thing.

The Nü Gua Jade, Mary said it contained the power of creation. A necromancer with the "power of creation" would be almost unstoppable. Sol said they sent word to collectors across the country. Hoodoo must have caught the scent and come running. He didn't come here for me. He came for the jade. Finding me was just the cherry on top.

I pull away from Julianna and head for the stairs.

"Mary Catherine!" Her voice cracks. "Where are you going?"

"To change. Get my gun. Then I'm going to get that jade before Hoodoo does."

"The jade?" Gudrun follows me to the staircase. "How does that—"

"It's what he's here for." I pause on the landing, looking back at them. "So I'm going to get it first. And then I'm going to use it as bait."

"And then what? You face him alone?"

"Nope. You're gonna send a note to Leona Freeman for me. Her direction's in my coat pocket. Tell her he's in town. And besides," my voice hardens, "he's not invincible, Jules. I knocked him down once before. And this time, I'm going to make sure he doesn't get back up."

I don't wait for her response.

In my room, I strip out of the borrowed gown. My hand shakes as I button my shirt, buckle my gun belt. The Colt's weight settles against my hip.

This is the woman I was in New Mexico. The Gleaner. The killer.

Good.

Chapter Twenty-Three

ABBY HOLDS THE PHOTOGRAPH like it might bite her. Her hands are steady, but her face isn't. She sits the photograph on the bar, smoothing it flat with both palms, and studies Hoodoo's blurred figure for a long time without speaking.

"You're saying Kollach's pet mystic is Hoodoo Jones?" she asks. "Hoodoo Jones is running around my city, has my boy, and he's under Isaac Kolach's protection?"

"Yes, Abby." I touch her arm. "But Hoodoo wants the jade. Once I have it, I'm gonna draw Hoodoo out, and he's gonna face me on my terms."

She reaches under the counter and pulls out the truncheon she keeps for rowdy sailors. Lays it next to the photograph.

"Right," she says.

Nico slides the photo over and squints at the image. "Sol and Loosh have traded antiquities out of Meiggs since the Rush. Sometimes even legitimate ones. Everyone on the wharf knew. But the real Nü Gua Jade?" He let out a low whistle. "That's a different animal all together. How did those two old fools even get their hands on something like that? "

"You can't write folks off on account of a gray beard. They've been running this game for decades, Nico." I shake my head. "Bet they knew every collector, every captain, every fence on the coast." I stare at the photo. "Poor Loosh was hoping for one last big score and it bit him in the ass. But I think Sol still has the jade."

Abby's already pulling on her coat. "There are three English ships in port. Every sailor who owes me a favor will be looking. Hoodoo Jones won't be able to take a piss in this city without me hearing about it."

Nico squeezes her shoulder. "We'll get Edison back."

"Damn right we will." She kisses him hard on the forehead, then pushes him toward the door. "Go help Mick get that jade. I'll handle the docks."

We leave her there, calling orders to the early morning regulars, her fear transforming into action. A woman mobilizing her army.

The scent of brine and coal smoke is heavy in my chest as Nico and I push north along the Embarcadero toward Meiggs. My plan is simple. Sol knows where the jade is. Last time I pushed him, the rusalka nearly drowned me. But Nico's known Sol twenty years and the rusalka's sung to him more times than he'll admit.

Nico is the lynchpin. My Gleaner's running on fumes. Whatever I'd pulled from the girl in the alley got burned fighting Brass and putting the fear of God into Kollach. All I've got left is enough juice to see by.

I scan the pilings as we walk, looking for pale limbs in the water. Avoiding the rusalka altogether would be ideal. The bay's empty except for bobbing debris and a few gulls working over a dead fish. Fingers crossed.

"You really think he'll just hand it over?" Nico asks, breaking the silence. "Sol's not exactly known for being generous with his treasures."

"He will." I adjust my coat, feeling the weight of my revolver. "Once he knows what Hoodoo did to Loosh. What he'll do to Edison."

Sol loved Loosh in his way. The old man's got a conscience buried under all that clutter and cobwebs.

He'll give me the jade.

He has to.

We round the bend, and Arachne's Castle comes into view. My steps falter.

Something's wrong.

The windows are shuttered. Heavy wooden slats latched across the wide glass panes that usually display Sol's collection to passing tourists. The door hangs slightly ajar, moving in the wind with a rhythmic creak.

And Werner's screaming. The gray parrot's shrieks carry into the street, frantic and continuous. High-pitched terror that makes my scalp prickle.

"Sol never closes up," Nico sounds worried. "Not unless there's a typhoon coming."

I hear the monkeys inside. Distressed calls overlapping in a cacophony of animal panic.

I draw my Colt, thumbing back the hammer. "Stay behind me."

"Like hell." Nico pulls a wicked-looking knife from his belt. "Sol's my friend. If something's happened—"

Approaching the entrance, a hum starts low in my belly. Death residue, thick as San Francisco fog, seeping from that open door. Someone died in there. Recently.

"Shit," I breathe.

I push the door wider with my boot, letting it swing inward. Werner's screaming gets louder.

Inside, the shuttered windows leave most of the space in shadow. Just thin strips of morning light slicing gaps in the dark, catching dust motes and cobwebs.

Werner launches himself at us in a flurry of wings. "Rum and gum! Rum and gum!" He awkwardly circles my head twice, then returns to his perch. His feathers ruffled, one wing bent at an odd angle.

The monkeys stop screaming and huddle silently on their totem pole perch, watching us. The one with the club foot clutches the tail-less one. Their eyes track our movement, wide and white-rimmed with fear.

The smell hits me next. Copper and salt, the particular smell of a death that's still fresh enough to be wet.

"Sol?" Nico calls out, his voice cracking. "Sol, you here?"

I already know the answer. Death's crawling up my spine like frost.

We find him behind the bar.

Sol Sonderling lies crumpled on the floor, his white hair matted dark with blood. His throat's been cut, nearly taken his head off. His stovepipe hat lies a few feet away, crushed under someone's boot.

Blood pools beneath him, dark and congealed at the edges. Rigor mortis has begun to set in. His jaw locked slightly open, his fingers curled like claws.

"No." Nico's knife clatters to the floor. He drops to one knee beside Sol's body, touching the old man's neck like he's checking for a pulse he knows isn't there. "Twenty years," he says hoarsely. "Twenty years I've been drinking his terrible grog."

I kneel beside Sol's body, forcing myself into the cold, analytical space I learned during the war. See the details. Read the story the dead tell.

The air beside his body shimmers.

Sol's shade flickers into view. Translucent, barely more substantial than the dust motes caught in the thin strips of light. I've been seeing strangers' ghosts for months now, faces I don't know drifting through crowds and clinging to doorways. But this one I know and I've got a suspicion it's my fault.

He's trying to pick up his crushed stovepipe hat. His fingers pass through the felt, and he jerks back, staring at his hand. Confused. He reaches for the hat again, more carefully this time, as if maybe he just missed.

Then he notices me kneeling beside his body and freezes. His eyes dart around the room, finally landing back on me and Nico next to his dead body.

His face crumples, frustration and grief and confusion bleeding across his expression. He studies his own body. The blood. The wound. The terrible stillness. His mouth opens in what might be a scream, but there's only silence.

His eyes widen and his shade fades. Flashes brighter. His jaw works, lips forming words.

Nothing. Not even a whisper of sound.

"I can't hear you." I shake my head at him, frowning.

"What?" Nico looks up from Sols physical body. "Mick, who are you—"

"Sol's shade." I keep my eyes on the wavering form. "He's here, next to the hat."

Nico follows my gaze, squinting at the empty air. "I don't see anything."

Sol's jabbing toward the back of the bar, past the shelves of bottles and curiosities, toward the far wall where the shuttered windows leave everything in deep shadow.

"He's trying to show me something." I mutter, pushing to my feet. My knees crack, protesting. "Stay here."

I move in the direction Sol's pointing, past the bar's overfull shelves, into the deeper dark at the back of the room. The floor feels sticky under my boots. It's darker here, the light through the shutters barely touches it.

Sol leads me. Flickering in and out. But he keeps pointing. Keeps jabbing his hand toward the floor near the back room entrance.

A glint. Low, near the baseboard, where one strip of light falls across the dark floorboards. Something metallic.

I crouch. My fingers close on a pocket watch. Gold case, the crystal cracked like someone stepped on it. I turn it over, holding it to the thin light.

An Irish harp engraved on the back. And the initials GTM.

"Nico," I say. "What do you make of this?"

He picks his way across the floor.

I hold up the watch.

"That's one of Mary's watches," Nico says, his grief transforming into something harder. "She gives them to her lieutenants when they make inner circle. Brass, Tommy, Connor, maybe half a dozen others. Marks you as one of her trusted men."

I glance at Sol's shade. He's barely visible now. A smudge of light, a suggestion of a man. But he's nodding, relaxed, easy. This is what he wanted me to see.

He reaches toward me one last time. Then he's gone.

Shit, I am responsible for this. I told Mary I was poking around Meiggs when she got suspicious at the dressmaker's. And of course, Mary would know Sol dealt in antiquities. Everyone on the wharf knew that. Stupid me, mentioning old men and oddity shops.

She sent one of her people here. Because of me.

I move to investigate the back room and my boot sticks to the floor. An unpleasant, tacky pull against the sole I barely noticed before. Looking down, I can't see anything. The floorboards are too dark, the light too thin. But I can feel it under my boot. And now the smell of blood reaches me, cutting through the dust and gin.

The Gleaner sight kicks in without conscious thought.

Another pool of blood. A few feet from where I found the watch, spreading toward the back room entrance. It's nearly invisible on dark wood without magical sight.

And drifting from it like a malaise, necromantic residue. The sickly violet taint I'd cut through when I severed Brass from his bindings at the party. Twelve hours ago. Less.

Two deaths in this bar. One body.

Mary's working for Kollach. Brass was one of her lieutenants. Did Kollach know Brass would be here? Did he send Hoodoo to eliminate one of Mary's people?

"Brass died here." I say it aloud, needing to hear it make sense. "Someone killed him and Hoodoo Jones, Kollach's 'Professor Nightingale,' raised him just in time for that party."

Nico's staring at the floor, poking his boot around. "You're saying Hoodoo Jones came here, killed Sol and Brass and then turned Brass into a zombie?

"Brass interrupted something," I say, piecing it together, the death hum louder. "Or he came here on business, and someone was waiting."

Could be wrong. Could be another of Mary's people walking around as a puppet somewhere. Could be there's a second necromancer running around the city. But the simplest read is the right one. Brass was supposed to be at Kollach's party. Never showed up alive. Because he was here, dying on Sol's floor while Hoodoo turned him into a weapon.

I straighten, scanning the rest of the bar. Even in the dim light there's evidence someone searched this place. Looking for the jade. I just don't know if he found it.

"We need more light." I move to the nearest window and wrench the shutter open. Morning light floods the room.

The bar looks worse in daylight. Every surface tossed. Sol's lifetime of collecting scattered and trampled. Werner huddles silent on his perch. The monkeys haven't moved.

"Where's the water woman?" Nico asks, voicing the thought I've been circling. "Ain't no way she'd stand by while someone killed Sol."

"No," I scratch my jaw. Why couldn't the rusalka save Sol?

Nico's scanning the floor near the back room. "Mick. Look."

Bare footprints. Small, delicate. Pressed into the tacky blood near where Brass died. They lead from the pool toward the back wall, then fade on drier floorboards.

She was here. She came in to find Sol already dead.

"I'll check the office. You keep looking out here. I don't want to be standing over Sol's body when the rusalka comes back."

Nico nods and I enter Sol's cramped office.

There's no way the jade is in here. Just more chaos. Papers scattered across a battered desk. Drawers yanked open, contents dumped. The strongbox is open. The lock forced, the hasp bent where someone had levered it with something heavy.

I pull out papers, scanning fast. Receipts. Bills of sale. Letters from collectors. Near the bottom, a folded document on heavier stock.

I open it. It's a mortgage note. Mary Elizabeth Hunter is Sol's mortgage holder. Sol owed Mary $1500 and was three months in arrears.

After I mentioned Meiggs Wharf she sent Brass here. Maybe to collect what Sol owed. Maybe she'd connected Sol to the jade and wanted Brass to investigate under cover of collecting money. Or to offer Sol a deal, the jade for his debts forgiven. Whatever the errand, Brass walked into something waiting for him.

I don't believe Mary wanted Brass dead. The grief on her face when she'd seen his revenant crumple in that hallway, that was real. But she set this in motion. And I gave her the push.

I tuck the mortgage note in my coat and return to the main room feeling dejected.

Leaning against the bar, I chew my lip in thought. Did Hoodoo find it? The place is ransacked. Every drawer, every shelf, every hiding spot an amateur would think of. But Sol wasn't an amateur. He'd been hiding things from customs inspectors and creditors for forty years. What are we missing?

"If it was here," Nico says, reading my face, "and that bastard found it, why'd he bother sending the dead man to the party with a note for you? He'd have what he wanted. He'd be gone."

He's right. Which means the jade is still hidden. Which means—

The temperature plummets, condensing moisture into frost that swirls across the window glass, the mirror behind the bar. Seemingly out of nowhere, water pools on the floorboards, seeping up from the bay.

Werner shrieks and buries his head under his wing.

The rusalka erupts through the floorboards. Water geysers up from cracks in the wood, spraying across Sol's collection, his animals, us. Her dark hair lashes the air in every direction, whipping bottles off shelves, scattering scrimshaw. Her eyes black pits.

"THIEVES." The words thunder through the room. "MUR-DERERS. LIARS."

Chapter Twenty-Four

WATER RUSHES ACROSS THE floor and coils around my ankles, locking them in place like shackles. The cold is immediate, savage, like being plunged into snowmelt. Within seconds it climbs past my boots to my shins, rising with purpose.

"We didn't—" I start, but she cuts me off.

"YOU CAME FOR THE STONE." Her voice fractures, grief and rage twisting together. "All of you, coming and taking and KILLING. The sweet-talking man came. My Sol said no. Fought him. He TOOK. TOOK MY SOL."

The water swirls up to my knees. Presses against me like a rip tide.

Sol's shade flickers into existence beside the rusalka—sudden and silent. He's barely visible even to me, his form wavering, weak. But he tries. He gets between me and the rusalka, as if he could shield me. Reaches for her face. His fingers pass through her pale skin without resistance.

She doesn't see him. Doesn't feel him. The one creature in this city she loved, and she can't sense he's here.

"I know," I say, forcing my voice to stay even despite the fear creeping up my spine. "The sweet-talking man—Hoodoo Jones, he's a necromancer. A murderer. I'm hunting him."

Her hair lashes out, wrapping around one of the ceiling rafters. Wood groans and cracks.

"LIES. You all lie with your pretty words." She drifts closer, and the cold becomes painful. "You came before. Asked and asked about stones and treasures. You BROUGHT them here."

"You're right." The admission is bitter. "I led them here. And I'm sorry. But I can make it right. I can stop the sweet-talking man. But I need the jade to do it."

The water hits my waist. The pressure is immense. I can't take a full breath. Feels like the entire bay pressing against my body.

Nico thrashes somewhere to my left, trapped in his own column of water. "Please," he chokes. "Sol would—"

"DO NOT SPEAK OF WHAT MY SOL WOULD WANT." The water surges to my chest. My ribs compress. "You left him. All of you. Left him alone with his treasures and his creatures. Only I stayed. Only I CARED."

Her hair snakes around my throat. Ice-cold, impossibly strong. I claw at it with my right hand, but it slides free. It's like trying to grip current.

"Then tell me what happened," I rasp through the tightening coil. "Tell me what he did to Sol. Help me understand."

"You want to know?" Her face is inches from mine, her breath cold enough to burn. "I will TELL you.

"I was in deep water. Hunting. When I felt it—" Her voice cracks. "Felt my Sol crying out to me. I came as fast as water flows. But I couldn't ENTER."

The hair around my throat tightens.

"The man KNEW. He knew me. He ringed this place with IRON. Casts his spells, made it DRY—so dry I couldn't form. Just mist and longing and SCREAMING."

I go still. Necromantic wards strong enough to lock out a furious rusalka. I'd been thinking of Hoodoo as a two-bit conjurer who got lucky with corpses. The man who animated Morgan's body in New Mexico had power, sure, but it was crude. Blunt force. Warding a building against a supernatural predator while simultaneously interrogating a man and preparing to raise a corpse from fresh death, that's three workings at once. That takes a kind of power Hoodoo didn't have a year ago.

Something changed. Someone elevated him. And I've been underestimating him at every turn, letting old contempt blind me to what he's become.

"I clawed at the prison he made. Threw myself against it again and again. Thought I'd scatter into nothing. But I couldn't reach him." Her voice drops to something almost human. Almost breakable. "I heard him. Heard my Sol begging. Heard your Hoodoo man's questions. Heard the blade."

She eases her grip on me. Just enough to breathe.

"And then the big man came." She glances at Brass's pocket watch, dangling from my hook. "He tried to fight. Tried to stop it. Brave. Stupid. Your man shot him. Like swatting a fly."

My chest heaves, dragging in frigid air. Brass walked into this. Sent by Mary on an errand, collecting a debt or squeezing Sol about the jade. He found Hoodoo already here, already working. And instead of running, he fought.

"When Hoodoo thing left—I came through. But my Sol was already gone." Her hair falls away as she collapses to the floor, wailing. "GONE. Already cold.

"The big man..." She shudders, her form flickering. "The sweet-talking man made him live, not live. Made him walk, made him follow like a dog."

Turned him into a revenant. To send him after me.

"The jade," I choke out. "Where is it? If Hoodoo didn't find it—"

The rusalka's laugh is the sound of drowning. "You think I would TELL you?" She peers at me through the curtain of hair covering her face. "You, who brought death to my door? You, who led murderers to my Sol?"

"Please—"

"Stupid death woman. The sweet-talking man searched. Ruined Sol's things." A terrible smile, showing small, pointed teeth, blooms across her face. "My Sol was clever. He hid it where none would DARE look."

"Where?" I gasp through chattering teeth. The stink of low tide is smothering me.

"You will NEVER know. And I will never tell." She begins to fade, sinking back into the water covering the floor. "Now GO. Leave my Sol. Leave this place. Or I will drag you down. You will keep me company in the deep dark FOREVER."

The water enshrouding me surges over my head. Forcing its way into my mouth, my nose, rushing down my throat. The weight of the entire bay crushing my chest. I can't breathe, can't see, can't think. Just cold and dark and pressure.

Then it breaks. Drains away fast as it came, leaving Nico and me on our hands and knees, retching salt water onto the floorboards. Werner huddles silent on his perch. Even the monkeys haven't moved.

She's gone. Only a puddle to mark where she stood.

Nico coughs, water streaming from his hair and beard. He doesn't speak for a long moment. Just kneels there on Sol's floor, catching his breath.

"Ever since I survived the Arctic I've listened to her sing," he whispers. "But I never understood Sol. Why he'd sit out on the pier in the cold, just waiting for her voice." He wipes his face with a shaking hand. "I understand now. She loved him. Only way she knows how."

I battle to my feet. The cold has sunk so deep I'm not sure warm is something I'll feel again.

But my mind's already moving to calculation.

The jade is hidden. Hoodoo doesn't have it. The rusalka won't give it up while her rage is this fresh. But rage cools. And when it does, she'll realize she can't reach Hoodoo alone. He warded against her once.

She'll come back to me. I just need to survive long enough.

A cold thought surfaces. Could Mary have engineered all this, even Brass's death? Her face when Brass's corpse crumpled in that hallway. The grief in her voice when she'd said *"He was with me for five years..."*

That was real.

Mary's a target. Not a player.

And right now, Mary doesn't know Hoodoo is hunting her people. Doesn't know her network is being taken apart by a necromancer who's slipped his employer's leash. If I don't warn her, she walks blind into whatever Hoodoo's planning next.

"We need to go," I say, pulling Nico toward the exit. "Now."

"We can't just leave Sol—"

"Sol's beyond our help. Edison isn't." I grab his arm. "Abby can send someone for the animals."

We stumble out into morning air that feels tropical after the rusalka's grip. My teeth chatter so hard I bite my tongue.

Behind us, Werner lets out one mournful cry. Then silence falls over Arachne's Castle.

We don't make it half a block.

Two men in dark suits, badges glinting on their lapels. Bureau, or I'm a monkey's uncle.

My stomach drops.

"Mrs. McClellan?" The taller one steps forward, hand resting on his revolver. "Niccolo Zigala? You're wanted for questioning regarding the death of Solomon Sonderling."

"Wait," I start. "How did you—we just found him—"

"Anonymous tip came in forty minutes ago." His expression radiates satisfaction. "Witness reported seeing you and Mr. Zigala enter the premises."

Forty minutes ago. Before we even arrived.

Someone called this in and then waited for us to walk into the frame.

Kollach. Has to be. He told me himself that Garrett answers to people who answer to him. And if Hoodoo convinced Kollach that Mick Kelly is the problem, that I'm the one who needs sidelining while the real game plays out, then this is Hoodoo clearing the board. Getting Mary's bodyguard locked up while he makes his next move.

"Are we under arrest?" I ask, trying to gauge how deep this hole is.

"Just questioning. For now." His tone suggests that could change. "Captain Garrett was very specific. You're to come with us immediately."

I could run, disappear into the city.

But that makes me a fugitive. Puts Julianna and Gudrun and Ylva in the Bureau's crosshairs. And it confirms whatever story Kollach's fed Garrett about me.

I raise my hands slowly. The pocket watch swings from my hook, Brass's blood tacky on the gold case. "Fine. Let's go talk to Captain Garrett."

Nico shoots me a look. I give him the smallest nod. He raises his hands too.

As they load us into the waiting wagon, I catch one last glimpse of Arachne's Castle. The door hangs open, cobwebs swaying in the breeze.

Hoodoo's clearing the board. Killing Sol, raising Brass, framing me for murder. Every move pushes Mary closer to the edge while stripping away anyone who might protect her. And she's the big dummy walking around the city thinking the threat is Chinese agitators, not the necromancer who's already inside the walls.

I need to get out of this interrogation. Warn Mary. Find Edison.

The wagon lurches forward, carrying us toward the BMI office.

Chapter Twenty-Five

THE INTERROGATION ROOM SMELLS like stale tobacco and old sweat. Garrett's been at this for what feels like hours. My teeth want to chatter, but I clench my jaw, lock it tight. Won't give Garrett the satisfaction.

He circles me like a vulture eyeing carrion. Stops. Leans against the wall behind me where I can't see him without turning.

Classic intimidation.

"Two murders in a week," he says. "Both connected to you."

I stare at the opposite wall. Someone's carved initials into the plaster. J.M. + R.K. Wonder if either of them made it out of here.

"Agent Temple. Now Sonderling." Garrett moves, heavy footsteps circling around to the front of the table. "Interesting pattern, Mrs. McClellan."

"I found Sol dead. Left when I heard someone coming." It's mostly true, but I keep my voice even, bored. "Already told your boys that."

"Your *temporary partner* winds up in the bay with his throat cut. Then you just *happen* to discover another body?" He plants both hands on the table, looms over me. Close enough I can smell his breakfast—eggs and onions. "You were suspended for a reason."

"For finding revenants you refused to believe in."

"For being a liability." His tone turns silky with malice. "For being *dangerous*."

I meet his eyes. "Careful, Captain. Your prejudice is show-ing."

His whiskers twitch. "You're a Death Eater. A *parasite*. You feed on death like some—" He breaks off, straightens. Adjusts his collar. "Your kind can't help yourselves. It's in your nature. Like a dog rolling in filth."

I breathe. Let it settle.

"I found Agent Temple's body," Garrett continues. "Exam-ined it myself. The cut was clean. Professional." He walks behind me again, places his hands on my shoulders. "Know what the coroner said? Said it looked like someone experienced did it. Maybe someone who's gutted enough men to know exactly where to slice."

"I was at the Grand Theater with my family when Loosh was killed." I keep my tone level. Reasonable. "Multiple witnesses. Even wrote a statement for your officers."

"Statements can be fabricated." His breath stirs my hair. "Witnesses bribed. And you have *motive*, don't you? Agent Tem-ple discovered something about you. Something you needed kept quiet."

My hand rests on the table, fingers laced through my hook. Don't move them. Don't react. "What do you think I'm hiding, Captain?"

"That's what we're going to find out." He circles back around, sits in the chair opposite. Studies me. "Forty-eight hours. That's how long I can hold you for questioning without formal charges. Forty-eight hours to keep you locked up. For your own safety, of course. Protective custody."

My pulse kicks up, but I don't let it show on my face. Forty-eight hours. Two full days while Hoodoo hunts for the jade. While Edison stays chained in some basement, running out of water, out of hope. While Mary walks around the city thinking she's safe, not knowing a necromancer is in bed with her boss.

Two days for Hoodoo to finish what he started.

"You can't hold me without evidence."

"Can't I?" Garrett smiles. Thin and mean. "You were found at a crime scene. Fled before authorities arrived. That's grounds enough for detention pending investigation."

"I came in willingly when your agents requested it."

"After attempting to leave the scene." He pulls out a notebook and flips it open. "According to witnesses on the scene—"

"Witnesses on the scene." I can't help it—I laugh. "You mean your men?"

He leans forward. "You were suspended. Told to stay away from active investigations. Yet here you are, neck-deep in two murders and God knows what else."

The room suddenly feels smaller. Walls closing in. I force myself to breathe steady, count the seconds. One. Two. Three.

Calculate.

If I'm locked up for forty-eight hours, Hoodoo wins. He finds the jade—wherever the rusalka's hidden it—and either sells it to the highest bidder or uses it himself. Either way, people die. Maybe Edison. Maybe Mary. Maybe my family if Hoodoo decides I'm a threat worth eliminating.

Everyone loses except the necromancer.

"Maybe Elizabeth Van Lew made a mistake," Garrett says softly. Almost gently. Like he's doing me a kindness by saying it. "Bringing you here. Giving you a second chance. Maybe leopards don't change their spots, Mrs. McClellan. Maybe a killer is always a killer."

My Gleaner roils. Hot and hungry. It wants me to kill him, ride his death, power up. I could maybe muster up one pulse of power, strong enough to stop his heart. Make it look natural. Stroke. Aneurysm. Happens all the time to men his age, stress of the job and all.

No one would question it.

Lie. Everyone would question it, but I'm past caring.

My fingers tighten. Knuckles white.

Don't.

Don't prove him right.

Hell. Who am I kidding? I would end up on the floor next to him. I don't have enough juice without knocking myself out cold. Taking a deep breath I force my hand to relax.

"I haven't killed anyone," I say. "Not Loosh. Not Sol. And you know it."

"Do I?" He stands. Walks to the door. Pauses with his hand on the knob. "We'll see what forty-eight hours of reflection can do for your memory. Maybe you'll remember something useful. Or maybe"—he glances back over his shoulder—"maybe you'll just sit here and think about all the people you've failed. All the deaths you couldn't prevent."

The door slams open, from the outside, cracking his knuckles. Garret yelps and jumps back, cradling his hand to his chest.

Leona Freeman marches in.

"Captain Garrett." Leona's voice cuts through Garrett's whimpers. "I require you to release Mrs. McClellan immediately."

His face flushes, his righteous investigator act broken. "This is *my* jurisdiction, Agent Freeman—"

"Mrs. McClellan is a federal witness in an active investigation." Leona poses in the doorway, spine straight as a rifle barrel. No hesitation. No apology. God, I love her. "You're interfering with a top secret task force operation."

"Federal witness?" Garrett's voice climbs half an octave. "She's a suspect in two homicides—"

"She's a *witness* to necromantic activity connected to my case." Leona steps into the room, producing a folded document from inside her jacket. "Russian artifacts with death magic residue. Same signature we found at your crime scenes. Mrs. McClellan has been consulting on the investigation."

A lie. Clean and sharp and delivered without a flicker of doubt.

Garrett snatches the paper. His jaw works as he reads, vein pulsing at his temple. "This doesn't give you authority to—"

"Section Seven of the BMI Charter grants task force commanders jurisdiction over local divisions when cases intersect." Leona's tone could freeze mercury. "My investigation predates yours by three weeks. Which means you're the one interfering, Captain. Would you like me to send my report to Director Van Lew?"

The blood drains from Garrett's face. He might taunt me with her name, but the real Van Lew's not to be trifled with. Even an idiot like him wants to stay below her notice.

"I'm conducting a murder investigation." But his bluster's hollow. "Two men are dead—"

"And Mrs. McClellan found one of them. I'm aware." Leona extends her hand. "Release her. Now. Unless you'd prefer to explain to the director why your turf war cost us our best lead on a necromancer trafficking enchanted artifacts."

Garrett looks at me. At Leona. Back at me again.

His hands ball into fists at his sides.

"You're making a mistake, Freeman." He bites off each word. "She's dangerous. Unstable. Her kind—"

"Her kind has been invaluable to federal investigations for decades." Leona's chin tilts up and she looks down her nose at him. "While you've been shuffling papers and collecting your paycheck, Gleaner agents have served the Union, dismantling four necromantic cults, and saved more lives than your entire division. Watch your mouth, Captain. Before I decide *you're* interfering with national security."

Silence fills the space.

Garrett breaks first, of course. "Fine." He jerks his head toward the door. "Get her out of my station. But she doesn't leave the city. First sign she runs—"

"She won't." Leona meets my eyes briefly. "Will you, Mrs. McClellan?"

"Nope." I practically chirp. "I'm staying right here."

"Good." Garrett gets in my face. Close enough I smell the onions on his breath again. "Because if you do? Federal jurisdiction or not, I'll hunt you down myself. Death Eater."

The slur hangs in the air.

Leona's hand moves to her hip. Not her weapon. Just a gesture. But Garrett sees it. Steps back half a pace.

"We're done here," Leona says.

She turns and walks out without a look back.

Garrett watches me like I'm a viper coiling to strike as I squeeze past him. Out into the hallway the desk clerk pretends he didn't overhear Garret's humiliation and ignores me filing past..

Rushing down the stairs to catch up to Leona I burst outside into the gray light. The sun is completely obscured by clouds, I can't tell if it's noon or three. I miss Colorado's sunshine, miss almost always knowing the time by the light. The flat gray days of San Francisco's spring unsettle me, leave me feeling disconnected.

Leona's already walking north on Kearny, away from the station. Doesn't utter a word as I catch up. Her spine rigid, her stride brisk. A delivery wagon rattles past, the driver shouting at his horses. A woman with a parasol gives us a wide berth on the narrow sidewalk.

We walk a full block in silence. At the corner of Kearny and Clay, she finally stops.

"A note." Her voice is emotionless. "You send me a fucking note telling me Hoodoo is alive?"

My stomach drops. "Yes."

"How long have you known?"

"Just since this morning. There was a photograph, from Woodward's Gardens. He was in the background the day Edison vanished."

"This *morning*." Something flickers across her face. Not anger. Worse. Hurt leashed beneath fury. "You send me a two-line, goddamn note and go get yourself arrested. That's all I get?"

"I've been a little busy being interrogated for murder."

"Deserved consequences of your own idiocy," she snaps. "Going to Sonderling's without backup."

"I was suspended, " I say, matching her pace as she resumes walking. "Who the hell was I supposed to inform?"

She stops so fast we nearly collide. "Me, you dunderhead!" Her eyes flash. She's well and truly pissed. "I thought after New Mexico—" She cuts herself off. Starts walking again, faster now.

I hurry to catch up. "Leona—"

"You've been investigating Loosh's death. Don't bother denying it." She doesn't look at me. "I knew it the second I got that note. Hoodoo's here, and you've been running around this city alone, chasing him. While I sat in my office, thinking you were sulking about your suspension."

The accusation in her voice stings. "I had a lead. On Edison."

That stops her. "What kind of lead?"

A businessman in a bowler hat glances our way, then hurries past. I lower my voice. "Someone with street-level connections. Intel the BMI couldn't access. She said she'd help me find him if I did a job for her."

Leona's eyes narrow. "Who?"

I hesitate. Know the second I say the name, everything changes.

"Mick." Her tone steel.

"Gold Tooth Mary."

For a moment, Leona just stares at me. Then she laughs—short, sharp, without humor. "Mary Hunter. You made a deal with *Mary Hunter*."

"She had information—"

"She's a *crime boss*!" Leona's voice rises, then drops as a pair of Chinese laundrymen pass by carrying a pole between them, baskets swaying. She waits until they're out of earshot. "Extortion, protection, smuggling, suspected involvement in three disappearances we could never prove. The woman runs half the illegal gambling in this city. And you made a deal with her?"

"For Edison—"

"What exactly did you promise her?" Leona steps closer, voice tight with something like fear. "What does she have on you?"

"Protection." The word comes out harder than I intend. "Someone's been following her. Killing her people. She needed someone who could handle herself."

"And you believed her?" Leona shakes her head. "Mary Hunter doesn't ask for help out of fear, Mick. She collects debts. She's been playing this game since before you and I were born."

"I've *seen* it, Leona." My hands curl into fists at my sides. "One of her lieutenants was murdered. Corrupted hoppies are following her through the streets. Someone's tearing down everything she's built, and she doesn't know who or why."

Leona studies my face. Something shifts in her expression. Is it concern? "You *like* her."

"I respect what she's done." The defensiveness in my voice betrays me. "She's built something in this city. Power, influence. Same as you did with the task force."

"You decided to play hero." Leona's tone softens slightly, but the edge remains. "Mick, she's a master manipulator. BMI's been trying to pin her down for fifteen years. You think you're special? You think you see the *real* her?"

"I think she's being hunted by a necromancer, and she doesn't know it yet." I pull Brass's pocket watch from my coat. The gold case catches the weak light. "This belonged to one of her closest people. Brass Murtaugh. Found it at Sol's murder scene."

Leona takes the watch and examines it. "Gold Tooth Mary's man?"

"Was. Sol owed Mary money. Maybe she sent Brass to collect, maybe to lean on him about the jade. I don't know." The words rush out. "But Hoodoo killed them both. Used Brass's corpse as a weapon. You hear about that revenant at Kollach's fundraiser? That was Brass."

"Wait." Leona's eyes sharpen. "The Nü Gua Jade? You're saying this is all connected to that jade rumor?"

"Loosh was fencing it. Sol had it or knew where it was. Mary's trying to acquire it." I watch her process the connections. "And Hoodoo's killing people connected to it."

"Jesus." Leona hands the watch back. Quiet for a long moment. A horse trolley clangs past on Clay Street, bell ringing. When she speaks again, her voice is careful. Professional. "Then bring her in. Protective custody. Let BMI—"

"No."

"Mick—"

"The second federal agents show up asking about Mary Hunter, she's done." Leaning closer, I need her to understand. "Her enemies smell weakness. Her people will think she's turned informant. You don't protect someone like Mary with a badge. It will paint a target on her back."

"She already has a target on her back!"

"But she doesn't know it's Hoodoo pulling the trigger!" My voice cracks despite myself. "She needs to know *now*. Before he kills her like he killed the others."

Leona's quiet. Watching me. "You're not thinking straight about her."

"I'm thinking fine—"

"I've seen this before." Her voice gentles, which is somehow worse than her anger. "Mick, you're a sucker for a tough woman making her way in a man's world. It's how we became partners." She reaches for my arm. "But you're walking into a trap. You have to see that."

Pulling away, I snap, "I know what hunted looks like, Leona. I've *been* hunted. And Mary's scared. Really scared. Whatever else she is—that's real."

"You don't *know* that."

"I know she's next on Hoodoo's list if I don't warn her." I hold her gaze. "Edison's been in Hoodoo's hands for five days, chained in some basement." My voice cracks despite myself. I see it again: the vision from the girl's death. Edison's split lip, the chains. "I *saw* him. I rode a death and it showed me. He's hurt. Terrified."

A hack rattles past, the driver cursing at his horse.

"Two hours," Leona says finally. Not a request. An order. "If I don't hear from you in two hours, I'm coming in. With my whole team. And I don't care who gets caught in the crossfire."

I nod. Can't speak past the tightness in my throat.

"Go." She says it gently. "Before I change my mind."

Turning, I walk toward Market Street. Toward the Barbary Coast. Toward Mary and whatever's waiting.

"Mick?"

I pause without looking back.

"I'm trusting you to be smart about this." Her words carry over the street noise. "Don't make me regret pulling you out of that cell."

I don't answer. Can't promise what I'm not sure I can deliver. Behind me, Leona's footsteps fade in the opposite direction, back toward the station, back toward protocol and procedure and doing things the BMI way.

Two hours. Enough time to warn Mary. Figure out what to do next.

Or enough time to prove Leona right about every damn thing.

I keep walking.

Chapter Twenty-Six

THE STRAUSBURG SLUMBERS ON the corner. Mary's territory. Mary's fortress.

I need to warn her. Before Hoodoo comes for her next.

Connor's at the door, slouching as usual. He straightens when he sees me. His face is drawn, exhausted.

"Miz Kelly." He glances at my rumpled clothes. "Didn't expect you back so soon."

"Need to see Mary. It's urgent."

He hesitates. "She's...she's not in a good way, miss. Been holed up in her office since we got back from the party. Won't see anyone."

"She'll see me." I hope. "It's about Brass. And what happened to him."

Connor's jaw tightens. "You know who did it?"

"I know who's doing all of it. And I know Mary's next on his list."

That gets his attention. He jerks his head toward the stairs. "Second floor. End of the hall. Knock first—she's got a derringer and she's jumpy."

"Thanks."

I climb the stairs, each step feeling like I'm wading through molasses. My wet clothes have dried stiff and uncomfortable since the showdown with the rusalka. I smell like bay water and death.

Perfect way to deliver bad news.

I knock. Three times, firm but not aggressive.

"Go away." Mary's voice is muffled but sharp.

"It's Mick. We need to talk."

Silence. Then footsteps. The door opens a crack, and Mary peers out. Her face is bare of cosmetics, hair unpinned and hanging loose around her shoulders. She looks older without the carefully maintained mask. Tired. Human.

"What do you want?" Not hostile. Just... empty.

"To warn you. Can I come in?"

She studies me for a long moment. Then steps back, opening the door wider.

The office is smaller than I expected. Elegant but practical with a small desk, a settee by the window, and a large bookshelf lined with everything from dime novels to legal texts. A half-empty bottle of whiskey sits on the desk beside a crystal glass.

Mary closes the door behind me and leans against it. "Well?"

"Sol Sonderling's dead."

Her eyes close briefly. "When?"

"Last night. Same time Brass died." I pull out the pocket watch and set it on her desk. "Found this at the scene. And evidence that Brass was there when Sol was killed."

Mary picks up the watch and turns it over in her hands. Her thumb traces the engraved harp. "I sent him," she takes a deep breath. "Wednesday night, before the gala. Told him to collect what Sol owed me. Find out if the old man knew anything about the jade." She looks up, and there's guilt in her eyes. Raw and terrible. "I sent him to his death."

"You couldn't have known—"

"Couldn't I?" Her laugh is bitter. "I knew Sol was desperate. Knew he was involved in the jade business somehow. I sent Brass anyway because I needed that information." She sets the watch down carefully. "Big, dumb kid. And now he's dead."

"It's not your fault. Hoodoo killed them both. He's the one—"

"Hoodoo?" Mary straightens. "You know his name?"

"Hoodoo Jones. Necromancer. Former Pinkerton agent, worked with Lafayette Baker." I watch her face carefully. "You know him?"

"I've heard the name." She moves to the desk and pours whiskey into the glass. Doesn't offer me any. "What's he doing in San Francisco?"

"Working for Kollach."

Mary's hand freezes halfway to her mouth, the whiskey glass suspended. "What?"

"Jones is Kollach's Doctor Nightingale. Has him doing séances for donors, but it's a cover. Hoodoo's his hired necromancer handling problems, eliminating competition." I pull my coat tighter. "Kollach tried to make a deal with me. Wanted me to deliver the jade in exchange for Edison's life. So much as admitted his Doctor Nightingale grabbed the boy."

Mary sets the glass down carefully. "Isaac hired the necromancer. Of course he did." Something flickers behind her eyes. Fear? Calculation? "That sanctimonious bastard lectures about moral decay while employing death magic."

"It's worse than that. Hoodoo's not just working for Kollach anymore. He's got his own agenda. People connected to the jade keep ending up dead." I meet her eyes. "Including your people."

"His own agenda." Mary repeats it slowly. "You're saying he's gone rogue."

"Kollach's scared of him. I saw it myself when he cornered me after the party." I think about those trembling hands in the carriage, the gun he couldn't hold straight. "Kollach hired a monster he can't control. And that monster is hunting the jade through anyone who gets close to it. Sol. Brass. The girl outside the Lotus Club."

"And you think I'm next." It's not a question.

"You're the biggest player still standing. Your people have been asking questions, making moves. Hoodoo knows you're in the game." I hold her gaze. "He killed Brass and turned him into a zombie delivery boy."

Mary drains the whiskey in one swallow. Sets the glass down so hard the crystal rings against the wood. She's quiet for a long moment, staring at Brass's pocket watch.

"Perhaps it's not this Hoodoo person we should worry about." Her tone shifts, takes on a careful measured quality. "Perhaps Isaac is the real threat. Using his mystic as a weapon while keeping his own hands clean. That's his style."

She's steering me. I can feel the gentle redirect. But the logic isn't entirely wrong either.

"Maybe Kollach's a problem too," I concede. "But Kollach wanted to make a deal with me. Offered Edison's safe return for the jade. A man cleaning house doesn't negotiate with the help. Hoodoo's the immediate danger, Mary. He's the one killing people."

She appears lost in thought, toying with the empty glass. "I won't hide," she says finally. "I've survived in this city for thirty years. I'm not going to let a pet necromancer scare me out of my own parlor."

"I'm not asking you to hide. Just be smart. Keep Connor and Tommy close."

"I can take care of myself, Mick."

"Brass could take care of himself too."

She flinches. Good. She needs to feel that.

She looks up at me, affection in her tired eyes. "You're a good woman, Mick Kelly. Better than I deserve."

Before I can respond, there's a knock at the door.

"Miz Mary?" Connor's voice. "Sorry to interrupt, but—"

"Come in," Mary calls.

Connor enters, hat in hands. He glances at me, then focuses on Mary. "The magpies just came in. Jimmy and Seamus. They found something."

Mary straightens. "What kind of something?"

"Near the Harrison Street pier, in the old Thompson cannery. Neighbors been complaining about screaming for two days. Someone saw a tall, thin man going in and out. Matches the description we been circulating."

My heart kicks against my ribs. "Did they see who's inside?"

Connor shifts his weight. "One of the neighbors says there's someone chained up down there. Young man, brown hair." He pauses. "Wearing spectacles."

Edison.

I can get there in 20 if I leave this minute. How could he be at a pier, I saw him in a basement? Somethings not right. It doesn't matter I've got to leave.

"Mick." Mary's voice cuts through my spiraling thoughts. She's writing something on a slip of paper. "Here's the address. But you should take Connor. Or wait—I can gather more men. We can go together—"

"No time." I snatch the paper from her hand. Every second I waste, Edison could be dying. Could already be dead. "If he's hurt, if he's—I have to go now."

"Then take Connor at least—"

"No." I meet her eyes. "He needs to stay here with you. This could be a trap to isolate you."

"Mick, you're exhausted. You've been running for days. You're in no condition—"

"I'll manage." I'm already moving toward the door.

Mary catches my arm. "Mick. If it's a trap—"

"Then I'll know soon enough."

She holds on a second longer than she needs to before letting go.

Chapter Twenty-Seven

THE PIER CREAKS BENEATH my boots. Old wood, half-rotted where the salt's gotten into it. Each step loud, echoing back off the shuttered cannery walls ahead, fading to nothing across the water to my left.

Thompson's place backs onto the bay. No other approach except straight down this pier with nothing but empty air on either side. Exposed as a barn door.

Nowhere to hide.

I scan the building ahead. Windows dark. Door hanging open. The screaming the neighbors reported has stopped, if it really happened. The lap of water against the pilings and the distant clang of a buoy bell the only sounds.

Movement catches my eye. High up, on the cannery roof.

A figure crouched there, maybe fifty feet away. Skinny frame silhouetted against the gray sky.

Our eyes meet.

That's when I recognize the rifle.

Time slows. I register the details in fragments even as I'm moving. Waxy skin reflecting the gray light. Hands locked on the weapon.

A hoppy. Kollach's muscle or Hoodoo's, doesn't matter which. Plenty of veterans on the streets, plenty hooked on opium. Wouldn't be that hard to find a rifleman.

The barrel swings toward me.

Best way to kill a Gleaner is from distance. Sharpshooters are my Achilles' heel. When my power's this weak, I can't ride what I can't touch.

I throw myself left as the bullet screams past my ear so close I feel the air split. Wood splinters behind me where my head was a second ago. The shot cracks across the water.

I make a break for the shore, running back the way I came. The pier's too narrow, too straight. I'm a target in a shooting gallery.

Fire explodes high across my left arm, near the shoulder. The impact spins me around like someone's grabbed my coat and yanked. The shot booms. My boots tangle. The world tilts.

Then there's nothing beneath me but air.

⁘∽∾∘∾∾⁙

Cold punches every thought from my skull when I hit the water. Salt burns my eyes, my throat. Blood clouds the murk around me in dark ribbons.

The pier pilings rise above like prison bars, blocking out what little light is filters through.

Thrashing I try to surface, but my coat drags me down. My boots fill. The current grabs hold and gently pulls.

My lungs burn. I need air. Need to breathe.

Which way is up?

Lafayette tried to drown me once. In the Elkhorn. Held me under while I screamed into the muddy water. I survived that. But I was strong then. Full of stolen death and fury. Now I'm empty. The Gleaner's got nothing left to give.

I struggle to kick a boot off, but I can't find any leverage.

My vision darkens. The cold doesn't hurt anymore.

Something warms against my chest. Thrusting my hand into the pocket, my hand closes on the charm from the Night Market. Jack's little fish-lady statue. I hold it tight and try to kick to the surface.

Protection from drowning, the old guy said.

I want to laugh. Stupid old man. Stupid trinket. Magic doesn't work like that—

Something wraps around my wrist. Cold and strong and alive, pulling.

The rusalka rises from below, her eyes find mine through the murk, and then she's inside my head without asking.

Not words exactly. More like pressure. Her thoughts push against mine, alien and uncomfortable.

Talisman calls. Calls and calls. Ringing in the deep like a bell.

Her face is inches from mine.

You owe me, breathe-and-bleed. You owe and owe.

She grabs my head between her hands and leans close. I think she's going to send me into the depths with a kiss.

Her mouth opens against mine.

She exhales, flooding my lungs with ocean wind, salt, and the cry of gulls, the musk of black sand, kelp forests swaying in current. My body convulses, trying to reject it. But my lungs stop screaming. The blackness at the edges retreats. And warmth spreads through my body.

She pulls away. Her hair floats around us, and those too-bright eyes hold mine with the regard of something deciding whether to keep a fish or throw it back.

Like quicksilver, she grabs my wrist and drags me down.

Not to drown.

The bay blurs past in ribbons of green-black water. The rusalka pulls me through, her hair streaming around me, flowing behind us like a comet's tail. The pressure in my chest builds. Whatever breath she gave me won't last forever.

A ship's hull materializes from the murk. Barnacled planking, half-rotted but still holding its shape. The rusalka doesn't slow. She drags me straight through a gaping wound in the ship's side.

Darkness swallows us and the need to breath becomes overwhelming. Just when I think I won't make it, a soft light appears above.

My head breaks the surface.

Air hits my throat like broken glass. Gasping, I choke, suck in another breath that tastes of bilge and rot. The Rusalka shoves. Rough wood under my hands, I pull myself out of the water and claw my way clear onto the floor of the ship's hold that's above the water line.

Water streams from my hair, my coat. My arm throbs in time with my heartbeat where the bullet tore through. Blood is soaking my sleeve, mixed with bay water. But I'm alive. Breathing.

I blink, try to focus. Cold blue moonlight peeks through cracks in the deckhead way above me. We're inside a scuttled ship, the rusalka's lair. Weak light paints everything in watercolor green.

The deck has listed hard to the stern which is under water. Everything's tilted. And everywhere, scattered across the canted floor, treasures.

Pocket watches tangled in chains. A ship's bell green with verdigris, children's toys, a wooden horse, rag dolls with button eyes. Jewelry glitters over navigation instruments. A wedding ring caught on a sextant. Combs and mirrors and spectacles. All the small, precious things people were carrying when they drowned.

The rusalka's head and shoulders is above the surface of the water, her hair spreading around her like a Sargasso Sea. She watches me cough and retch and shake without a glimmer of empathy.

I push myself back on the deck to give her room as she pulls herself, spider-like, to crouch beside me.

Her head tilts as she watches. "Talisman called me," she says, her physical voice strange after the invasion of her thoughts. "Rang and rang in the deep. Could not ignore."

"Is that why you saved me?" I manage between chattering teeth.

"Wanted to watch you drown." Small, pointed teeth gleam, her hair writhing around her in wet coils. "But Sol spoke your name. Before the end. Said you would come. Said you would make right." Her eyes narrow. "And I want the sweet-talking man, your Hoodoo. He wards against me. Iron and death magic. I claw and claw and cannot reach." Her fingers curl against the wood, gouging it. "But you walk in the dry world. You walk where I cannot."

Ah. a trade.

"You bring sweet-talking man to water." Her voice is low, intimate, hungry. "Leave him where the waves break. I take him. Make him bleed every lie his pretty mouth told. Every scream my Sol screamed."

"And in return?"

She reaches into the shadows of the bulkhead beside us and pulls something forward. A small wooden box, maybe the size of an almanac. Even in the poor light I can see it's beautifully made. Old. A box for precious things.

"Sol gave me this. Before the Hodooo man came. Said keep safe. Said with me none would dare to take." She strokes the lid possessively.

My pulse stutters. "The jade."

"Sol's last treasure." She holds the box out but doesn't release it when my fingers close on it. Her grip is iron. "You take the stone. Give to the dragon's daughter."

My brain must still be waterlogged. "Dragon?"

"The one who came across great water. Who built empire from ash of burned beds." The rusalka's eyes go distant, one hand traces patterns across her own face "Who wears power like second skin but hides fire behind silk and painted face." She focuses, her gaze finds my face. "Fire in her blood. Old fire. Runs deep, deep, deep."

"Ah Toy." I say, understanding.

She releases the box.

It settles onto my hand heavier than I expected. My death sense is quiet, no dark magic rolling off it. Makes sense I suppose, since the jade's tied to creation and my senses focus on endings. Maybe there's a tiny hum, like a tuning fork, faintly vibrating.

"Yes, Ah Toy. I told you *dragon-child*." She's exasperated with my dullness. "Her blood runs true. Sol knew. Jade belongs with dragon's daughter. Keeps city safe from earth's anger. From fire and shaking ground." She grips my arm. "Sol's last wish. You honor it."

I'm shivering for reasons beyond cold now. This is it; with the jade I can fix everything.

"You bring the sweet-talking man to me." She leans closer, her grip on my arm painful. "You give the stone to the dragon's daughter. Simple, simple. Even breathe-and-bleed ones understand this." She scowls, releasing my arm.

"But I can't promise, what if—"

"Then I come for you." No anger in it. Just fact. "The bay takes what it's owed. And I am the bay."

A strand of her hair crawls up my body to stroke my face while she studies me a moment longer before sliding into the black water without a splash.

Gone.

I sit there on the tilted deck, the box in my hand, saltwater dripping from my hair. The hold creaks around me. Drowned people's treasures glint in the green half-light.

I'm alone. Wounded. Bone-weary. No idea how I'm gonna get back to shore.

On the upside, everyone thinks I'm dead.

And I'm holding the Nü Gua Jade. Finally.

I push myself back to rest against the bulkhead. My arms and legs are so heavy. I think I'll rest for a moment, just to catch my breath... My eyes drift close...

The cold has sunk so deep into my bones that I can't remember what warm feels like. But cold might be better than warm. Cold means I can still feel. The wool of my coat saved me.

I lie on the tilted deck with the jade box clutched against my chest and try to convince my body to move. My arm throbs all the way down to the stump. Blood's stopped flowing but the sleeve of my coat is stiff with it, glued to my skin.

Can't stay here.

I push myself to sit up. Nausea rolls through my gut. I swallow it down, force myself to breathe.

The box. Still have the box.

I tuck it inside my shirt, against my skin, and button it securely. My fingers fumble the buttons three times before they catch. Stupid hook makes everything harder than it should be.

Gray light filters down from above. Dawn, maybe. Or close to it. How long was I out?

Edison's been captive since Saturday. I went off the pier Wednesday evening. That makes this Thursday morning. Five days.

Christ.

I grab one of the tilted support beams and haul myself up. My legs fold on the first attempt. I hang there from one arm, the good one, breathing hard, waiting for the strength to try again.

Second attempt gets me vertical.

The ladder to the upper deck hangs at an angle, half the rungs rotted through. I test the first one. It groans but holds.

I start climbing.

Every rung is a question. Will it break? Will my hand hold? Will the hook slip? My shot arm won't bear much weight. My good hand is clumsy with cold. The hook scrapes against wood, trying to find purchase on surfaces rotten through.

Halfway up, a rung cracks under my boot.

I drop, catch myself on the rung below. Pain detonates through my shoulder. I hang there, gasping, feet dangling over the hold.

Below me, the drowned treasures gleam. Wedding rings and children's toys and all the small things that went to the bottom with their owners.

Easier to let go. Slide back down. Curl up among the dead's keepsakes and let the cold finish what the bullet started. I'm so tired. Tired of fighting. Tired of chasing.

Would serve everyone right.

But then Edison dies in whatever hole Hoodoo's stashed him. And Julianna has to explain to Ylva why Auntie Mick isn't coming home.

I reach up with my hook, jam it in a crack in the hull, and pull.

The next rung holds.

My arms burn. My shoulder feels like it's tearing open. I keep climbing because stopping means dying and I've decided I'm not done.

One rung. Another. Another.

The hatch above me hangs loose on broken hinges. I shove it wider with my good shoulder and drag myself through onto the upper deck.

Fresh air. Warm and salt and real.

I collapse on my back, chest heaving, and stare up at the sky. Gulls wheel overhead, their cries sharp and mocking. The sun's peaking above the eastern horizon.

My Colt's gone, lost somewhere when I fell in the water. Miraculously I still have my boots.

I roll onto my side, then push myself up to hands and knees. The deck's slick with kelp and bird shit. I crawl to the railing.

I'm in the middle of a ship's graveyard. I recognize the mud-flats just west of Meiggs where the bay's being filled to make new shoreline. Skeletons of scuttled ships punch above the mud, like rotted teeth. Some are half-buried in debris. Others list at ridiculous angles, their masts snapped or stolen, hulls crushed.

And there, less than two hundred yards away, is solid ground.

Two hundred yards of mud and shallow water.

And it's not gonna get easier when the tide comes in.

My body informs me in no uncertain terms that two hundred yards might as well be two hundred miles.

My body can go to hell.

I climb down the outside of the hull. The ship's listed so far starboard it's a short drop to the mud. Barnacles tear my palm on the way down. I barely feel it. My hand is beyond registering new complaints.

The flats suck at my boots with each step. Cold mud, broken shells, things I don't want to think about working past my boot tops. The smell of decomposing sea life fills my nose with every huffing breath.

I focus on the shore. One foot in front of the other.

Fifty yards. My legs threaten to fold.

A hundred. My vision narrows to a tunnel.

A hundred and fifty. I'm weaving like a drunk, leaving a crooked trail through the mud behind me.

Two hundred.

I reach the shore and collapse against a low dune, gasping. Everything hurts. Everything's cold. I haven't slept in over thirty hours. I've been shot, drowned, rescued by something that wanted to watch me drown, and given an artifact that's gotten at least four people killed.

I went off that pier with a bullet in me. No one saw me surface. By now, Garrett's probably writing up the report. "Suspended agent Mary Catherine McClellan got what she deserved." Case closed. Problem solved.

And not one of them knows I crawled out of the bay with the jade against my ribs and a bargain with the thing that lives in the deep.

For the first time since Loosh's death, I have an advantage.

Chapter Twenty-Eight

A TRIO OF CLAMMERS working the low tide stop mid-dig to stare. Can't blame them. I'm a sight, clothes torn and mud-caked, coat stiff with blood and bay water, hair hanging in kelp-tangled ropes down my back. Hell, I've even got a hook, like something that crawled out of a sailor's nightmare.

"You all right, miss?" The youngest one takes a half-step toward me, then thinks better of it.

"Fine." My voice comes out like gravel. "Am I headed toward Meiggs?"

He nods, pointing east with his clam rake, eyes wide.

Nodding my thanks I keep walking.

"Ghost," I hear one of them mutter. "White ghost lady."

Close enough.

Following the shoreline east, my path transforms from a single wagon rut to a really wide dirt path. My body and will are duking it out. My body wants to lie down right here on the sea grass and sleep for a week. My will reminds it that Edison's still chained somewhere, and Hoodoo's still breathing.

Will wins. It always does.

Within a few minutes, Meiggs is in sight, already crawling with activity. Too early for tourists, but the lumber yard is buzzing. Only a short jaunt to Calpurnia's. Should take fifteen minutes. I think it takes me thirty. Maybe forty. Time gets slippery when you're this tired.

Most folks give the wild-eyed, blood-covered woman limping through the crowd a wide berth. Ignoring fishmongers setting up their stalls, my spirits lift at the scent of coffee drifting over the perfume of fish guts. Wish I had the two cents for a cup.

Even in this chaos, I'm garnering stares. Some curious, some wary, some downright alarmed. A cop takes one look at me headed in his direction and crosses to the other side of the street.

Good. Last thing I need is to answer questions about why I look like I've been dragged backward through the bay.

Which I have been, technically.

Blessedly, Calpurnia's, squat and solid, finally comes into view. Abby's probably been up all night, coordinating her network, gathering information about Hoodoo's whereabouts.

I push through the front door.

The warmth greets me first. Then the smell—coffee and frying bacon, tobacco, stale beer, and lamp oil. Normal things. Human things.

The handful of early customers scattered around tables go silent. Every head swivels towards me.

Abby's behind the bar, pouring rum into someone's coffee. The bottle stops mid-pour when she sees me.

"Sweet, merciful Christ." The bottle bangs on the bar. She's around the counter in three strides and grabs my good arm. "Mick? We thought—everyone said you were—"

"Dead?" I let her guide me to a chair near the stove. My legs give out gratefully. "I heard."

"There was a shooting at Thompson's cannery. Blood on the pier. You went in the water." Her hands flutter over me, checking for wounds, cataloging damage. "Nico sent word to the docks. Everyone's been looking—"

"Let 'em keep thinking that. It will give us a little time. But I'm fine."

"You're not fine. You're half-drowned and bleeding." She's already calling out. "Emma! Get me clean water and bandages. And the good whiskey. And blankets."

Emma scurries off toward the back.

Abby walks into the middle of the room, surveying the early morning drinkers. "Out." Her voice brooks no argument. "Everyone. Now."

A grizzled sailor tries to protest. "But I just—"

"I'll stand you a beer next time you're in." She jerks her thumb toward the door. "Go on. And keep your traps shut and we'll make it two beers."

Chairs scrape. Muttered complaints, but they go.

The door swings shut behind the last of them. She bars it, locking it from all comers.

She slumps against the door, for an instant. She's about done in if the dark hollows under her eyes tell the story true. Her worry for Edison must be eating her alive.

Emma's footsteps returning with supplies break the momentary silence.

Nico rises from his table as Abby composes herself and joins me by the stove.

She crouches in front of me, her face pale beneath the rouge. "What happened? Where have you been?"

"Long story." I exhale a long breath as Emma drapes my shoulders in a wool blanket. "Short version is I got shot off the pier. Went in the bay. Got out again."

"What's the longer version? How'd you even get loose from Garret?" Nico asks. "I figured you were headed for lockup."

"Garrett held me for at least a couple of hours. Leona pulled strings to get me released." Gratefully accepting a glass from Emma, the delicious scent of whiskey fills my head. She smiles and nods at me to drink.

Abby waves at Emma to hand her the basket filled with bandages and unguents. "But why were you on that pier?"

I take a long sip of the brown liquor, letting it sends warm tendrils throughout my chest. "I went to warn Mary. I think Hoodoo's gonna go after her next. While I was there, her team got a report about a possible Edison sighting at the cannery. I went to check it out."

She sits back on her heels, and scowls. "Gold Tooth Mary sent you into a trap?"

"No, it's not like that..." Is it? I drain the rest of the whiskey. "No. She offered to send one of her boys with me. She was misled. Hoodoo must have set it up. He knows the best way to kill a Gleaner is with a sharpshooter. It had to be him."

Nico and she exchange glances. My temper flickers. Like I'm a child, too stupid to know I'm being played. Shit. *Get a hold of yourself, Mick.*

"It was Hoodoo." I meet her eyes. "Loosh, Sol, Brass—all killed by Hoodoo. And he's still hunting. Still searching for the jade."

She starts briskly unbuttoning my ruined coat. I let her, too tired to argue. Pulling me forward, she peels my coat down off my shoulder and hisses when she sees the wound on my upper arm. Glancing down I grimace. It's ugly. Bullet went clean through-and-through, but the edges are ragged.

"This needs proper stitching, Mick." She clucks her tongue and tries to pull the frayed shirt fabric away.

"Quit poking at it." I catch her wrist gently. "We've gotta move fast while we have an advantage. Everyone thinks I'm dead, but they're gonna figure out the truth pretty quick." She shakes me off and continues picking at the bullet wound. I flinch away.

"We haven't found Hoodoo." Her voice cracks, but she puts one hand on my shoulder to hold me still. "Nico's had men searching. Every warehouse, every boarding house, every crimp hole. But it's like he's a goddamn ghost."

"It doesn't matter—ouch, stop!" I slap at her hands.

Handling me like a recalcitrant child, she pulls me to my feet, strips me out of the coat altogether, and tosses it over a chair. After settling me back down, she picks up the scissors from the basket and starts cutting the bloody sleeve off my shirt.

Glaring at her, I continue, "Right now, I need to get everyone together. Mary, Kollach, Ah Toy. All of them."

"Why?" Nico asks, leaning forward to take the scissors dangling from Abby's hand as she rolls the sleeve down to my wrist.

Glaring at her, I reach into my ruined bodice. My fingers brush the cool, distinct hum of the box. "We don't need to find him. He's gonna come to us."

Pulling the box out I flip the latch and the lid springs back.

The Nü Gua Jade nestles in scarlet silk padding. It's about the size of my palm, milky green with darker veins running through it. Serpent and tortoise are intertwined in a single masterful carving. Centuries of handling has worn the edges smooth. My Gleaner sight picks up the faintest shimmer of power worked into the stone.

It's pretty but I expected more somehow.

"Is that really it?" Abby pauses her torturous ministrations, and color floods her face. "The Nü Gua Jade. You really found it."

"Yeah." Snapping the box shut.

"Sol hid it with the rusalka?" Nico asks, running his index finger over the boxes gold hinges.

"Yeah." I don't elaborate on the bargain I made, on the debt I owe. "And Hoodoo wants it."

Abby pours an amber astringent onto a rag. The smell overwhelms the the coffee. "So, what now? If Hoodoo knows you have it..."

"He doesn't. Not yet." The burn of the alcohol-soaked rag against the bullet hole is momentarily blinding, but it wakes me up. Hissing through my teeth, I squawk, "But he will."

Abby hmms and starts wrapping linen around the injury. I try to be grateful for her steady hands despite the pain. "I need messengers, Abby. Fast ones. Boys who can keep their mouths shut."

"I've got them." She doesn't look up, focusing positioning a bandage over the exist would. "Who are we writing to?"

"Everyone."

Nico frowns. "Everyone?"

"Mary. Kollach. Ah Toy." Ticking them on my fingers I explain, "I want them all here. Tonight. Midnight."

Abby stops wrapping the bandage. She looks up, eyes wide. "Here? Calpurnia's?"

"Said it yourself, your territory. Your rules." I take another hit of the whiskey. "Tell them I have the jade. Tell them I'm ready to deal. Whoever brings me Edison alive and unharmed gets the box."

She's quiet for a long moment, thinking. Then she smiles. "All right. But we do this smart. I'll have sailors around the block. Anyone tries to start trouble, they'll regret it."

"And Hoodoo?" Nico asks. "You think he'll just show up?"

"He's Kollach's man, isn't he? Or pretending to be. If Kollach comes for the jade, Hoodoo won't be far behind." And I can deliver him to the bay. "He won't be able to stay away."

"It's suicide," Nico says. "Three crime lords and a necromancer in one room?"

"That's why I need one more message." I look at him. "Go find Leona. Tell her I'm alive. Tell her to get here now. With her badge."

"You want the BMI involved?" Abby finishes tying off the bandage, gentle despite the tension radiating off her. "Garrett will hang you."

"Not Garrett. Leona." I sway slightly in the chair. The adrenaline is fading, leaving nothing but a deep, hollow ache. "Just...get her here. I'll explain the rest later."

"Mick—"

"I can't, Abby." My head droops. "I need two hours. Maybe three. Just...send the messages. Midnight."

Abby exchanges a look with Nico. A long, heavy silence stretches between them. Then she sighs, a sound of resolve.

"Eat something first," she orders. "Then sleep. If you fall over dead before midnight, this whole thing goes tits up."

"Fine."

She helps me to my feet, guiding me toward the back room. "I'll bring you some dry clothes. We're about the same size, more or less."

I sink onto the narrow bed in her private quarters, the jade box still clutched in my hand. Every muscle in my body sings with relief as the mattress welcomes me.

"We'll get my boy back, Mick." She smiles, sad and fierce at once. "One way or another."

The door closes behind her.

Lying back, I press the box against my ribs. Outside Abby's giving orders, Nico's heading out, the sound of the front door opening and closing. The messengers are running. The clock is ticking.

Tonight we end this.

Chapter Twenty-Nine

VOICES DRAG ME FROM sleep like hooks in flesh. Abby's voice first, sharp with protective anger.

"She's resting, and you're not—"

"I don't care that she's sleeping off a resurrection." Leona's voice cuts through, hard as winter iron. "I need to see her. *Now*."

I'm already swinging my legs off the bed when the door crashes open. Leona fills the doorway, hair escaping its pins, coat buttoned wrong like she dressed in a hurry. Her eyes find me and relief flashes across her face before it's buried under a scowl that would make a lesser woman cower.

"You died." She crosses the small room and pulls me into a hug that damn near cracks ribs. "Word came down last night. Agent McClellan, shot and drowned at Thompson's Cannery. I spent twelve hours thinking you were at the bottom of the bay, Mick. Twelve hours."

"Clearly exaggerated." I pat her back awkwardly with my good arm. She's shaking slightly. "I'm fine."

"You're not fine." She pulls back, grabs my bandaged arm without asking and turns it to examine the wound. I hiss and try to yank it back. She holds on tighter. "Bullet?"

"Through and through. Abby patched it."

"Abby's a bartender, not a surgeon." She prods the edge of the bandage. I swat her hand away. She swats mine right back and keeps poking. "This needs proper stitching."

"You sound just like Abby. Quit it."

"Then stop getting shot." She releases my arm, but only to grip my shoulders and look me dead in the face. "Nico wouldn't tell me details, just said to get here before you did something that would actually kill you this time."

"It's not that stupid—"

"Don't." Her voice cracks. "Don't do that thing where you downplay nearly dying. I've had a shit couple of days, Mick. Garrett's been crowing about closing your case, Thatcher's breathing down my neck about this Russian smuggling bullshit, and then I hear you're *dead* and I—" She stops, jaw working. "Just don't."

The anger's really worry underneath. I know the tune, sang it myself a time or two.

"I'm sorry." I sit back down on the cot. "Truly. Didn't mean to scare you."

"Well, you did." She drops onto the narrow bed beside me, the frame groaning under our weight. The tiny room barely fits the bed and a chair. With Leona's long legs and my borrowed trousers showing three inches of ankle, we must look like scarecrows crammed into a hatbox. "Now tell me everything. Start with how you're alive."

"I went to warn Mary, like I told you—"

Leona's head snaps up. "Huh, so you went to Mary. The thing I specifically told you was a terrible idea."

"You said to be smart about it."

"And getting shot off a pier is smart?" She's on her feet again, which means she's pacing, which in this room means two steps, pivot, two steps back, narrowly avoiding the washstand each time. "Gold Tooth Mary. The woman I told you was a master manipulator. The woman I warned you about hours before you—"

"She had a tip about Edison, Leona. A sighting. I wasn't going to sit on my hands—"

"Mary says jump and you jump right off a pier." She spins on her heel, nearly clipping the washstand. "Brilliant strategy. Really top-notch."

"Are you done?"

"Not even close."

The door pushes open. Abby leans in, coffee cups on a tray, eyebrow raised. "Can you two keep it down? My regulars are starting to think there's a bar fight back here."

"There is," Leona and I say simultaneously.

Abby looks between us, shakes her head, and sets two mugs of coffee down on the tiny bedside table. "Sort yourselves. I'll be behind the bar pretending I can't hear every word." She pulls the door shut with a click.

Leona snatches one of the coffees before I can reach it. Takes a long swallow. Grimaces.

"That's terrible."

"It's Abby's. Her Majesty's sailors swear her grog is excellent, but her coffee is sludge." I grab the other mug. "And no, I'm not certain Mary knew about the sniper. She sent me on her people's intel."

"So you admit—"

"I admit I don't know." The words are bitter. I admired Mary. "I admit you could be right about her."

Leona stops pacing. That's not what she expected. She studies me over the rim of her mug.

Something almost like a smile tugs at the corner of her mouth. She kills it fast but I catch it. Then she sets down the coffee and leans against the washstand, arms crossed. Professional mode engaging.

"You know what I've been doing while you were busy drowning? Following up on your mess."

"My mess—"

"Sol Sonderling's murder. Reports of corrupted hopheads attacking people on the waterfront. Three separate sightings of revenants near the docks." She ticks them off on her fingers with the air of someone who's been building a case while her partner was off getting killed. "I pulled customs records, shipping manifests, cross-referenced every artifact dealer between here and Portland."

I open my mouth. She holds up a hand.

"I'm not done. Every single lead circles back to your old partner Aloysius Temple and the goddamn jade. The same jade that connects to the Russians I've been chasing for six months. Temple was working with my smugglers, Mick. I've been building that case for half a year and your dead friend was sitting right in the middle of it."

She delivers this with the quiet satisfaction of someone laying down a winning hand. And damn it, she's earned the right. While I was getting dragged through the bay by a vengeful water spirit, Leona was doing actual detective work.

"Impressive," I say, nodding.

"I know." No false modesty with Leona. Never has been. "Imagine my feelings when Nico shows up this morning telling me you're alive, you've got the artifact, and you're cooking up some lunatic scheme. How did you get your hands on the jade?"

"The rusalka gave it to me. Sol delivered it to her keeping before Hoodoo killed him."

"The rusalka." Leona pinches the bridge of her nose. "The San Francisco Bay Rusalka is real?"

"Very real. Very angry. Very willing to drown me if I don't keep my end of the bargain."

Leona pushes off the washstand. "Bargain?"

"I promised to bring Hoodoo to her. In exchange, she gave me the jade and didn't drown me."

"Didn't drown you. That's a generous spirit." Leona's voice is dry but her eyes are sharp. She knows what deals with elemental beings mean. Shifters learn early that the old things don't negotiate like people do. There's no renegotiation. No appeal. You keep your word. "And if you don't deliver?"

"She drags me to the bottom of the bay and keeps me there forever. Her words."

"Naturally." Leona folds her arms, leaning back against the doorframe. "So your backup plan, is to feed a wanted necromancer to a rusalka."

"Well, not the backup plan."

"That's not justice, Mick. That's a sea monster."

"It's a sea monster who watched Hoodoo murder the person she loved. She's earned her shot at him." I hold Leona's gaze. "And he's slippery. I don't want him pulling another disappearing act."

Leona's quiet for a long beat. Looks like the agent is wrestling with the woman. Wrestling with the memory of New Mexico, what Hoodoo did to those women, what he did to Morgan.

"If it comes to that," she says carefully, "I didn't hear any of this."

"Hear what?"

"Exactly." She turns to a fresh page in her notebook, pencil poised. Her expression changes. The competitive energy bleeds away and something vulnerable takes its place.

"We need to talk about Hoodoo."

I set down my coffee.

"He's stronger." She says it calmly, but her fingers are clenched around the pencil. "Much stronger than the man we fought in Las Vegas."

She carried the scars out of New Mexico same as I did.

"The revenants my people spotted on the waterfront? They're not shambling wrecks. They're coordinated. And those hoppies aren't just addicts, he's layering power into whatever he's dosing them with." She paces to the far wall and back, slower now. Thinking. "That's not the Hoodoo Jones we fought."

"It's worse than you know." I lean forward. "When he killed Sol he warded the entire building against the rusalka. He was strong enough to hold her at bay while he was interrogating Sol, killing him and Brass, and raising a fresh corpse."

Leona stops pacing. "Three simultaneous workings."

"At least three. The Hoodoo we knew couldn't manage one without being propped up by stronger mages."

"Someone or something is backing him." Leona says chewing on the end of her pencil. "Feeding him power."

"Lafayette's dead. So, who's holding his leash?"

We look at each other across the cramped room.

"I'll pull the Eastern Division files," She says. "Everyone connected to Lafayette's circle after the war. Anyone who walked away from Las Vegas that we didn't account for."

"Good. But right now, I need you focused on tonight."

"Tonight." Her eyes narrow. "Why do I already hate this?"

"Because you know me." I shift on the bed, trying to find a position that doesn't make my arm throb. "Kollach doesn't know Nightingale is Hoodoo Jones. He knows the man's dangerous, suspects he raised Brass. But he has no idea he's harboring a wanted federal fugitive."

Leona's pencil taps the notebook. Once. Twice. I can see her working it through. "That's leverage."

"Damn right it is."

"Assuming they don't just shoot you first."

"That's where you come in."

She snorts. "It's always where I come in. 'Leona, clean up my mess. Leona, bring the cavalry. Leona, make sure I don't die—'"

"I saved your life in Las Vegas."

"I saved yours first." She drops onto the bed beside me, which protests loudly. "Fine. What's the play?"

"I bring everyone to the table. I tell them whoever delivers Edison alive and unharmed gets a shot at the jade. The others get nothing."

"You said everyone. Mary, Kollach. Who else?"

"Ah Toy."

Leona's eyebrows climb. "Ah Toy? Are you serious? The Bureau's had a file on her since the war. She's fought off coups, lawyers, arson, and three deportation attempts in court all while amassing the largest magical artifact collection on the West Coast. Chinatown's power brokers treat her like a bleeding emperor."

"A dragon's daughter," I correct. "According to my sources. The jade belongs with her." I meet Leona's eyes. "And I promised I'd get it to her."

"Mick, she's dangerous. Anyone who crosses Ah Toy either winds up on a boat to Hong Kong or in the bay."

"Maybe. But the rusalka says the jade belongs with her. Sol wanted it that way."

Leona chews the end of her pencil. "That's lunatic—" She trails off. I watch her do the math. Three agents against Kollach's muscle, Mary's boys, and a necromancer. Then add a powerful woman with personal stake to our side of the equation.

"She's got resources," Leona says slowly. "Ships. Men who know how to fight."

"And she'll come."

"You already invited her." Her tone clipped. "Before talking to me."

"I invited everyone before talking to you. I was working fast."

"You were working recklessly. As usual. But all right. Ah Toy could be useful," she concedes.

"Kollach's Hoodoo's meal ticket. If Kollach comes for the jade, Hoodoo won't be far behind. He can't resist."

"Where is this meet?"

"Here. Calpurnia's. Midnight tonight. Abby's territory, Abby's rules."

Leona tilts her head back against the wall and stares at the ceiling. "Three crime lords and a necromancer in a bar at midnight with what? Abby's pewter mugs and a rusty derringer?"

"Naw, Abby'll loan me her Colt." I punch her in the arm. "I want to put them in a room where I control the exits and you control the perimeter."

"Agreed." No hesitation. She straightens, pulling the notebook into her lap, pencil moving. "Three agents minimum. My people only." She underlines something. "Nobody from Garrett's division. Nobody who reports to Garrett. Nobody who's even had coffee with Garrett."

"Perfect. Your team. Your chain of command. Nobody else."

She stands, tucking the notebook away, and nearly knocks the coffee mugs off the table. I catch one. She catches the other. We look at each other and for half a second, despite everything, I almost laugh.

"Mick?" She's at the door now, hand on the frame. The worry's back under the professional mask. "Don't die tonight."

"I'll do my best."

"Your best usually involves losing a limb, getting shot, or drowning."

"Then I'll aim for none of the above. New personal record."

She shakes her head, but she's grinning. Sharp and fierce and ready for a fight. She pulls the door open.

"I'll be back at nine. We can figure out how we want to deploy everyone."

The door swings shut behind her. Her footsteps recede down the hall, quick and purposeful.

Abby appears in the doorway almost immediately, cloth in hand, eyebrow raised. "You two always like that?"

"Like what?"

"Like a pair of cats sharing a fence." She crosses to collect the mugs. "You trust her?"

"With my life." I look down at my hands, one flesh, one steel. "Already have. More than once."

Abby nods, satisfied. "Then let's get to work. Nico's waiting with the maps."

The afternoon passes in a blur of messages sent and received. Mary confirms her attendance through Connor. Kollach sends a letter so smug I want to frame it. And Ah Toy responds on paper fine enough to sleep on, formal and careful, confirming she'll attend with "appropriate escort."

Appropriate escort. Coming from a woman who's survived coups and deportation, that probably means a lawyer and a small army.

Good. We're going to need one.

Leaning back in the chair, every bruise and scrape from this morning's swim in the bay vie for my attention. The borrowed shirt Abby gave me is too tight across the shoulders, and my bandaged arm throbs with each heartbeat.

I reach for my other sight without thinking. The knack that lets me see vitae and animus, all that pretty pink and ugly purple. Would be nice to know what I'm working with before tonight.

Static.

Or almost. A faint shimmer at the edges, like trying to look through dirty glass. I push harder, trying to force it to sharpen.

Pain spikes behind my eyes.

"Mick?" Nico's voice sounds far off.

Letting go the room snaps back to plain wood and lamplight and scuffed floorboards. My hand is shaking.

"You all right?"

"Fine." Voice hoarse.

He studies me with knowing eyes. "You're not fine. You look like you're about to hit the floor."

"Just tired." Not entirely a lie.

"Tired don't make you go that color." His mouth twists. "What were you doing?"

I flex my fingers, trying to work the tremor out. "Leaning on my sight. The bit that sees power."

"And?"

"And it didn't go so well." I look at the table without really seeing it. "I'm running low. Spent most of what I had on that revenant at Kollach's party. Haven't had a chance to build it back up."

He's quiet a beat. "How bad?"

I think about lying. Decide against it. Nico's walking into this with me. He deserves the truth.

"Bad enough. I've got maybe one good shove left in me." Sure, if I'm willing to risk unconsciousness. "After that..." I shrug. "After that I'm just another woman with a gun and a bad attitude."

"Could be worse I suppose." But his tone's serious. "There a way to...I don't know, top off? Before tonight?"

The question sits between us like a loaded gun.

"Yeah," I say, low. "There's a way."

"But you ain't doing it."

"No."

He waits. Doesn't push. Just watches.

"The slaughterhouses run all night. Down past the Mission. Cattle, pigs. Always something dying down there." My jaw tightens. "I could go. Stand close when the hammer falls. Take what shakes loose."

Nico doesn't blink. "But you're not going to."

"No."

"Why not?"

I meet his eyes. "Because animals barely give me anything I can use. Trickles. I'd need a whole yard of 'em to equal one hopped-up hophead. Hours standing in blood and shit, riding panicked deaths for pocket change." I swallow. "Last time I tried something like that was in Philly. Going up against a nasty warlock cabal and needed some quick juice. I came out so full of dying I didn't sleep for a week. Squealing in my head every time I shut my eyes."

His jaw works, but he says nothing.

"Going down there just to feed?" I shake my head. "That's treating death like a pump you crank whenever you feel like it. That's Lafayette. That's Hoodoo. Once you start thinking that way, power's all you see.

"And even if I did it, I'd walk into tonight jittery as a cat in a room full of rocking chairs. Wired on ugly slaughterhouse panic. Last thing we need is me twitching the wrong way in a room already thick with fear."

He turns that over, then nods slowly. "You're walking in tonight half-empty."

"More like nine-tenths." I wish. More like nothing.

"Against three of the biggest power brokers in the city and a rogue necromancer."

"Yeah."

"That's either real brave or real stupid."

"Probably both." My mouth quirks. "Story of my life."

He huffs, almost a laugh. "At least you're consistent."

Through the front window, shards of early evening light slant gold through heavy clouds. Normal folks heading home from normal jobs, thinking about supper.

I wonder what that's like.

The door bangs open and Connor stumbles in, breathing hard like he's been running.

"Mick." He braces himself against the doorframe, chest heaving. "Message from Mary."

Chapter Thirty

My heart kicks against my ribs. I'm on my feet before I consciously decide to stand. "What is it?"

He pulls a folded paper from his pocket, hands shaking slightly. "She's got your man. Says you need to come now—tonight, not midnight. Says she heard Garrett's people are moving on Calpurnia's within the hour."

Now.

Not midnight. Now.

I take the paper and unfold it. Mary's handwriting—elegant but rushed:

Mick—

I have Edison aboard the Norn, anchored off Meiggs. Plans have changed. My sources say Garrett's marshals are moving on Calpurnia's before midnight—likely within the hour.

Bring the jade. I'll give you the boy. Then I'm gone before this whole mess comes down on my head.

Slack water ends at 7:15. After that, the current runs too hard to board safely. Miss it, and you won't see me or Edison again.

Connor will bring you. Don't be late.

—M

The words blur for a second as my mind races.

Garrett's people. Moving tonight. Could be true. Could be Mary manufacturing a deadline. Doesn't matter either way. She's got Edison.

Slack water at seven fifteen.

I look up at Connor. "What the hell is slack water?"

"The turn of the tide," he says quickly. "Between the flood coming in and the ebb going out. Water goes still for maybe fifteen, twenty minutes. Only time you can bring a skiff alongside a boat safe, otherwise, the current'll smash you into the hull or drag you under."

Abby's come around the bar, reading over my shoulder. "She's anchored off Meiggs?

"Yes, ma'am."

"Currents run mean there." Abby's voice is tight. "Exposed berths, water moving fast once the tide turns. If Mary says you can't board after slack—"

Nico clears his throat and gives Connor side eye.

"I'll just step outside." He tips his bowler. "I'll be waiting when you're ready, Miz Kelly."

Nico waits for the door to close behind Connor. "She's not lying about the tides." He's already at the shelf behind the bar, pulling down the worn Pacific Coast Tide Tables. His finger traces down the columns, stopping. "Slack before ebb at seven fourteen. Seven fourteen p.m." He looks up. "Thirty minutes from now. Maybe less." "And after that?" I ask.

"Ebb starts running. By seven thirty, it'll be pulling hard toward the Gate. Peak current around eight p.m. Probably four, five knots. Maybe more with the moon we've had." He sets the book down. "You miss that boarding window, you're not getting on that boat. And once the ebb's running strong, Mary can weigh anchor and ride it straight out the Gate. Be in open water before anyone can stop her."

"Smart," I say. "If she's got Edison and she's really planning to run, this is how she'd do it."

Abby's gripping the back of a chair, I imagine I can hear the wood creak. "You think it's real? You think she's really got my boy?"

"Maybe." I fold the letter and tuck it in my pocket. "Or maybe it's bait to get me out in the open. But either way—"

"Either way, you're going," Nico finishes flatly.

"Yeah." I meet his eyes. "I am."

"Mick—"

"I know it could be a trap. Probably is. But what if it's not?" I turn to Abby. "What if Mary does have him, and she's legitimately offering a straight trade, and I don't go?"

Abby's eyes shine wet in the lamplight. "Then my boy stays in the dark."

"Then your boy stays in the dark," I echo. "And Mary sails, and we're back to nothing."

Nico slaps the tide tables down. "And if it *is* a trap? Mary shoots you in the head the moment her hand touches the jade?"

"She's not gonna shoot me." I head toward the back room where I left my coat and weapons. "She likes me. And I'm not sitting here wondering if I let Edison die because I was too scared to take a chance."

Behind me, Nico swears inventively in Greek.

In Abby's room, I strap on her gun belt and check the revolver. Fully loaded, six rounds.

I pull the jade box out of my pocket bounce it in my hand.

Will Mary keep her word if it serves her interests?

It's a calculated gamble.

I tuck the box inside my coat and button it.

When I come back out, Nico's already at the door, coat on.

"You're not coming," I say.

"The hell I'm not—"

"You're staying here," I say urgently. "Garrett's people might still hit Calpurnia's. Hoodoo or Kollach might show up mad as hell that Mary flew. You keep the men in place. You make sure Abby's protected."

His jaw works. "And you go alone onto a boat in the middle of the Bay with the most dangerous woman in San Francisco?"

"I go with Connor to a boat. Mary wants the jade more than she wants me dead." I hope. "There's a difference."

"Not much of one."

"Piffle." I turn to Abby. "Soon as Leona shows up, send her after me. Tell her—" I pause. What do I tell her? "Tell her to come carefully. Tell her if I'm not back by nine, assume it went wrong."

Abby nods, swallowing hard. Then she moves around the bar, grabs my shoulders, and pulls me into a fierce hug.

"You bring my boy home," she whispers against my ear. "I don't care about the rest. Just bring Edison home."

"I will," I promise, hoping it's not a lie.

Connor's practically vibrating outside the door. "Miz Mick, we need to go. Current won't wait."

"I know." I pull away from Abby, meeting Nico's eyes one more time.

"You'll be back," he says roughly. "You're too damn stubborn to die on some boat."

I manage a smile. "That's the spirit."

Then I'm out the door, Connor at my heels, and there's no more time for second-guessing.

⁂

The Embarcadero's a long rib of timber, stone, mud and old ambition. Under the gas lamps the puddles shine slick-black. The air tastes of salt and tar, creosote and wet rope, with a sour edge of fish guts from somewhere down the line and a faint coal-smoke breath when the wind shifts.

Out in the dark, masts scribble thin lines against a low ceiling of cloud. Halyards *tap-tap-tap* like nervous fingers, restless in the light breeze. The bay talks, the tide slapping pilings, sucking at seaweed, and then going oddly quiet in pockets.

Connor leads the way north along the wharf edge, cutting away from the main streets where the evening crowds mill. Fewer eyes here. More shadows. The kind of route you take when you don't want to be followed.

My hand stays near my gun. My senses stretch out—listening for footsteps that match our rhythm, watching for shapes that move inhumanly, feeling for that cold prickle that means something dead is nearby. I'm a plum ripe for Hoodoo's picking out here.

Just the wharf sounds: a dray clattering in the distance, a watchman's lantern swinging slow on its hook, somewhere a tug giving a blunt whistle that echoes between warehouses and hulls. Gulls mutter half-awake on pilings, annoyed at being disturbed.

"You ever been on the Norn?" I ask Connor, keeping my voice low.

"Once. When Miss Mary first bought her." He doesn't slow his pace. "Two-masted schooner, gaff-rigged. Fast. She keeps a small crew—four, maybe five men."

"Armed?"

"Always."

Of course.

We pass a sailor sleeping it off against a coil of rope, a cat hunting rats between crates, a woman in a tattered shawl selling something from a basket I don't look at too close. Normal wharf business at twilight.

Except none of it feels normal.

My neck prickles. I glance back over my shoulder. Nothing but fog and lamplight and the long empty stretch of planking we just crossed.

"You worried, Miz Mick?" Connor asks quietly.

"Terrified," I admit. "You?"

"Some." He grins, quick and nervous. "But Miz Mary says you're the toughest woman in San Francisco. Says if anyone can walk onto that boat and walk off again, it's you."

"Mary says a lot of things."

"She does." His grin fades. "But she means that one. She respects you. Even if she don't always show it."

Respect. Sure. The kind of respect one predator gives another before deciding whether to fight or flee.

I'm betting Mary's planning to flee.

I'm betting my life on it.

We cut through a gap between warehouses and come out onto the north end of the wharf where the berths are less protected and the water runs meaner. The fog's thicker here, muffling sound, turning the world soft and gray.

Ahead, a numbered piling: Berth 7-N.

A man waits beside it, lean and weathered, hand on the painter of a low skiff that bobs in the oddly still water. He doesn't speak when we approach. Just nods once at Connor, then jerks his chin toward the boat.

"Paid in advance," Connor says to me. "He'll take you out and wait as long as the tide allows to bring you back."

"Understood." I step down into the skiff. It rocks under my weight, then settles. The jade box presses against my ribs under my coat.

Connor stays on the wharf, hands shoved in his pockets. "Good luck, Miz Mick."

"Thanks, kid." I sit and balance my weight.

Then the boatman pushes off, and the oars bite water.

The crossing is fast and quiet.

The boatman rows hard, muscles working smoothly under his canvas jacket. The water barely resists—slack current, just like Mary promised. The reflections of distant lights don't smear or ripple. The oar blades pull clean.

It's eerie, actually. The Bay this calm. Like it's holding its breath.

Ahead, the Norn takes shape out of the mist: two masts, dark hull, riding easy at anchor. Minimal deck light, just a single lantern near the stern. No movement I can see.

But someone's aboard. Someone's watching.

I can feel it.

The boatman brings us alongside, smooth as silk. Throws a short line up. A hand catches it—male, quick—and the skiff pulls in tight against the hull.

A Jacob's ladder unrolls down the side. Rope and wood, old but solid.

The boatman doesn't look at me. Just holds the skiff steady, waiting.

This is it. Last chance to turn back.

I stand, grab the ladder, and start climbing.

The rope's rough under my palm. My boots find the rungs. The skiff rocks below me, already starting to drift—the boatman's not holding it anymore, I realize. He's pulling back. Leaving.

First crack in the plan.

I climb faster.

My hook catches the rail. I haul myself up, swing a leg over, and drop onto the deck.

The skiff's already ten feet away, the boatman rowing hard into the dark. Not looking back. Not waiting to see if I need a ride home.

Gone.

I straighten, turn.

And I find myself staring at Gold Tooth Mary, standing near the mainmast with a lantern in one hand and a pistol in the other. Several of her boys ring her, on the edge of the lantern's light.

She's smiling.

"Welcome aboard, love," she says. "So glad you could make it."

Her boys shift, making room. A man steps forward, flashing that cadaverous smile I hate so well.

Hoodoo Jones. He's thinner since I last saw him. Purple shadows ring his glittering eyes.

The deck shifts under my feet. The current's starting to run. The slack window closing.

The Norn's beginning to swing on her anchor as the ebb takes hold.

Mary's smile doesn't waver. "Nothing personal, darling. Just business."

Chapter Thirty-One

THE DECK LURCHES UNDER my boots again as the Norn swings on her anchor. Tide's turning, current grabbing at the hull like cold fingers pulling us toward the Gate. Glancing behind me, the skiff's vanished.

No way off. No way out but through.

The light catches the gold in Mary's sharp smile. Beyond her, slumped against the forebitt, chain wrapped round his wrists, Edison raises his head. Bruised face. Split lip. His eyes find me.

He's alive.

"Well now," Hoodoo drawls, stepping fully into the lantern light. "Been a while, Mrs. McClellan, since I've had the pleasure of your company. You still collecting dead men like trading cards?"

My hand moves toward my gun. Mary smoothly levels her pistol at my chest.

"Don't," she says. Not loud. Doesn't need to be.

I freeze. The sickly hum of necromantic death vibrates through the ship. People have died here, then turned, recently.

Mary and Hoodoo. Together. My mind scrambles for an explanation that doesn't make me a fool. Maybe she's double-crossing Kollach. Cut a deal with the necromancer behind his back, grabbed Edison, plans to sail before Kollach knows he's been played.

The cabin door swings open.

Kollach sashays out onto the deck like he's entering a god-damn parlor. Stupid topcoat, hair slicked.

"Mrs. McClellan." He inclines his head. "Punctual as promised. Mary, Doctor Nightingale, well done."

Kollach still doesn't know Nightingale is Hoodoo Jones. His pet necromancer who made revenants dance at his rally. Who raised Brass and sent him stumbling into Kollach's own house

I'm facing all three of them, power players with guns and muscle, and me standing alone in the middle with nothing but a Colt, the jade, and my hook. But they don't know I'm weak. They have no idea if I'm gonna blast them all into the bay.

I look at Mary. "You sold me out."

She tilts her head, appraising. The lamplight softens her face, makes her look younger, almost kind. Then she speaks.

"You're charming when you're naïve, love." Her voice is silk. "Come now, Mick, a woman of your years understands. There's no friendship in war. Only alliances that sour past their prime."

I thought—God, I don't know what I thought. That we had some kind of understanding. Some crooked kinship between women who'd clawed their way up from nothing. Mutual respect, at least.

"I thought we were on the same side of self-interest," I say and hate how vulnerable I sound.

"We were. Until your interests stopped aligning with mine." She lowers the pistol slightly. "You're useful, Mick. I'll give you that. Stubborn, loyal, surprisingly competent. But you're not my equal in this game. You never were."

Hoodoo chuckles, low and wet. "Told you she'd come, Mary. Told you she couldn't help herself."

I turn on him. "Hoodoo Jones. Working for Kollach? Thought you had standards."

Kollach's head snaps toward Hoodoo. "Jones?" His voice sharpens. "What is she talking about, Professor?"

Hoodoo's smile doesn't slip, but a shadow flits behind his eyes. "Professional names, Mr. Kollach. You know how the spiritualist trade works. Clients like a bit of mystery."

"Hoodoo Jones," I repeat, louder. "Wanted by the Bureau for necromancy, murder, and about a dozen other charges. Last seen in Las Vegas, New Mexico, where he murdered men, women, and children."

Kollach goes very still. His gaze slides from me to Hoodoo, recalculating. "Is this true?"

"Mrs. McClellan has a colorful imagination," Hoodoo says smoothly. "And an old grudge."

"Not that old," I shoot back. "Morgan Jackson ring any bells? Or should I mention what you did to the women?"

Hoodoo's smile thins. Kollach's jaw tightens, but he doesn't press. The seed's planted, though. I can see it working behind his eyes.

Mary steps between us, voice pitched to soothe. "Gentlemen. We're here for business, not old grievances. Mick has what we want. We have what she wants." She gestures toward Edison. "Let's keep this civil."

Kollach clears his throat, reasserting control. "Indeed. Ms. Kelly, you have the Nü Gua Jade. I am prepared to pay handsomely for it and ensure you and the boy leave this vessel unharmed."

Hopefully, Abby got word to Leona. Hopefully, Leona will commandeer a ship and roll up to save the day. All I need to do is keep them talking.

"Handsomely," I echo. "What's your plan, Kollach? Parade it at your next rally? Tell the crowd it'll drive the Chinese into the sea?"

His expression hardens. "I intend to restore the natural order of this city. The jade will ensure a San Francisco where honest working men need not compete with coolie labor—"

"You mean a San Francisco where you get to decide who counts as human." I look at Mary. "And you're helping him?"

She shrugs elegantly. "You knew Isaac's vision aligns with my interests."

"And yours?" I turn to Hoodoo. "What do you want it for? Gonna raise another vampire?"

His grin widens. Shows too many teeth. "Why yes, my dear. Among other things. Imagine what a relic of true creation could do in the right hands. Heal the dying. Raise the fallen. Give power to those who've been denied it." He coughs, wet and rattling, and presses his hand to his chest.

Damn it. I thought I was being ironic. But that's Lafayette's scripture coming out of Hoodoo's mouth. Heal the dying. Raise the fallen. Last time someone preached that gospel, Morgan ended up the sacrificial guest at Hoodoo's party.

And Hoodoo's stronger than he should be. Much stronger. Despite the ugly cough. Someone's backing him. Feeding him power. That question can wait. Edison can't.

I might not be all alone. I glance hopefully toward the black water sloshing against the hull. No pale hands. No kelp hair. Just mist and cold. Jack's fish-lady charm presses against my ribs next to the jade box. It called her when I was drowning. Not sure "drowning in trouble" counts the same way.

A week ago I wouldn't have imagined myself praying for a rusalka.

Keep them talking. Buy time.

"I want to see Edison," I say. "Up close. Hear his voice. Then we talk terms."

Kollach nods to Hoodoo. "Show her."

Hoodoo jerks his chin and a scarecrow figure with the waxy skin and twitchy hands of a hophead emerges from the shadows around the cabin. Looks like maybe half a dozen are crouched there. With Kollach's guards and Mary's boys, might have a dozen bodies between them. The man drags Edison forward a few steps, chain clinking.

Edison's voice is hoarse, cracked. "Don't, Mick—don't give them anything."

Hoodoo yanks the chain hard. Edison chokes, stumbles. It's a horrible déjà vu of Morgan at the end of Hoodoo's chain in Las Vegas. Jesus, living my worst nightmare all over again. I failed Morgan then. Not gonna fail Edison this time. I need to kill Hoodoo and be done with it.

"That's enough," Mary says sharply, glaring at Hoodoo. To me, "You've seen him. He's alive. Now show us the jade."

I'm hoping lightning will strike and I have some brilliant idea to get us both out of here. "Not yet." I look at Kollach. "You really trust Hoodoo with something this powerful? A man whose real name you didn't even know until five minutes ago?"

"You will deliver the jade to me." Kollach's mouth tightens. "Besides, Doctor Nightingale has been in my employ for weeks. His credentials—"

"Are lies. He's a rogue necromancer who'll gut you the second you're not useful. Two nights ago, you wanted me to remove him for you." I shift my attention to Mary. "And you think Kollach's going to let you keep any power once he's got the jade? He'll toss you aside like yesterday's laundry."

Mary's expression doesn't change, but her knuckles whiten on the pistol grip.

I turn to Hoodoo. "And you. You really think these two won't turn on you? Kollach's a politician. He'll hang you out to dry the moment the law gets close. Mary's a survivor. She'd auction you off and sleep sound that same night."

For a moment, nobody speaks. The ship creaks as the tide shifts. Water slaps the hull. Wind hisses through the rigging.

Kollach glances at Hoodoo, suspicion plain. Hoodoo's smile stays fixed, but his eyes narrow. Mary watches both of them, calculating.

Not enough. The cracks are there, but they're not breaking. Not yet.

Mary steps closer, lowering her voice. Intimate. Almost tender. "Mick. Listen to me. You're exhausted. You're out-gunned. You're out of moves." She reaches out, fingertips brushing my sleeve. "Hand over the jade. I'll make sure Edison walks. You both walk. No one has to die tonight."

I meet her eyes. See the plea beneath the venom. She *wants* me to believe her. Is it the siren talking to me now?

But I also see the desperation. The fear. The woman who's been losing her grip for years and sees this as her last chance.

The Norn lurches again, harder this time. The anchor's dragging. Current's pulling us toward open water, toward the Gate, toward the cold Pacific beyond.

Time's running out.

"All right," I say firmly. "Let's do this."

I touch the jade's box under my coat. Feel its weight.

Over their shoulders, Edison's eyes find mine. Terrified. Trusting.

I lost Morgan. Not this one.

Chapter Thirty-Two

KOLLACH'S PATIENCE SNAPS LIKE a dry twig.

"Enough." He steps forward, hand extended. "We proceed at once, Mrs. McClellan. I've indulged enough delay."

The tide pulls harder now. Through the deck, I feel the Norn straining at her anchor, wanting to swing toward the Gate. Every second, we drift farther from shore, from help, from any world where Leona might stumble into this mess in time.

I'm out of moves.

My hand goes to my coat. Fingers close around the box. Whatever's inside—whatever Sol died protecting, whatever the rusalka guarded in her sunken ship, whatever everyone in this godforsaken city has been killing each other over, is the only card I've got left.

I pull it out.

Kollach's eyes light up like a man seeing salvation. He reaches—

Mary steps between us, smooth as silk.

"Isaac, darling." Her voice is honeyed reason. "Let's do this properly. You wouldn't buy a racehorse without looking at its teeth first, would you?"

Kollach's hand freezes mid-reach. His jaw tightens.

"What are you suggesting?"

"Let the professor verify the stone's authenticity." She gestures toward Hoodoo with the languid grace of a woman arranging flowers, not bartering over a kidnapped boy and a relic of dubious providence. "Then we release the boy. Everyone gets what they want, and you don't parade a dud in front of your friends."

The word *dud* lands like a fishhook. Kollach's face darkens. "You think I'd be fooled—"

"I think you've sunk a small fortune and your reputation into this venture." Mary's smile doesn't waver. "Better to know now, in private, than to discover it on a podium with a thousand witnesses."

His vanity and his paranoia wrestle for control. I watch it play out across his face—the civic leader who wants to look shrewd, the politician who can't afford to be made a fool.

Vanity wins.

"Fine." He stabs a finger at Hoodoo. "Verification. But the moment you confirm it's genuine, Professor, you hand it over. No more games."

Hoodoo's smile spreads wider. "Of course, Mr. Kollach. Purely procedural."

I clock the new order of operations: verify jade, *then* release Edison.

That pushes everything farther down the line. More time for things to go wrong. More time for them to realize my power's about tapped out. Right now, they think I'm dangerous.

Mary's gotta be playing an angle here. She didn't *need* to suggest verification. Kollach was ready to take the box and hand over Edison. But she *wants* the jade in Hoodoo's hands.

Why?

Hoodoo tilts his head, that cadaverous grin showing too many teeth.

Mary leans close to my ear. "I'm the only one here who gives a damn whether you and the boy live through this." She peels my fingers from the jade's box.

"We'll want quiet," Hoodoo says. "For delicate work."

He flicks two fingers. A pair of his waxy-skinned, twitchy, strung out on whatever cocktail of opium and necromancy he's dosing them with hopheads disappear below deck.

Within moments comes the wet slap of something heavy hitting wood, is bouncing up from the hold.

The hoppies reappear, hauling sacks up through the hatch. They return to the hold multiple times until three, five, ten lumps, wrapped in burlap that reeks of brine and rot are dumped on the deck.

Hoodoo murmurs something low and guttural. Snaps his bone-white fingers.

The sacks twitch.

Gray bloated hands emerge from the gathered tops, fingernails black, tearing the burlap away. Ten revenants lurch upright, swaying like sailors three sheets to the wind. Their eyes are milky. Their mouths hang slack.

Hoodoo gestures. They shamble to posts around the deck, taking up positions like sentries.

Oh hell. I hate zombies. He's padding the room. More bodies between me and him. More fuel for whatever he's about to do.

Me and Hoodoo go back a good fifteen years. I taught him to fear me. Since I set foot on this deck, he's kept his distance. No doubt remembering Las Vegas. Remembering what I did to Lafayette and his whole rotten cabal.

I need him to keep remembering.

Mary's boys close around Mary. Kollach's men tighten the ring. I'm boxed in.

"Secure her," Kollach says. "Bring me the boy."

Two of his thugs move toward me, one on each side, reaching for my arms. I don't think. Just react.

Scraping together every scrap of animus I've got left, fragments I've conjured from my own vitae in desperation, I *shove*.

The force hits the thug on my right. He stumbles backward, arms windmilling, and crashes into the rail hard enough to crack wood. The one on my left steps back, off-balance. Shit, it wasn't enough.

I lunge for Edison anyway, three steps, maybe four, reaching for the chain—

Pain explodes behind my eyes. White-hot. Blinding.

My knees buckle. Waves of nausea flood my throat. The rebound for trying to use more power than I have.

Someone slams into me from behind and drives me face-first into the deck. My cheek hits planking. Blood floods my mouth from teeth meeting cheek. Stars in my vision.

Hands grab my arms, yank them behind my back. My hook scrapes wood, useless.

I try to pull more power, try to *move*—

Nothing.

The well's truly dry. Not even fumes left.

That's it. I'm done.

The thug hauls me upright, pins my arms. I sway on my feet, vision graying at the edges, every breath a razor.

Hoodoo's staring at me.

For a long moment, he just watches. Eyes narrowed. Calculating. Then his shoulders drop. Tension bleeds out of him. And he smiles. "That all you've got these days, Mary Catherine? Quite a sorry showing." He chuckles, then exhales in relief. He's grinning at me like I'm a Christmas pony. "But never fear. I just need a couple drops of blood from this healthy young man."

He's not afraid of me anymore.

Mary sees it too. Of course she does.

"See?" She says it lightly, taking Kollach's arm and pulling him back to make room for Edison to join the circle around Hoodoo. "Our girl's spent, Isaac. Let the professor work. You'll have your prize and everything else you were promised before the night's out."

Our girl.

Hoodoo turns back to his work, unhurried, practically cheerful.

Taking the box from Mary, he opens it with a theatrical flourish. Asshole loves to show off.

He lifts the jade out.

It's beautiful in the lantern light. The green stone appears to glow from within.

The rusalka pulled it from her hoard, pressed it into my hands, and sent me topside with a bargain and a threat. I have no idea how it works. But I'm guessing it takes energy, Big Magic always does.

Unfortunately, Hoodoo doesn't seem to share my ignorance. He slips the box into his coat pocket and starts snapping orders.

"Kneel. Circle up."

Half a dozen of his hopheads shuffle in, eyes glassy. They drop to their knees in a rough ring aft of the foremast. Another six revenants lurch up behind them, and gray hands settle on living shoulders.

He steps into the ring, fishing a small tin from inside his vest, and dips two fingers in something black and greasy. Tar, maybe, mixed with blood. He works his way around the circle, smearing crooked sigils on each hophead's brow, then on the gray flesh of the revenants behind them.

When he's done, he winces as he kneels in the center and bows his head. The hopheads link hands, making a solid ring of flesh and chain around him. The revenants' dead fingers tighten on their shoulders.

Pulling the jade from its box, Hoodoo holds it in cupped hands. He closes his eyes and starts to chant words that scrape like gravel.

The air thickens. It feels like a million ants are crawling over my skin. He's pulling vitae, life force.

It comes off the revenants first. I feel the tug as their life-stain yanks free, threadbare and sour. It runs through their hands over the hoppies, flowing toward Hoodoo in a foul stream.

Then the hopheads themselves. Their vitae hums with whatever filth he's been feeding them, bright and wrong. It bleeds out of them, into a swirling mix around Hoodoo.

Pausing in his chanting, he crooks a finger at Edison. I tense, waiting for the worst.

"A drop of the boy's blood. To prime the working." Hoodoo grabs Edison's wrist and pulls him close.

He flicks a knife across Edison's wrist, not deep. Dropping the knife, Hoodoo positions Edison's bleeding wrist over the jade. His blood drips onto it, trailing bright yellow threads of vitae, Edison's life force.

I struggle pointlessly against the men holding me.

Pushing Edison away, Hoodoo's chant resumes. The syllables scrape the inside of my skull.

The deck shudders under my knees.

Sickly purple light seeps along the ring of joined hands, crawling up the hopheads' arms, through the revenants' fingers until it crests over their heads, spilling inward toward Hoodoo, spiraling up around the jade resting in Hoodoo's hands.

The air feels heavy. Pressing me down. Like the whole sky's leaning on us.

Sweat beads on Hoodoo's cadaverous face.

Mary's taut as a drawn bow, everything she's gambled riding on this. Kollach's got his greedy eyes locked on the stone, fists clenched.

The revenants have gone still. Their mouths work soundlessly.

Because there's something *wrong* with the way the energy Hoodoo called is flowing.

A hum starts in my bones. Not the usual background static but something sharper, a wrongness I feel in my teeth, my spine, my blood. Something's off with the working. I can't see it, not with my sight burned to ash, but I feel it all through me. The energy Hoodoo's calling should be settling, anchoring, finding purchase. Instead the jade's hum is thin, hollow.

Mary and Kollach lean closer, expectant. Waiting for salvation. For victory. For whatever they think this thing will give them.

The purple light flares brighter.

Hoodoo's voice rises to a shout.

And somewhere out in the dark, I swear I hear the sound of oars cutting water.

Chapter Thirty-Three

HOODOO HITS THE PEAK of his chant, and the jade hums under the pressure of all the power he's summoned.

Then it chokes.

The purple glow gutters. The death-rattle wheeze of something failing wails in my head.

A crack skitters across the carved tortoise's shell.

One of the revenants standing sentry just...collapses. Strings cut. It hits the deck with a meaty thud and doesn't move again.

Hoodoo staggers. His chant breaks off mid-syllable, and a wet, rattling cough explodes from his mouth. When he pulls his hand away from his lips, there's blood speckling his palm.

The jade gives one more feeble flicker.

Then the glamour sloughs off.

In that last dirty light, we can all *see* it changing. The rich, deep green dulls by a shade, then two, sliding down into a muddy olive. The fine etching on the serpent's scales blurs, edges softening like someone's wiped chalk off a board. The tortoise's shell loses its crisp expert carving. What's left is a squat little beast with clumsy lines and a lopsided head.

Not some god-touched treasure from an emperor's altar.

A tourist trinket.

Stones and stories, the rusalka had said. All the same to her. We'd spilled blood across half the city chasing the story surrounding this one.

The light dies. The thing in Hoodoo's hands is as ordinary as it ever was.

He stares at it like it just insulted his mother.

"You sons of bitches," he snarls. "This isn't it." His voice is hoarse, shaking with disbelief.

He hurls the jade down. It hits the planks and splits, two dull halves spinning apart, nothing special about either piece.

It all comes back to me: Garrett's sneer, him telling me how Loosh lost his tenure at the University, *antiquities scams*. Jack at the Night Market warning me that Loosh was yanking the wrong tiger's tail. Sol's cobwebbed palace full of junk and the odd real prize.

Loosh didn't fence a stolen treasure. He *made* one. Took a nice old turtle, wrapped it in a cheap glamour, and let the city's greed do the rest. Sol never knew. Sol died protecting his friend's con, and never once doubted it was real.

The whole bloody coast has been tearing itself apart over a forgery.

Hoodoo wheels on the nearest hoppy.

"Useless!"

His boot catches the man's ribs. The hoppy curls inward, but Hoodoo's already turned to the next one, fists swinging wild. The addicts scatter like roaches, scrambling for cover behind masts and rigging.

He kicks at a revenant. It doesn't even flinch. Just stands there, dead eyes tracking nothing.

Hoodoo spins back to Mary, chest heaving. Bloody spittle stains his cheeks.

For a heartbeat, nobody moves. The deck creaks. Water slaps the hull. The night presses in close and cold.

Then Kollach speaks.

"What"—his voice is strangled, barely above a whisper—"did you just say?"

Hoodoo turns on him, eyes wild. "It's a *fake*. A gods-damned *glamoured souvenir*." He's wracked by a chest-deep cough. "Someone sold you glass beads and called them diamonds."

Kollach goes white. Then red. Then a mottled purple that makes the veins stand out on his temples.

I watch him put it together, the truth he could deny when he thought he would win.

The money he's spent. The political capital he's burned. The necromancer he hired is a *wanted criminal*, as it turns out.

All of it for *nothing*.

His gaze swings to Mary.

She's frozen, eyes locked on the cracked jade. For the first time since I met her, the mask is completely gone. No gold-tooth smile. No languid confidence.

Just naked, animal terror.

Her last chance at restored power, at keeping her place, her influence, her *self* just shattered.

"You knew," Kollach breathes, closing the gap between them.

Mary's head snaps up. "Isaac, I didn't—"

"You *knew*." His voice rises, cracking with fury. "You and your pet corpse-raiser. This whole time. You've been playing me for a fool."

"Isaac, listen—"

But he's not listening anymore. He needs a target. Mary, stepping between him and the jade. Mary, insisting Hoodoo verify it first. Mary, keeping him placated while she and Hoodoo worked their own angle.

She was never the lick-spittle lap dog he wanted.

"You whore," he spits, grabbing her shoulders. "You scheming Barbary Coast *whore*."

Mary's chin lifts, meeting his eyes in a flash of defiance. "Careful, Isaac. You're showing your breeding."

The knife flashes as he draws it from his coat. A gentleman's blade, slim and silver, drives into her side, just below her armpit.

Mary gasps. Not a scream. Just a small, shocked sound.

Hoodoo shouts something. "She's *mine*, you damn fool!" Not grief in his voice. Whatever he wanted Mary's siren for, Kollach just put a knife through it. But he's still reeling, still coughing blood, still trying to recover from the ritual, the glamour's backlash, and his own temper.

I don't think. Don't weigh options or calculate revenge.

I see Mary folding, her hand pressed to the wound, blood already soaking her dress. Every bit of anger I've been nursing evaporates.

The thug holding me is distracted, staring at Kollach and Mary. I twist, wrench free. I'm on my knees before I've consciously decided to move, catching Mary as she falls. She's heavier than I expected. Or maybe I'm just that weak. We go down together on the blood-slicked planks.

Her eyes find mine. The raw fear hurts to see.

"Mick—"

"I've got you." My voice is steadier than I feel. "It's going to be all right."

Her heartbeat thuds fast and thin and losing ground. Blood soaks through my shirt where I'm pressing her against me.

I should hate her. A minute ago, I did. Now I see her, without the mask, without the gold-tooth smile, and I want to save her.

The quiet is cut by a heavy thump from the starboard hull as the Norn lurches hard to port. Kollach stumbles. Hoodoo falls to his knees. Then the waves still.

"Bureau of Magical Investigation! Stand down!" More shouting erupts in a language I don't recognize.

Leona.

I twist just enough to see a Chinese junk materializing from the fog, her hull pressing tight against the Norn's starboard side. She's half our length at best, sitting low and dark in the water. Her battened sail hangs furled tight to the mast; she came in silent, under oars, to mask her approach.

The small deck is crowded with men, some bracing against the gunwale, others swinging grappling hooks overhead in widening arcs. In the bow, silhouetted against the soft glow of a hooded lantern, two figures stand side by side, one in a long coat with a rifle, the other in silk and fur, both shouting orders that cut through the chaos like thrown knives.

Leona and Ah Toy.

Together.

How in hell—

Kollach's men whirl toward the starboard rail, guns coming up as grappling hooks arc up from the junk, biting into the Norn's deck. Ropes go taut and men swarm the lines.

I count fast. Eight, maybe ten men, in dark coats and queue braids, some with long poles, some with swords. Three more figures in civilian jackets. Gotta be Leona's team.

Leona stands, rifle braced, voice cutting through the noise. "Drop your weapons and step away from the prisoner!"

Ah Toy barks an order in what might be Cantonese and her men move faster, throwing more hooks, fighting the chop to keep the two ships tight together.

One small boat. A dozen boarders at most, counting the crew.

Against Kollach's hired guns, Mary's boys, Hoodoo's hopheads and revenants.

As the first of Ah Toy's fighters hooks an arm over the Norn's side and hauls himself over, someone fires. He topples backward off the rail and hits the junk's deck with a sick thud.

More are coming.

Leona is up the rope in three hard pulls, boots finding purchase on the Norn's planking. She swings over the rail and drops one of Hoodoo's hoppies with the rifle butt to his head.

Ah Toy holds the junk's deck, one hand on the rail, eyes sweeping the chaos while snapping fresh orders to her men.

Leona and the first men aboard scatter. Bullets chew the masts as Kollach's shooters take aim. The hoppies and Mary's boys try to close distance, fists and blades out.

Hoodoo's already moving, hands weaving patterns in the air, dragging at every scrap of death within reach.

And Mary—

Mary's breath hitches against my arm. I feel her weight sagging heavier against me, her life spilling fast. I pull her to the leeward side of the main mast, hoping to shelter her there so I can join the fray.

Mary's hand is pressed to the wound, her breath coming in shallow gasps. She's dying. I feel it: she's got minutes. Maybe less. The gleaner within roils, hungry, wanting to taste this death.

Her fingers close on my sleeve. Grip tight despite the blood loss.

"Don't," she whispers. "Don't leave me alone."

Bullets crack across the deck. Someone's shouting orders. Leona, I think, but I can't make out the words over the chaos.

Edison's by the bitt twenty feet away, trying to make himself small as gunfire rips the air above him.

Hoodoo's gathering power, purple light beginning to coil around his hands again.

Kollach's backing toward the cabin, shouting for his men to protect him.

And I'm kneeling in the center of it all, holding a dying woman who sold me out an hour ago, torn between—

Between what?

Between vengeance and mercy?

Mary's eyes lock on mine. Terrified. Pleading.

"Please."

The word breaks something in me.

Chapter Thirty-Four

KOLLACH'S VOICE CUTS THROUGH the chaos. "Protect your mayor! Shoot the Chinamen!"

Hoodoo's hands weave patterns in the air, yanking power from whatever corpses he can still reach. Two bodies lurch from the deck, victims of bullets. They shamble into position, meat shields between him and the incoming fire.

A BMI agent vaults over the rail, rifle up. Gets tackled by one of Mary's boys. They go down in a tangle of fists and curses.

On the port side, Ah Toy steps onto the Norn's deck like she's entering her own parlor. Silk robes, fur collar, a sword in her hand that gleams in the dim lantern light. She decapitates the nearest revenant.

One clean stroke. The revenant's head tumbles across the deck.

Mary's breathing is ragged, wet. I clutch her tighter. Each breath sounds like it costs her something she can't afford to spend.

"Always thought I'd die in bed," she says, voice thin but still with a sardonic edge. "Pretty boy beside me. Not on a blood-slicked deck with a half-dead Gleaner."

Despite everything, I almost smile. "Could've picked better company than me."

"Could've. Didn't." Her fingers tighten on my sleeve. "Story of my life, really."

A bullet cracks overhead. Someone screams—can't tell whose side.

Mary's eyes find mine. A scared woman running out of time.

"I was terrified," she says. "Of being useless. Of being the one they pat on the head and ignore." She coughs and blood flecks her lips. "I thought if I could just get the jade..."

"Wish you'd picked a better partner than Hoodoo Jones."

"I thought I was clever enough." A bitter laugh turns into a gurgle. "Turns out I was just desperate."

I glance around. Can't tell shit from where we're sitting. The fighting still swirls around us.

"I do admire you," Mary says. Her hand finds my face, thumb brushing my cheek. "You're better than I deserve, Mick Kelly."

"Mary—"

"I'm scared." The words come out small. Childlike. "I've seen so many die alone in back alleys, forgotten. I don't want—" She breaks off, breathing hard. "Stay with me," she whispers. "Ride with me into the dark. Just this once. Please, love."

The Gleaner growls, wanting this. It's animal need, not thought.

My throat closes. Mary can't understand what she's asking. The closer I am, in love or hate, to the person whose death I ride, the stronger the tie afterward. If I do this, I will not be free of Mary.

"Mary, you understand this means you'll be stuck with me, can't tell for how long, but your soul won't cross over like normal folk do."

"I know." She stops to try and take a breath, but it comes out a gurgling sigh. I can barely make out her words, her voice breathy. "Take it...use the power...give these assholes what they deserve." She tries to say more but chokes, blood and foam clinging to her lips. She manages a small nod.

The power of Mary's death would let me save Edison, halt Hoodoo in his tracks. Maybe it wouldn't be so bad to have Mary dogging my steps for a while.

I feel her heart slowing, stuttering. Now or never.

I grip her hand. Lock eyes with her.

"I've got you," I say as I unleash the Gleaner. Her shining pink Animus rises as her heartbeat slows.

My focus narrows to the blazing core of her life force. The Gleaner seizes her, latches on. Her final heartbeat shudders through me.

The world drops away.

I'm falling through darkness. Like slipping into someone else's dream, her life plays before me.

A parlor in Belfast. Young Mary—ten, maybe twelve—standing straight-backed while her mother's employer inspects her like livestock. "She'll do for the companion position. Teach her to keep her mouth shut."

A ship's hold. Sixteen and sick as a dog but singing anyway because the sailors toss pennies when she does.

A closed door. A man's hand. The sound of fabric tearing. Then silence, and the road to the docks.

A San Francisco stage. The first time she opens her mouth and the whole room goes quiet. The first time she realizes she can make them do anything if she sings it sweet enough.

Building her empire one smile, one song, one carefully placed threat at a time.

The night she realizes it's fading. Standing in front of a mirror, watching a younger woman steal the attention she used to command without effort. The terror of irrelevance creeping in.

And underneath it all, a current of loneliness so deep it hurts.

Never trusting anyone. Never building anything that wasn't transactional. Never letting anyone close enough to see the fear.

Except—

We're laughing over whiskey in the Strausburg. I see myself through her eyes, Mick, looking at her as an equal instead of a mark or a threat. Mick, who she could've—

Mary's voice in the liminal space, clear as bells, *I ruined it. I ruin everything. But don't let me go alone.*

You aren't, I tell her. I promise.

Use it, she says fiercely. *My power. End this right. Make my death worth something.*

One last bargain. Even here, even now.

But I'll take it.

Her Animus Mortis floods into my veins like liquid fire, and I swallow it down—half-siren charisma, half criminal ruthlessness, everything Mary was and everything she wanted to be. It fills the hollow places inside me, roaring through veins and bone and soul.

I feel her settle. Not gone. A shade. My shade now.

I snap back to my body.

Well then, love, she murmurs beside me, peering down at her corpse, slack in my arms. Eyes open, staring at nothing. *Let's see if you can make this mess worth my trouble.*

Around me, the fight rages. The tide has shifted in the minutes I rode with Mary.

A BMI agent screams, a revenant's hands locked around his throat, dragging him toward the rail. Leona fires, but the bullet punches through dead flesh without effect. She's bleeding from a gash on her left arm, backing toward the gunwale with nowhere left to go.

On the port side, Ah Toy's facing three revenants at once. Her sword is buried in one corpse's ribs, stuck fast. She yanks, can't free it, dodges as another swings a boat hook at her head.

Kollach's men have regrouped, emboldened by the chaos. Two of them have Edison in their sights, pistols raised.

And Hoodoo—

Hoodoo stands near the foremast, both hands raised, purple fire coiling around his fingers like living smoke. He's grinning despite the blood on his teeth, despite the way his body shakes with fever and consumption.

He's rallying. Pulling more power from the fresh corpses, from the corrupted hopheads, from the very air. Building toward something big.

Now, love, Mary's voice whispers in my ear. *Before we lose them all.*

I lay her body down gently.

Then I stand.

The world sharpens with Mary's gift humming through my veins, power and purpose wound together like rope. My Gleaner sight floods back with it. For the first time in days, I can actually see the lines of power on this deck.

Purple-black lines of necromantic control stretch from Hoodoo to every corpse on deck, a dozen, maybe more. They pulse and writhe like veins carrying poisoned blood, bright as burning wire in my amped-up vision.

I reach out with everything Mary gave me and *seize* the nearest thread.

Pain explodes through my skull.

It's like grabbing live electrical wire. Hoodoo's will fights back instantly, thrashing against mine, trying to keep his grip on the dead. The thread burns in my grasp, searing hot and freezing cold at once. This is ten times more power than I felt with Brass, fired by ten times as many fresh deaths.

I don't let go.

Hoodoo feels it. His head snaps toward me, eyes wide with shock that curdles into fury.

"You can't—"

"Watch me."

I wrap my will around every thread at once.

A dozen corpses. A dozen lines of control. All tethered to him like a marionette master's strings.

And I *pull.*

The threads fight. Each one writhes and burns and screams, echoes of Hoodoo's rage and desperation, his need to *own* even death itself.

Blood is dripping from my nose, hot copper taste at the back of my throat.

My vision whites out at the edges, narrowing to a tunnel.

One of the threads nearly slips free. I feel it sliding through my mental grip like a greased rope.

Pull, Mary's shade snarls in my ear. *Pull, damn you. PULL.*

I brace myself, feet planted on blood-slick deck, teeth gritted hard enough to *wrench*.

For a heartbeat, nothing happens.

Hoodoo's laughing, thinking he's won.

Then something inside his working *snaps*.

Audible. Like a rope breaking under too much weight. Like bone cracking.

The threads come apart all at once.

The revenants collapse. The corpse choking Leona's agent drops like a sack of wet sand. The agent gasps and crawls backward, alive.

The three surrounding Ah Toy crumple mid-swing, limbs folding, hitting the deck in a tangle. She yanks her sword free, breathing hard, and looks at me across the deck.

All across the Norn, Hoodoo's puppets just...*stop*.

The hopheads stagger, gasping, suddenly freed from whatever cocktail of chemicals and necromancy was driving them. One drops to his knees and vomits. Another sobs, hands pressed to his face.

The purple fire around Hoodoo's hands gutters and dies.

The deck's quiet for a single, suspended heartbeat. Then chaos erupts.

Leona's voice cuts through, sharp and commanding, "Now! Take them down *now*!"

Her agents rally. One tackles a Kollach thug. Another disarms a hophead who's still trying to fight on muscle memory alone.

Ah Toy moves like water, sword flashing. Two of Kollach's men go down in as many breaths, disarmed and bleeding but alive.

The remaining hoppies scatter, diving overboard or fleeing toward the bow.

Kollach himself is backing toward the cabin, face pale, shouting something about unlawful arrest and diplomatic immunity that nobody's listening to.

Hoodoo staggers, his meat shields gone. His power gutted. Blood running from his nose and ears, the backlash from losing all those threads at once hitting him like a mule kick to the skull.

I see *fear* in his eyes.

"You—" He's coughing, bent double, hands braced on his knees. "You can't—you shouldn't be able to—"

I step over a fallen revenant, moving toward him.

"I just did."

Mary's voice purrs at my shoulder, *Finish it.*

My vision's swimming. My hands shake. Even with Mary's boost, ripping apart a dozen necromantic bindings damn near emptied me again.

But I've got enough left for one more trick.

Hoodoo sees me coming and tries to run, stumbling toward the rail, hands scrabbling for purchase.

The Bay waits below. And somewhere in those black waters, the rusalka is waiting too.

I can feel her. Like a cold current running through my bones. I just think her name. Think of Sol. Think of the bargain I made in that sunken ship.

I've got him. Come take what's yours.

The water alongside the Norn goes still.

Dead calm, even though the current should be running hard toward the Gate.

A pale hand breaks the surface, long bone-white fingers, nails black as pitch. Hair swims across the water.

Ah Toy freezes mid-strike against one of Kollach's men. Her head turns sharply toward the water. Her eyes narrow as she sees. Her dragon-blood knows when old spirits move.

Hoodoo sees it too.

"Mick—" He backs up another step, hands raised. "We can make a deal. I can give you power."

"You're done," I say plainly, the heat wrung out of my words.

Morgan. Sol. Brass. The girl in the gutter. Edison in chains. All the dead and broken people this man left in his wake.

All of it.

Mary's shade urges me on. *Do it.*

I gather the last scraps of her power, my power now, and *shove.*

Hoodoo flies backward.

Arms windmilling, mouth open, boots leaving the deck.

He crashes through the rail, wood splintering, and hits the water with a splash. Even as he falls, I hear a last attempt at a spell, maybe a ward.

But the rusalka's ready. Eyes white and wide and filled with fury. Her mouth is open in a scream that echoes in the hollow places where the dead live.

She's beautiful.

She wraps arms and hair and cold bay water around him.

The water churns once. Twice. White foam and dark shapes twisting together. Sinking back into the black, dragging Hoodoo Jones down to the deep, then the current resumes rocking the Norn.

I chose that. Chose to feed him to the deep. I'd do it again.

The only sound on deck is the creak of rigging and the labored breath of the living.

Ah Toy sheathes her sword with a soft *snick* and looks at the water where Hoodoo disappeared. Then at me. Understanding passes between us.

She knows what I did. What I *called.*

Leona's standing over Kollach's men, breathing hard, blood running down her arm, but her rifle steady. They kneel, with their hands behind their heads.

Kollach himself is backed against the cabin wall, still sputtering. "This is unlawful! That quack Nightingale—that madwoman Mary—they forced me into—"

Any chance you could toss him over as well? Mary chuckles. *I owe him after the knife in my heart.*

Leona walks over, calm as Sunday morning, and slaps iron cuffs on his wrists.

"Isaac Milton Kollach," she says, voice flat and official. "You're under arrest for conspiracy to procure illegal magical artifacts, accessory to kidnapping, and about a dozen other charges I'm going to enjoy listing in my report."

She glances past him at me. Then at the water.

"Where's Jones?"

I meet her eyes. "Gone."

She holds my gaze for a long moment. Finally, she nods once. "Good."

Ah Toy steps over a headless revenant and picks up a piece of the jade from the deck.

She turns it over in her hands, examining it. "Forgery," she says. "Fine work, beautiful in its way." She glances at me, her eyes flickering to where Mary still hovers at my shoulder. Can Ah Toy see her? "Your friends were ambitious. They fooled a city."

She lets it fall from her hand.

"The real Nü Gua Jade is elsewhere." A slight incline of her head. "But you kept this counterfeit out of the hands of men who would have used it to destroy my people. That is...a service I will remember."

I'm too tired to answer. Too wrung out to do anything but nod.

One of Ah Toy's men cuts Edison hands free and helps him over the rail to the junk below. His face is bruised, his wrist bandaged where Hoodoo cut him, but he's *alive*.

On the deck behind me, Mary's body lies in a pool of cooling blood.

But her voice is loud and clear.

Not bad for a half-drowned Gleaner, she murmurs.

I almost smile.

Almost.

Chapter Thirty-Five

THE DECK OF THE Norn creaks beneath my boots. Dawn grays the Bay, night thinning, pulling back to reveal the mess we've made. My mouth tastes of blood and salt.

Leona's already organizing the aftermath, barking orders at her agents. Kollach sits slumped against the cabin wall in chains, looking like a man whose world just ended. Which it has.

I push off the rail, every muscle protesting. Need to move before my body figures out how badly it wants to stop.

Leona catches my arm. "You did good tonight. Don't let Garrett's bullshit make you think otherwise."

I glance across the deck where Ah Toy is directing her men, sword cleaned and sheathed at her hip. Her silk robes are stained with seawater and blood at the hem. She looks like she's done this before.

"How?" I ask Leona.

Leona sighs, wiping blood from her cheek. "Garrett refused to authorize resources. Called it 'a local matter between foreign gangs and a disgraced Death Eater.' Said the Bureau shouldn't waste federal assets on Barbary Coast politics. So, I went to someone who had a ship and a reason to use it."

"And she just said yes?"

Leona smiles. "She had a junk crewed and armed inside of an hour. Fastest mobilization I've ever seen."

"But how did you make it against the tide? When slack ended I figured me and Edison were gonners for sure."

"Turns out the whole 'daughter of the dragon' thing is real." She grins in Ah Toy's direction. "Did you know dragons have an affinity for water?"

Ah Toy catches us looking. Inclines her head slightly.

Careful, love, Mary's shade murmurs. *That woman doesn't lend ships out of kindness. She's buying a seat at every table you'll ever sit at.*

Maybe. But tonight, she bought Edison's life. That earns her whatever seat she wants.

I nod. Can't speak past the tightness in my throat.

I join Edison in the junk, climbing over the railing on legs that shake like a newborn colt's. Edison's wrapped in a blanket, I sit next to him.

The little boat carries us to shore. Nobody speaks much. Edison dozes against my shoulder. The city materializes out of the fog, gray and solid and real.

We reach Pier 10 just before dawn, that deep gray-black where the world feels suspended between night and morning. My boots hit the familiar planks and Edison stumbles slightly beside me.

The bar's lights glow warm through the front windows. Sounds like a party's happening inside.

The familiar smells hit first. Then the noise. Calpurnia's is packed. Abby's English sailors, dock workers, folks from up and down the waterfront, all crammed in shoulder to shoulder. Word travels fast on the docks. Every eye turns to us when we walk in.

Abby's behind the counter, talking low with Nico. The moment she sees Edison, her face lights up, mug in her hand forgotten.

"Edison."

She's at the boor before he can take two steps inside. Her arms go around him, fierce and trembling, and Edison—tall, gangly Edison who tries so hard to look professional and capable—folds into her like he's a child again.

"You scared ten years off me, boy." Her voice breaks on the words.

"BMI protocol states that agents in the field should—" He tries for levity, but his voice shakes and the joke falls flat.

Abby pulls back just enough to cup his face in her hands, turning his head gently to examine the bruises. He winces when her thumb grazes over the split lip, then lets out a wet laugh that's half sob.

"I'm all right, Ma. I'm all right."

Abby leads him over to a table, her customers cheerfully make way, cheering and patting him them both on the back settles on a chair.

I take a spot at the bar nearby. Mary's shade materializes on a stool beside me, watching them with an expression I'm surprised to see. Something soft. Almost wistful.

That's what I never had, love. She's quiet for a moment. *No wonder you turned out better than me.*

The door bangs open loudly.

"Where is he? Where's that idiot boy?"

Spanish Kitty storms in, flying skirts and fury. She stops dead when she sees Edison in Abby's arms, and relief flickers across her face, so naked it hurts to witness.

Then the mask slams back down.

"You stupid, reckless—" She races across the floor and Edison stands to meet her. She smacks his shoulder. Not too hard. Just enough to make her point. "I didn't know if you were dead or—"

"Kitty—"

"Don't 'Kitty' me." But her hand stays on his shoulder, gripping tight. "You owe me a steak dinner. With champagne. The expensive kind."

Edison manages a real smile. "Deal."

She turns to me, eyes narrowing. "And you. What took you so long to get him back?"

"You're welcome," I say dryly.

Her lips purse. Then, grudgingly, smiles. "Thank you."

Abby's watching this exchange closely. She gives Kitty the faintest nod. Probationary acceptance.

I lean against the bar, exhaustion hitting me all at once. Nico sets a glass of whiskey in front of me without being asked.

"Good." I drain half the glass. The warmth spreads through my chest, cutting the cold that's been dogging me since I went in the bay yesterday.

Emma appears from the back room, eyes red like she's been crying. She goes straight to Edison and presses a clean cloth into his hands. "For your face," she says kindly.

The bar settles into something like normalcy. Low voices. The creak of floorboards. Someone putting coffee on to brew.

Then Nico gestures toward a covered cage in the corner. "Almost forgot. That's for you."

I blink. "What?"

"Sol's animals. Had to be placed. Ah Toy's taking the rare birds. She's got aviaries, apparently. Mrs. Chen from the herbalist meeting took the monkeys. Father Donnelly agreed to take the snakes for the parish oddities cabinet." He pauses. "But this one's yours."

"I don't want—"

He pulls the cloth off the cage.

Werner the gray parrot cocks his head, bright eyes fixing on me. Then he explodes into sound.

"Give me a rum and gum! Pour a grog while you're at it!"

The bar erupts in laughter. Tired, slightly hysterical laughter.

I stare at the bird. The bird stares back, unrepentant.

"You're joking."

"Nobody else would take him," Nico says. "Too foul-mouthed for polite company. Figured he'd fit right in with you."

Mary's shade laughs outright, delighted. *Finally, someone in your life with worse manners than yours.*

Werner ruffles his feathers and starts preening, clearly pleased with himself.

"Wonderful." I take another drink. "Just what I needed. A foul-mouthed parrot."

"Could be worse," Emma offers. "Could be the monkeys."

Fair point.

Werner launches into a bawdy drinking song, the kind sailors sing three sheets to the wind. The lyrics are spectacularly obscene. Then he stops mid-verse, cocks his head, and announces in his best imitation of Sols voice, "Free chowder on Sundays! No exceptions!"

Nico goes still. Abby's hand pauses on Edison's shoulder.

Then Nico raises his glass. "To Sol."

The room echoes it. Werner resumes his song and the crowd joins in the chorus.

Edison slips away from Kitty and Abby and comes to stand beside me at the bar. His hands shake slightly as he picks up the coffee Emma offers.

"You all right?" I ask quietly.

He's silent for a moment. "Keep seeing it. The cellar. The revenants. That ritual, watching him cut my wrist, knowing he was using my blood for..." He trails off.

I don't give him platitudes. Don't tell him it'll fade or that he'll forget. That would be a lie.

"Nightmares come," I say instead. "They will for a while. Don't fight them. Just breathe through and remember you're not there anymore. And don't drink yourself stupid trying to stop them. That just makes it worse."

He looks at me, something grateful in his eyes. "Bureau teach you that?"

"Experience." I meet his gaze. "And Edison? If BMI hangs you out to dry over this, if Garrett tries to blame you for getting grabbed, or questions your judgment, or any of that bureaucratic horseshit, you come to me first. Understand?"

He nods slowly. "Thank you."

Mary's shade, watching from her perch, sounds approving. *See? Building your own little bureau. Much more sensible than begging scraps from theirs.*

I drain my whiskey and push off the bar. "I should head home. Family'll be worried."

Abby catches my hand. "Thank you. For everything."

I squeeze back. "Get some sleep. All of you."

Outside, dawn's finally breaking. Real dawn, not that gray half-light. The city's waking up. Vendors setting up. Sailors heading to their ships. The normal rhythm of San Francisco carrying on despite necromancers and revenants and women dying for jade that wasn't even real.

Mary's shade walks beside me, hands in her pockets.

Not a bad night's work, she says. *All things considered.*

"You died."

Details, love. Details.

I shake my head, too tired to argue with a ghost.

Werner's cage swings from my hook as I walk. He's gone quiet, feathers ruffled against the morning chill. Even the bird's had enough excitement for one night.

The townhouse. Lights in the windows despite the early hour. Julianna's probably pacing. Gudrun, making tea.

I reach for my key, but the door flies open before my fingers find it.

"Aunt MC!"

Ylva barrels into me with the force of a small cannonball. I stumble back a step, catching her with my good arm while Werner's cage swings wildly from the hook.

"Easy, cub. I'm still in one piece."

"You're back! You're really back!" She's got her arms around my waist, face pressed into my coat. "And you stink."

Julianna appears in the doorway, hair coming loose from its pins, apron dusted with flour. Her eyes are red-rimmed, and when she pulls me inside, her hands shake as she straightens my collar.

"You're bleeding," she says, touching my sleeve.

"I was. It's fine now."

"It's not fine." She cups my face, checking for damage. "None of this is fine. We got Abby's note. That you were safe, that Edison was safe." Her voice catches. "Don't you dare do that to me again."

"Julianna, I can't promise that."

"I know." She pulls me into a hug, fierce and brief. "But let me pretend you can."

Gudrun appears from the kitchen. One long, assessing look.

"You look half-dead." She says, taking my arms and leading me to the kitchen.

"Only half? I'm getting better at this."

She doesn't smile. Just points at the kitchen table. "Sit."

Werner announces himself the moment the cage hits the table. "Give me a rum and gum! What'll you have?"

"What," Julianna says faintly, "is *that*?"

"Werner. Sol Sonderling's parrot."

Werner starts up a sea shanty—thankfully, one of the cleaner ones. Ylva dissolves into giggles. Gudrun mutters something in Norwegian about chaos and feathered demons.

The kitchen fills with the sounds of a normal morning. Gudrun at the stove. Julianna slicing bread. Ylva peppering me with questions I half-answer while Werner provides commentary nobody asked for.

It's domestic. Safe. Mine.

Ylva leans against my shoulder, small and warm and trusting. "I'm glad you're home."

"Me too, cub."

And Mary's shade, watching it all, says softly, *This is what you fought for, isn't it? This mess of life and noise and people who won't let you disappear.*

"Yeah," I say, too quiet for anyone but her to hear. "I guess it is."

She nods once. *Good. Don't forget it when the next disaster comes knocking. Because it will, love. It always does.*

"I know."

But for now—just for now—I let myself be home.

Chapter Thirty-Six

THE STRAUSBURG IS PACKED shoulder to shoulder, air thick with cigar smoke, whiskey fumes, and the particular humidity that comes from too many bodies pressed into too small a space. Candles ring Mary's closed coffin on its bier near the bar, their flames guttering in the draft every time the door opens. Someone's hung her portrait above it. It's Mary in her prime, gold tooth catching the light, eyes sharp enough to cut glass.

"To Gold Tooth Mary!" A sailor hoists his glass, voice already slurred. "May Hell brace itself!"

The room erupts in agreement, glasses raised, whiskey sloshing.

That portrait's five years old, at least. Flattering angle, though." Mary's shade stands beside her own coffin, arms crossed, surveying the crowd with the critical eye of a woman inspecting troops. *Flowers, music, half the Coast in tears. The boy pulled it together. I'll give him that.*

I edge through the crowd, nodding at faces I recognize from the Night Market, from Pacific Avenue, from a dozen other Coast haunts. Half the Barbary's underworld is here: pickpockets and madams, dock workers and smugglers, all united in their respect for the woman who'd kept a kind of peace among them.

Connor spots me and makes his way over. He's dressed better than I've ever seen him, though his eyes are red-rimmed and exhausted. He's trying to look the part of Mary's successor and mostly pulling it off.

"Mick." He grips my hand. "Glad you came."

"Wouldn't miss it."

He glances around, then pulls me toward a quieter corner near the back stairs. "Walk with me a minute?"

We slip into the relative quiet of the hallway. The noise from the wake becomes a dull roar behind us.

Connor leans against the wall, some of the mask dropping. "I'm stepping up. Most of Mary's boys are backing me. Say they'd rather answer to someone who knew her than watch the whole thing fall apart in a turf war."

"You ready for that?"

"Hell no." He laughs. "But someone's got to. And I was with her longest. Learned the routes, the contacts, who owes what to whom." He rubs his face. "I'm terrified I'll bollocks it up, but I'm more terrified of what happens if nobody tries to hold it together."

Mary's shade appears beside him, studying him with something almost like pride. *If he sells my routes cheap, I'll haunt him worse than you.*

"You've got enemies," I say to Connor. "People who'll test you. Kollach might be finished, but there are others—"

"I know." He straightens. "I'm not Mary. Can't charm men into doing what I want with a smile and a song. But I've got something she taught me: know who's useful, who's loyal, and who's just waiting for a chance to stick a knife in your back." He meets my eyes. "I'm watching the politics. Already reached out to some of Mary's old contacts, people who'd rather deal with the devil they know than risk chaos on the Coast."

I study him. Still young. Still grieving. But there's steel underneath.

He'll do, Mary says. *Not what I'd have chosen. But he'll do.*

"You need help, you know where to find me."

He nods. "Appreciated."

We return to the main room. Someone's started singing an Irish ballad, mournful and defiant. The crowd joins in, voices rising and falling in waves.

On one of the tables near the door, I spot a copy of the *Chronicle*, folded but visible, already ringed with whiskey stains. The headline screams in bold type:

"CIVIC LEADER ARRESTED IN ARCANE PLOT"

Beneath it, smaller: Isaac Kollach Charged with Murder, Conspiracy. Claims of Mystical Influence.

I pick it up and skim it. Lots of quoted outrage from Kollach's lawyers about "unnamed foreign actors" and "entrapment by mysterious federal agents." A denial that sounds like exactly what a guilty man would say. It mentions a Federal raid, though Leona's name is conspicuously absent—the Bureau's way of keeping their cards close.

I fold the paper and set it down.

A couple of Coast regulars nearby chuckle darkly. "Always was a sanctimonious bastard," one mutters.

"Couldn't have happened to a nicer fellow," another adds, raising his glass.

Kollach's fall is complete. Public, humiliating, permanent. The kind of ruin that doesn't allow for comebacks.

Good.

The noise in the room dips suddenly, conversations stuttering to a halt.

Ah Toy stands in the entryway.

She's dressed in deep charcoal gray silk embroidered with white chrysanthemums. A trusted man stands half a step behind her, hand resting near his coat in a way that suggests a weapon close at hand. Two more are behind him, arms full.

Mutters ripple through the crowd. "Chinawoman doesn't belong here." "What's she doing?" "Nerve of her, showing up—"

Connor moves immediately, crossing the room to greet her. The crowd parts, uncertain, watching.

"Miss Ah Toy." He bows slightly, the gesture respectful. "Thank you for coming."

She inclines her head. "Mrs. Hunter and I understood each other. One does not ignore the passing of such a woman."

She gestures, and her escorts step forward. One with a massive wreath of white roses, and the second holds a wooden case of what looks like very expensive whiskey.

"For the wake," she says simply. "In respect."

Connor accepts them, visibly moved. "Mary would've appreciated that."

"Perhaps." Ah Toy's expression doesn't change, but there's humor in her eyes. "Or perhaps she would have thought me presumptuous. But the gesture is offered nonetheless."

She turns, scanning the room until her gaze finds me. A slight beckoning gesture.

I make my way over.

"Mick Kelly." She moves toward a quieter corner, away from the crowd's prying eyes. "A word, if you will."

We step into the narrow space between the bar and the back wall. Her escort positions himself to give us privacy while keeping watch.

Ah Toy produces a small, elegant box from within her robes—lacquered wood, inlaid with mother-of-pearl in a pattern of cranes and clouds. She hands it to me.

"What's this?"

"Open it when you have privacy," she says. "Inside, you will find instructions to a workshop in Chinatown. A craftsman awaits you; he has been commissioned to create something for you."

I frown, starting to protest. "I can't—"

"A hand," she states. "Not a hook. A proper hand. Mechanical artistry combined with...certain enhancements. The craftsman is very skilled. The work has already begun; he merely requires you for fittings."

I stare at her. "Why?"

"I began arrangements after our luncheon," she says. "I saw what you were, what you might become. Useful women should not be hampered by inadequate tools." She pauses. "And because Mrs. Hunter, before her death, expressed...concern. She wished you better equipped and knew a my artificer specialized in this this art."

Mary's shade materializes beside Ah Toy, looking smug. *Of course I did. Can't have you swinging a butcher's hook forever, love. You're meant for better.*

The box itself is beautiful, and strangely heavy. A gift from two underworld queens—one dead, one very much alive. An investment.

"This isn't a bribe," I say, the last thing I want is to offend her but I gotta be clear.

"No." Ah Toy's expression is cool. "You are...useful to many, Miss Kelly. I prefer my useful friends whole."

I'm being claimed. Equipped. Made more valuable.

Meeting her eyes, I tell her, "Friends I can work with. Not masters."

She regards me cooly for a moment. Then the faintest smile touches her lips.

"Friends," she agrees. "I believe we understand each other."

She inclines her head once more, then turns and makes her way back through the crowd. The crowd notes her departure, whispers following her to the door.

I tuck the box under my arm, Mary watches the Coast toast her name.

Don't let them tidy me into legend just yet, she says. *We've work to do.* Drifting toward the door she ask. *Coming? Or are you going to sit here all night congratulating yourself?*

"Where are we going?"

The Bay, of course. She turns, that gold tooth catching the lamplight. *You made a bargain with a rusalka. Best make sure she's satisfied.*

I grab my coat and follow her out.

Chapter Thirty-Seven

MEIGGS IS PRACTICALLY DESERTED when we get there. My breath ghosts in the chill air, footsteps hollow on wet planks. The waves against pilings are a slow, patient rhythm.

Mary's shade walks beside me, quieter than usual. Her hands are in her pockets, chin tucked against the wind she can't actually feel.

I walk past Arachne's, all the way to where the pier juts into the bay. The water stretches black and infinite, fog obscuring where it meets sky. Somewhere out there, Hoodoo Jones went down screaming.

I speak to the darkness.

"You asked for the sweet-talking man. I delivered him."

The usual harbor sounds—creaking boats, distant foghorns, rats scuttling between crates, all fade. Even the wind dies.

Then the water around us goes still.

Not calm. *Still*. Like glass. Like the tide itself has paused mid-breath to listen.

Hair like kelp swirls up from the depths. The rusalka rises just enough to rest her arms on a low piling, water streaming off her shoulders. Her eyes are fathomless pools.

She looks at me. Through me.

"Death-touched." She sings. Then her gaze shifts, fixing on Mary's shade. "Drag them behind you like nets."

Mary straightens, meeting the Rusalka's stare without flinching. *Some of us prefer better company than drowned sailors and rotting timber.*

She answer through a toothy smile, "Sad. Tethered like seaweed to rock. Cannot let go."

"Do you have him?" I cut off their little jab fest. "Hoodoo Jones."

The rusalka's attention swings back to me. "I have. What is left. It thrashes, begs. Calls names nobody answers."

My stomach turns. "Is he dead?"

Something amused slides behind her eyes. "Men like sweet-talking man do not end. They rot. Rot spreads. Even in deep water." She pulls herself higher, water dripping from her chin. "Bay keeps what it is given. Until something stronger pulls."

Not dead. Not alive. Something in between, trapped in her grip until someone, or something, wants him badly enough to fight her for the scraps.

"Our bargain," I ask, holding my breath. "Is it settled?"

"You kept your word." One pale finger slides along the piling. "You gave me Sweet-talking man. Debt paid."

Relief tries to take root, but her next words cut it off.

"But you stirred deep mud, Death-touched. Others smelled it." Her eyes gleam. "Things wake. Things hunt. You made noise. Noise carries in water. Far. Far."

Mary steps back from the edge of the pier. *Cheerful creature, isn't she?*

The rusalka's gaze snaps back to her. "You should sink, little siren. Down where drowned things go. That is where you belong."

I prefer a higher vantage. Mary's voice is cool. *The view is better out here.*

They stare at each other. Two powerful things that shouldn't exist, circling.

The rusalka laughs, low and bubbling and points at me. "Dead siren uses you. I use you. You stand between living and dead, Death-Touched. Cannot refuse either side. That is your nature."

"Maybe," I say. Then standing straighter, I tug on my collar, "Or maybe I'm the one doing the using."

She considers that, head tilting. Then nods once and circles the piling, lithe as a seal. "Bring me monsters. I take." Her smile widens.

Generous, Mary murmurs.

"Yes," the rusalka says. Her shoulders slip beneath the surface. "Bay remembers. Remembers who gives. Remembers who takes." Her face is the last thing visible. Pale as moonlight, that terrible smile.

Then she's gone. The water returns to normal, choppy, dark, moving with the tide. The harbor sounds resume. Wind picks up, cutting through my coat.

Mary's shade stands at the waterline, looking down at her own reflection that isn't there. *Well. That was unsettling.*

"You get used to it."

Do you? She turns, walking back to shore. *Or do you just get better at pretending you're not terrified?*

I don't answer.

She's right, you know, Mary says after a long silence. *About being used. About being the fulcrum.* She glances at me. *Ah Toy sees it. Leona sees it. You're not just a Gleaner anymore.*

"And you?" I ask. "What do you see?"

Mary's quiet for a few steps. *I see a woman who could've walked away a dozen times and didn't. Who keeps choosing the hard path because she thinks it's right.* She pauses. *I see someone I could've been, if I'd been braver. Or stupider. Hard to tell which.*

The city spreads before us lights in windows, smoke from chimneys, the distant clatter of a late-night trolley. San Francisco, carrying on despite everything. Despite necromancers and corrupt politicians and water spirits guarding drowned men.

I think about Leona's offer. Ah Toy's gift waiting in China-town. Connor trying to hold together Mary's fractured empire. My family sleeping safe in the townhouse, Ylva curled up with dreams that don't include revenants and blood.

"They want to use me," I run my hand over my brow. "Fine. But it's going to be on *my* terms now. No more begging. No more crawling. They want my help, they ask. They want my power, they negotiate."

Mary's shade grins, gold tooth flashing. *There she is. There's my girl.*

We walk into the night together. The dead woman and the living one, both of us changed by the same cursed city, both of us bound to it in ways we've yet to learn.

Behind us, the Bay keeps its secrets. And somewhere in its depths, Hoodoo Jones screams prayers nobody's listening to.

For now.

And San Francisco dreams on.

⁓⌁∿⌁⁓

Want more Mick Kelly?

If you're new to Mick's adventures, you can grab the first book in the Bad Magic series,

Bad Magic and Whiskey
here on Amazon

More →

As a special thank you for Mick's readers, you can check out the free prequel!

The Phantasm Prism

Book Funnel

THANK YOU

Thanks for riding along with Mick Kelly through a world of death magic, double-crosses, and ghosts!

I'd love it so much if you have a moment to leave a rating or review on Goodreads, Amazon, Barnes & Noble, Kobo or wherever you discovered ***Necromancers and Navy Grog***. Reviews are a big shot of **Big Magic** for indie authors like me. They are the single most powerful way to help new readers find stories like this one, and they help writers keep writing. Reviews are more heady than a shot of the best whiskey!

And yes, I read them. Every single one.

The next story in the Bad Magic series is underway! Initially my plan was to send Mick down to Galveston Texas following rumors of Confederate gold but I had so much fun writing in San Francisco (one of my favorite real life cities on the planet,) that I figure she might need one more adventure there. I promise Mick will be spending more time with Leona, Edison, Ah Toy and of course Gold Tooth Mary!

If you'd like to hear when the next book drops (and maybe snag a few extras along the way), come join me at melissajaco bsonauthor.com. I'd love to keep in touch.

And don't forget your free copy of ***The Phantasm Prism*** – on Book Funnel!

Thanks for spending your time with me and Mick.
Melissa

Acknowledgements

I am so lucky to have people in my life who love and support me, this book would never have come to life without them.

Shout out to my beta readers, those intrepid readers who evaluated an early draft and provided invaluable feedback – Steve, Mel, Tracey, Still and Gary! THANK YOU SO MUCH for your time, energy and thoughtful criticism.

Also big thanks to Rocky Mountain Fiction Writers, Littleton Critique Group. The kindness, generosity and knowledge in this group is immense, and I'm so lucky to have found them. (Well actually my husband found them.)

I owe a huge debt to fellow author T.A. Caldwell who continuously cheers me on, promotes me and in general helps keep imposter syndrome at bay.

Thank you Lawrence Editing for line edits and Hosang Quality Editing for proofreading.

And finally, as always, my loving husband who still seems to think becoming an indie author was a valid career choice for me.

Despite all this help and support, typos are my superpower. I can seemingly introduce them into text I haven't touched. That said, any remaining errors are all my own and in no way a reflection of anyone who assisted in the publication of this novel!